AN *Amish* DILEMMA

JERRY EICHER

ELK LAKE PUBLISHING INC

PUBLISHING THE POSITIVE
Plymouth, Massachusetts

Cover and Interior Design: Derinda Babcockww
Editor(s): Cristel Phelps, Deb Haggerty

PUBLISHED BY: Elk Lake Publishing, Inc., 35 Dogwood Drive, Plymouth, MA 02360, 2021

Library Cataloging Data

Names: Eicher, Jerry (Jerry Eicher)

An Amish Dilemma / Jerry Eicher

362 p. 23cm × 15cm (9in × 6 in.)

ISBN-13: 978-1-64949-461-0 (paperback) | 978-1-64949-462-7 (trade paperback) | 978-1-64949-463-4 (e-book)

Key Words: Amish, Marriage, Courtship, Romance, Unrequited Love, Cozy, Family

Library of Congress Control Number: 2021951787 Fiction

CHAPTER 1

The trees on the Miller farmstead had blossomed again, brought to life after the hard winter by the warm breezes of spring blowing in from the Nebraska prairie. The grass in the distant fields moved slowly in the soft movement of the winds. Cows grazing by the stream lifted their heads momentarily to stare at the horizon as if they too saw and appreciated the blaze of glory revealed by the rising sun. Bright blue, red, and purple cut broad swaths across the dawning sky.

Rose was an Amish girl known by reputation as an excellent gardener among a people noted for their gardening talents and for their devoutness to God and the soil. A people who grew things, who produced healthy plants shooting from the ground, who sought to produce people sound in body and mind, living with an uplifted face under an open heaven.

At the moment, Rose stood holding a piece of wet wash in her hand, gazing toward the rising sun. There was coldness on her fingers from the touch of wire wash line and the chill of the dripping water. While warmth touched her cheeks, the rays bursting through the low bank of brightly colored clouds flooded her face with light. She closed her eyes and breathed deeply.

"My Lord and my God," she whispered, remembering the words having been uttered by the doubting Thomas before he saw the risen Christ.

"I don't doubt you," she said, barely breathing the words.

They seemed unspeakable in weight. Their wings unable to lift the implied doubt which haunted her mind. Why had God taken Wilmer when her heart had been so young and unbroken? How did God expect her to ever love a man again?

God had his reasons, unfathomable to man. Her people's faith was strong on this point, and so was hers. Her heart was simply frozen and wouldn't respond.

"I don't doubt," she said, a little louder. "I just wish God had chosen otherwise."

Rose sang softly gazing at the still glorious sunrise. "Praise to God immortal praise. For the love which crowns our days."

The memory of Sunday evening's hymn singing with Mary Bontrager seated beside her returned. They had poured their hearts out in song, along with the rest of the community's young people. She was moving on with life, just slower than some people wished.

God was a gracious God, even if he handled the human heart a little roughly at times. How brightly his sun shone this morning and this display of colors. Truly the Lord touched their lives each day with fresh grace. She was happy, deep down she was, living here in this lovely Amish community on the prairie. She belonged in this place. She had been born here. Near the time the community had been founded. This was her home.

Rose stared at her brother Edwin's shirt. Her reverie broken. She snapped on the clothes pins with quick motions and let go. Edwin wasn't the problem. His shirt reminded her Robert Bontrager was waiting for an answer. He had sent smiles her way several times on Sunday during the hymn singing.

To make matters worse, *Mamm* had asked again when she arrived home with Edwin. "When are you are letting the man do the driving for you on a Sunday evening?"

Her entire family knew of Robert's frequent requests for a date. The man was waiting—had been for a year, which said a lot for his character. Not every Amish man had such patience.

"He's quite a catch." Mamm had encouraged once more, and quickly followed with a gentle chide. "Remember! You're getting no younger."

Rose winced. What Mamm said was true. She was nearly twenty-one years of age and had not opened her heart to a man after Wilmer's premature death. There had been requests, many requests since she had turned sixteen, but she had always found a reason to say, no.

"Is there someone else?" Mamm had probed last night.

"I'm waiting." Rose had responded, when she felt like saying, *I'm not in love with the man. I'll never be in love again.*

Her sister Esther had been the only one who knew about Wilmer, about the sixth grade, the notes, the looks, and the smiles. Rose blocked the churning memories. No one else had paid them any mind at such a young age. School year infatuations happened constantly—to blow over when maturity arrived. Only what had arrived was the news of a drowning, delivered to the Miller family late on a Friday evening, followed by a funeral and a casket lowered into the ground. Wilmer had never been her boyfriend—not a real one, but they had been in love. Puppy love, Esther had tried to convince her, but Esther knew, as Rose knew. Their love had been the real thing, the kind which would have grown beyond note passing in school and shy smiles behind desktops, to dating and eventually marriage. Followed by a home kept together and doubtless children given by the Lord and in their old age grandchildren.

Now she was waiting, but waiting for what? There would never be another Wilmer. Never! There couldn't be. No face would grip her heart like Wilmer's had. With his lopsided grin. His lop of loose hair floundering about his forehead, hanging at an angle from his cowlick. She would never forget Wilmer. Waiting wasn't going to solve the problem. Neither did weeping or crying or turning down dates from eligible Amish men.

She had to say yes to Robert. She had to because he was a decent man. A poor excuse to date a man, but the situation couldn't be helped. If she must marry a man, Robert was the best choice. When the other men had asked for dates, she could always think of reasons to turn them down. Usually some silly thing, with roots in the memory from the past. So alive the boy had been, so into her life, so all consuming. Her breath would leave her body when their eyes met. Memories, always memories. Only memories left. Rose forced herself to pick up another piece of clothing. The only way she could find peace was praising the Lord. Something akin to happiness would sweep through her when she sat on the wooden bench at the hymn singing and lifted her voice in adoration to the Lord. Those memories were precious ones. There was the feeling of being alive, of being lifted upward, of wanting to dwell in this place of glory forever. Only one couldn't. There came the hour— quite quickly when the hymn singing ended, and the drive home began. She must forget Wilmer. She must after all these long years. She must move on, she often resolved, and a measure of peace would come only to drift away again.

"Be practical." Mamm had said. "The feelings will come. You need a man who keeps the church *ordnung and* doesn't crowd the fence. Together, you can create a life, one in which the Lord is pleased to dwell with his presence."

Rose sighed and pinned another shirt on the line. She studied the frazzled cotton shirt. *Daett*'s this time. Mamm must know of what she spoke. Never did she hear an unkind word pass between her parents. They had married young. Mamm had been only eighteen, and their oldest daughter, Esther, was born within a year. No child could remember anything of the move to Nebraska, but she had heard the stories of how Daett and Mamm had left their prosperous farm back east in Lancaster County and set their faces westward to begin a new life far from the faster pace of the older communities. Daett and Mamm had never regretted their move, and neither had anyone else. Esther was married and lived with her husband, Jesse, on a small farm a mile below the small town of Table Rock. Edwin, her younger brother, would soon date Mary Bontrager if she didn't miss her guess. How happy the two were already, the perfect couple, as Esther and Jesse had been. No doubt there. No one could have made a better frau for Jesse than Esther. There were moments like this morning when she was ready to acquiesce and accept her lot when it came to marriage. Offers of marriage didn't grow on trees. Robert was well beyond breaking the ice. He sent her constant smiles, and his standing offer of a formal date was over a year old. He had approached her again two Sunday evenings ago outside the barn with the lantern light flickering on his shaven face.

"Have you thought about my request lately, Rose?"

"I'm still thinking." She had forced a smile.

"I hope I'm not asking again too quickly."

"It's okay."

"You'll let me know when you decide?"

"Yah." She had sought for the right words. Ones which wouldn't hurt his feelings. "Let's both pray on the matter and wait on the Lord."

"Of course." Robert had agreed, but still looked worried. "You know I can't wait forever."

"I enjoyed my time with you at Esther's wedding." She had encouraged him. Mamm had insisted. Esther had to ask Robert to fill one of the table waiter spots with her. The remark had brought a smile to his face. "I'll let you know then," she had said. Robert had nodded and drifted into the shadows. How different things would be if Robert was Wilmer, his grin glowing under the gas lantern. She would have been trembling, no doubt, holding herself back from clutching his hand to keep him near her forever. Wilmer was a dream, an angel in heaven, and she was on the earth destined to marry another man. How could the Lord have willed such cruel suffering? Yet, he was God, and men did not question the Almighty. Surrender was the only proper response, but surrender tore at her heart and left the wound fresh and bleeding.

"Rose!" Mamm's voice called from the house. Rose jumped and grabbed at the laundry basket to hurry back across the lawn.

Mamm greeted her with a smile. "I didn't mean to startle you. Can you call the men? Breakfast is almost ready."

"Certainly." Rose came far enough up the steps to set the laundry basket on the floorboards.

"It's a beautiful morning," Mamm said, gazing toward the rising sun. The low bank of clouds had turned a deep red with streaks of orange and dark blue darting upward. "But there will be rain in a day or two, I'm guessing."

"At least I finished the garden last week," Rose said.

"You're always on time and a *goot* daughter," Mamm replied. "The Lord has blessed us with so many things we can't begin to count them."

"I know. Thanks for reminding me."

"You're a sweet daughter," Mamm said. "Be assured that you have Daett and my blessing when you accept Robert's offer of a date. At his age, he'll have a quick wedding on his mind, and Daett and I also have no objections."

"Thanks." Rose moved away from the porch. "I should call the men."

Mamm nodded and disappeared inside.

Rose hurried across the lawn. What would Mamm say if she decided to turn down Robert? She didn't plan to, but the option had remained as a comforting thought. Which was now gone—at least it felt gone. Rose opened the barn door and called inside. "Breakfast!"

"Be right there." Muffled male voices answered. Rose retreated to pause near the front porch for one last look at the horizon. The clouds were almost gone, and the sun was a ball of fire in the sky. She banished thoughts of Robert from her mind and took joy in the moment. What a sign of hope the Lord had painted in the sky. Troubles might arise and cloud the horizon of life, but the light always broke through. Rose turned her head when she heard a vehicle coming up the road from the valley below. She waited, still caught in the morning's peaceful musings. A dark blue pickup truck came into sight. Rose took a step toward the house but stopped mid-stride when the vehicle slowed down, and the turn signal came on. Likely someone was arriving to see Daett. The driver had to have caught sight of her. Hurrying into the house might appear rude. Rose waited and waved as the pickup truck turned into the driveway. A young English man was driving, a handsome young English man. He looked like a farmer, but she had never seen him before. Rose felt the urge to run into the house, but she held her ground. She had met and spoken to English men before. There was nothing to fear from this encounter.

CHAPTER 2

Conrad Wisner placed the pickup in park, his gaze fixed on the young Amish girl who stood in the yard staring at him. She was pretty in an earthy sort of way, not unlike his sisters. They were daughters of the prairie. Her peace, despite her startled look drew him, soothed him in ways he couldn't explain. The entire Amish community had this effect on him. He had no right to draw from their strength or from her strength, for he could tell the girl had great strength. He could tell from her face, from the clear look in her eyes, from the unmarred spirit she carried about her. These people knew little of the world's troubles. Not like he did. Service in Iraq hadn't been against his convictions or his desires. He wasn't marred or scarred as some of the soldiers had been. What he had seen was death—immediate and violent death—and poverty, hopelessness, a country and a people lost in despair. Maybe he was in denial. Why else did the Amish community overwhelm him with such peace. Conrad stepped down from the pickup truck and called out. "Good morning. Is your father around?"

The young woman pointed wordlessly toward the barn.

"Should I knock?" He asked, more to make conversation than anything. She looked speechless, but he couldn't be this intimidating. She knew nothing of soldiers or what soldiers did in combat, yet he was no longer a solider.

"Just walk in." She finally answered.

"I'm Conrad Wisner, the new county extension agent." He offered a smile.

"You must know Daett." Her voice croaked.

"We've never met," he said, wondering how to put her at ease. "I'm looking for Enos Miller."

"Daett is Enos Miller. In the barn." She was pointing again.

"It's a lovely morning, isn't it?"

She looked ready to dash away.

"Are you the culprit who put those long lines of wash on the lines this morning?" He motioned with his chin. Her gaze turned to move up and down the lines of laundry stretched across the yard.

"I—yah. I was up early."

"Must have been quite early," he said. "My parents taught us to rise early. Sort of goes with prairie life."

A ghost of a smile crept into her face. "There was a beautiful sunrise to greet me."

"Certainly was." He agreed. "I took a moment to enjoy the sight while my coffee was brewing."

"I should go." She looked frightened again.

"Of course. Sorry to keep you."

"Daett is in the barn," she said.

He couldn't help himself. "Your name, Miss?"

"Rose," she said, already turning to leave. He watched her vanish into the house.

"Rose," he said, out loud. "An Amish girl named Rose."

"Can I help you?" A man's deep voice asked from behind him.

He turned to face the bearded figure. "Ah, yes. I'm Conrad Wisner, the new county extension agent."

"I see," the man said. "You must be the young man who lives next door to my daughter, Esther. Jesse was telling me about you."

"Hopefully nothing bad." Conrad forced a laugh. "I didn't know Esther was your daughter."

The man smiled. "They enjoy having you as a neighbor."

"Thanks," Conrad said.

"I see you've met Rose. What can I do for you this fine morning?"

"I thought I'd stop by early and catch you before you hit the fields."

"Well, here we are." Enos turned as the barn door opened. "And this is my son, Edwin. He's more into these newfangled farming methods than I am. I'll let you speak with him, and my other son, Charles, is somewhere."

Conrad offered his hand to the younger man. "Good morning, Edwin."

"Good morning, sir."

"Conrad, please. I'm looking forward to speaking with you at length when you have the time."

"You're not from the area, Jesse tells us." Enos observed.

"Raised up north on a cattle ranch. Not that far from here, but I never ran into the Amish until I took the job for the county."

Enos chucked. "There aren't many of us around here. There's an Amish community up near the state line, but they're small like we are."

"You're hardworking and industrious farmers by reputation."

"Did you expect to find reality otherwise?"

"Of course not!"

"I was just teasing." Enos's eyes twinkled.

"Why don't we invite Conrad in for breakfast?" Edwin asked.

"Why not?" Enos agreed at once. "If young Conrad can stomach Amish cooking?"

"I've heard good things about Amish cooking," he said, "but I wouldn't want to impose on such short notice."

"There's always room at an Amish table." The older man's smile filled his face. "Let's go see what the women have prepared for breakfast this morning."

"You sure?" he asked. This he hadn't expected, but he couldn't resist either.

Enos slapped him on the back. "You rent a place from my daughter. Glad to have you stop by, son. Come on in and make yourself right at home."

CHAPTER 3

Inside the house, Rose stood frozen at the kitchen window, her voice barely above a whisper. "*Daett's* bringing the man right into the house."

"Bringing who?" *Mamm* asked from the stove.

"The county extension agent. A young English man." Rose's heart started pounding in her throat again. What was happening to her? These feelings. She hadn't felt them since the sixth grade, since the news arrived the night of Wilmer's death. The heat in her face, the hope rising in her heart, the light shining from a man with the strength of heaven. She couldn't. She couldn't here, not now. He was not Wilmer. He didn't even look like Wilmer. There was no connection. There couldn't be. Her heart was lying, being deceived.

Mamm came over to the window for a look. "Have you seen him before?"

Rose tried to keep her voice from breaking. "He drove into the lane before I came in looking for Daett."

"He must be decent," Mamm said, glancing at Rose. "Daett wouldn't bring him in if he wasn't."

Rose felt weak, her fingers nearly slipping from the egg plate.

Mamm noticed. "He's safe. I'm sure he is, or have you met him before?"

Rose's face flamed. "I—of course not."

"There's no harm done if you would have." Mamm appeared puzzled. "Did he say something inappropriate in the yard?"

"No. He was—I mean, quite decent."

Mamm didn't look convinced. "What is he again?"

"The new county extension agent."

"What exactly is an extension agent?"

Rose drew a long breath, trying to still the rapid beat of her heart. "They help the farmers in the area with tips and farming advice, I think."

"With your gardening skills, you would know." Mamm muttered. "You young people are more up-to-date on the English ways these days. Since you've met him, and he's decent, go welcome him in. I'll set another plate at the table."

Rose set down the egg plate with a clatter. She forced her feet to move toward the front door. Daett liked visitors, but he had never invited an English man to their breakfast table. Would he, if Daett had known about the moments she had spent transfixed on the front yard, her heart pounding—still pounding. Conrad had to have noticed. What must the man think? Rose stilled her rapid breathing before she opened the front door and stepped halfway out of sight. She needed a big solid barn door to hide behind. Somewhere she could wait out of sight until the storm had passed.

"Rose." Daett peered around the door frame. His face lit into a smile. "Don't be shy, daughter. This is Conrad. I believe you two have met."

"We have." Rose managed. She kept her gaze on the floor. She didn't dare look up at either Daett or Conrad. Her face was red enough.

"Good to meet you again," Conrad said quite loudly.

"And you." Rose kept her eyes fixed on the floor. They were moving toward the house, as waves of shame filled her. She had to get control of her emotions before she embarrassed everyone. But how? She couldn't stay behind the door forever or away from the breakfast table. There would be conversation. She would have to look up and catch glimpses of his face. His eyes. They were sorrow filled—deeply—as if the man had seen great pain, and yet he was so young. He couldn't be much older than she was. Rose again stayed behind a door while she heard introductions being made in the kitchen. There was the sound of Daett and her brother trooping into the washroom. She couldn't move, listening to the banging of boots on the tile floor.

"Rose," Mamm called, and she jumped. "I need your help."

Rose forced her feet to move and nearly tripped over the kitchen threshold. Mamm gave her a strange look. Conrad was seated on a chair with his back turned toward her. Rose rushed past to grab a loaf of bread and vigorously began to slice. Edwin reappeared from the washroom before anyone could say anything, his hair wet from the water basin.

"Wipe you face dry." Mamm chided. Edwin rubbed both hands on his smooth chin. "Better?" He looked around, grinning.

"Look at you, dripping water over the kitchen floor!" Mamm exclaimed.

"I'm used to wet farmhouse floors." Conrad's voice rumbled.

Edwin's grin grew. "There are only two drops." He leaned down to rub with his finger. "Gone."

"Now your hand is dirty." Mamm scolded.

"How can they be dirty from touching your clean kitchen floor?" Edwin turned the tables on Mamm.

Conrad was laughing good-naturedly. "A man after my own heart, I would say."

Rose could see Mamm's face soften. "Sit down, the both of you," she said, when Daett reappeared, "or the food will be cold."

"Ah—" Daett stopped to draw a deep breath over the bacon and eggs plates. "What a breakfast this will be."

"Indeed. I agree." Conrad chimed in. "Thank you so much for having me, Mrs. Miller."

"Anna to you." Mamm brushed her hands on her apron. "No Mrs. Miller when you're a guest at my breakfast table."

"Anna then." Conrad ducked his head politely, smiling.

Rose had dared to look up in the middle of their light banter and caught of glimpse of his eyes again. The sorrow was in them, but something else took her breath away. Her heart began to pound in her throat again. Thankfully, everyone bowed their heads for a prayer. Conrad seemed to know the routine.

When Daett said amen, Rose began to pass the food, only half listening to what Daett was saying to Mamm.

"Conrad has rented a place next to Esther and Jesse's."

Mamm's face lit up. "You're living beside our daughter."

"I didn't know until this morning," Conrad said, helping himself to the eggs and bacon. "They're a lovely couple and very kind to me."

"We try to bring our children up well," Mamm said. "I'm glad you're comfortable in their rental house."

Conrad was smiling, his eyes losing some of their sadness. "I tilled their garden spot with my tractor the other evening. Your daughter will share a few of her vegetables with me as payment."

Mamm's face darkened. "There, I must admit, I failed. You might as well know the truth. I never could teach Esther how to grow anything. Rose, here, is our gardener."

"I'm sure Esther can handle a garden since she's married." Rose forced herself to speak.

Mamm shrugged. "Jesse might have the green thumb."

Daett was chuckling. "Just to fill you in on the details, Conrad. Our eldest daughter apparently left all her gardening skills to her sister. Rose has a reputation for gardening throughout our community, which says much since we're Amish."

Conrad was grinning. "I knew Amish had their farming skills. I'm glad to hear some of them don't. I was beginning to think they might be the ones teaching me, instead of the other way around."

"I'm sure we can learn from you either way." Edwin was laughing. "But if my sister Esther were the guide, you'd never find the garden plot."

"Now, now," Daett said. "Your sister tried."

"She did." Rose spoke up, feeling the need to explain. "I took care of the garden while Esther worked in the house. She was in her element—household things."

"To each his gift." Conrad agreed, giving Rose a smile. "I guess I'll be coming to you for lessons on gardening."

They all laughed, and Rose felt her face grow red again. Inside, though, she felt happier than she had in years. Conrad's voice soothed her, and his smile had healed something she hadn't known was torn. Or had she? This was horribly wrong, though—completely, utterly, and unthinkably wrong. Receiving touches of love in her spirit from an English man.

"I'm serious," Conrad was saying. "Even with my training I'm open to lessons on gardening, especially from an Amish woman who is an expert."

"Well," Daett said. "You may have to settle for Esther's advice, little though she knows. Rose sticks around the house pretty close."

They all laughed, and Rose ducked her head as the conversation around the breakfast table continued. She waited for Conrad to say the wrong thing, but he never missed a beat, smiling and nodding his head. Rose let her mind drift, seeing herself walking through a garden plot with Conrad by her side, glancing up at him, hearing his voice rumble above her, running her fingers through the soil, telling him the secrets of the earth. Rose saw the kitchen walls shimmer and dim. She pinched herself twice, hard. She couldn't pass out at the kitchen table thinking about an English man. This was not Wilmer. Her heart was playing tricks on her.

"This is amazing," Conrad was saying. "I can never repay your kind welcome this morning."

"We'll be expecting special deals from the county." Daett deadpanned. Everyone laughed again.

Outside, a buggy rattled into the driveway. Mamm stood for a peek out the kitchen window. "It's Esther!" Mamm exclaimed. "She's out early this morning."

Rose jumped to her feet, glad for an excuse to escape, but Daett motioned her back down. "I'll go help Esther unhitch."

"Maybe Esther has come to spend the day with us." Mamm whispered to Rose after Daett had left. "At least, go welcome Esther at the door."

Rose stood quickly and went outside to wait on the porch. Esther was talking with Daett beside the buggy. She needed this moment alone in the fresh air to clear her mind, after sitting across from Conrad at the breakfast table.

Esther saw her and hollered. "Goot morning."

"Goot morning." Rose called back. She rubbed her cheeks with both hands. Mamm had noticed her burning face and so would Esther. She turned away from the rising sun and willed the cool morning air to blow across her cheeks. This was beyond embarrassing. What a reaction to have! Conrad was an English man and way out of her reach—if he even noticed her or thought of her as a woman he could be interested in. Rose's cheeks burned again. What awful thoughts were rushing through her mind. Something was terribly wrong with her.

"It's so goot to see you." Esther called out from behind Rose. "Looks like you already have a visitor."

Rose forced herself to turn around. "Yah! Your renter. How come we never heard a peep?"

"Rose." Esther chided gently. "What is wrong with you? He's the local county extension, and a good friend, but—"

"Daett invited him for breakfast," Rose said, between her teeth.

"I'm not surprised." Esther stopped short. "Why are you blushing?"

"The sun is shining brightly." Rose avoided the question.

Esther was staring at her. "So, you did—I mean, I kind of thought so, but—"

"You what?" Rose demanded.

"He's an English man," Esther said.

"Of course." Rose rubbed her face. "I know he's an English man."

"You're—" Esther grabbed Rose's arm. "I can't believe this! Not quite like this. I mean, I thought, but—"

"You keep on saying—and I'm not—"

"You're red in the face."

"Being red in the face—"

"This is why I didn't tell you," Esther said. "There's something about him. I don't know what, but—"

"Don't keep saying he's like—"

"I know, but he does remind me of Wilmer, in some way I can't explain."

Rose paled. "There's nothing about him which is like Wilmer."

"I know." Esther agreed. "And yet—"

Rose clutched the rail. "He's not Wilmer. He never was, and he never will be. There was only one Wilmer."

"I know." Esther reached for Rose's arm. "Come, let's go inside."

Rose nodded, holding open the door. She followed Esther, a cold numbness circling her heart. Conrad wasn't like Wilmer. He couldn't be. Rose waited at the kitchen doorway while Mamm gathered her eldest daughter in her arms.

"So goot to see you." Mamm cooed. "What brings about this early morning visit?"

"We'll talk later," Esther said before she turned to Conrad with a smile. "I didn't except to find you here."

"Is the garden growing?" He teased.

Esther made a face at him. "I see you've been talking to my family."

"They assure me there will be an abundant harvest." Conrad tried to keep a straight face but couldn't with the hoots coming from Edwin and Charles.

Esther glared at them. "Since you know my little secret, do you want cash payment for your work, Conrad?"

He waved his hand in dismissal, caught in the throes of laughter.

"The garden will be fine with Jesse around." Mamm jumped in. "Have you eaten?"

"I have." Esther didn't look placated.

Mamm rushed on. "It's so sweet of you to come over. We can keep you busy for the day. I have a pile of mending, and the laundry will be dry soon."

Esther drew a long breath. "Does Rose have her garden in?"

"I didn't mean to cause problems with my comments." Conrad spoke up.

"You didn't." Mamm assured him. "Are you sure you don't want to eat, Esther?"

"You have to eat," Daett said, reappearing in the washroom door.

Esther gave in quickly, seating herself at the table. "You do make the best breakfast, Mamm."

"Agreed here," Conrad said. "A meal like this would keep any husband satisfied."

Mamm beamed. "I'm sure Esther keeps Jesse very happy, but thank you, Conrad."

Esther looked ready for the subject to change. "So, how are my handsome brothers this morning?"

"Goot here." Charles called out.

"Mary is doing quite well." Edwin grinned from ear to ear.

"You don't have to flaunt your success." Esther chided.

"Mary's the prettiest girl in the community." Edwin retorted. "Why wouldn't I?"

"You should thank the Lord for your blessings." Mamm chimed in. "He's the one who gives great grace."

"Of course." Edwin agreed, but he didn't look very repentant.

"How is love treating you, Charles?" Esther turned to her younger brother.

Before Charles could speak, Edwin answered for him. "There is Susie Byler, but word is out she burns the breakfast toast."

Charles sputtered in his rage at the insult.

"We don't take such rumors seriously," Mamm said at once.

"I assume the boy is teasing." Daett added, still appearing worried.

"I would hope so!" Mamm exclaimed. "Susie would be a great catch for Charles."

"This is so wrong." Charles managed to get out. Conrad was laughing along with everyone else.

"Still holding your goot opinion of my family?" Esther asked him.

He chuckled. "Nothing's changed, but I should be going."

"Not before you answer my questions." Edwin rose to his feet. "Maybe we can talk outside."

"Perfect." Conrad agreed. "Thanks so much for the breakfast, Anna."

Mamm gave him a kind smile. "You come again, now."

"I certainly will," Conrad said, and the two left.

Daett got to his feet. "We should also be going."

Charles gulped his last bite of food and followed Daett. Rose jumped at the slam of the washroom door. Her nerves were completely on edge. Thankfully, Mamm didn't notice, but Esther had.

"We have missed you so much, Esther," Mamm was saying, "but life moves on, as it should."

"And I've missed you," Esther grimaced, "but I can speak freely now that Conrad is gone. The truth is, I need help."

"Help with what?" Mamm asked.

"My horrid garden," Esther said. "I haven't planted anything yet, and it might rain tomorrow."

"You came—" Mamm was staring.

Esther wrung her hands. "I know. I wanted to visit, but yah. I need help. Desperately. This is my first year of gardening alone, and I'm frozen with fright. If nothing grows, Jesse might even regret he married me."

"Nonsense." Mamm scoffed.

"I feel so helpless." Esther continued. "Maybe a pep talk is what I need before I get busy. I really was planning to get right back and set myself to work, but my courage failed me."

"You just put the seeds in the ground, and they sprout." Rose couldn't resist.

Esther gave her a glare. "Says the gardening expert."

Mamm clucked her tongue. "Jesse will not think ill of you if things don't grow too well the first year."

Esther didn't look convinced.

"Why don't I go back with her and help." Rose offered.

"You would?" Esther's face glowed.

Rose shrugged. "Why not? If Mamm can bring in the wash after lunch. We're not very swamped today."

"Can she?" Esther looked pleadingly at Mamm.

"You're have to learn these things sometime," Mamm said. "I should have insisted you help Rose with the garden the year before you married."

"I will learn." Esther promised. "I just need a little help this year."

"Okay then." Mamm gave in. Esther jumped up from her chair and did a little jig on the kitchen floor. Mamm looked mildly amused. "I'll clean up the kitchen, just go."

They left, and Conrad Wisner was no longer in the front yard when Rose followed Esther out of the front door. Edwin grinned when they told him their plans, but he had Brownie hitched for Rose in record time. She threw in some string and stakes before hopping in and following Esther's buggy out of the lane.

CHAPTER 4

About the same time, Robert Schlabach drove his team of horses out of his Daett's barnyard. He took a quick backward glance over his shoulder. His Daett had the other team ready to go and would follow him soon. If things went well, they would have the last of the spring plowing done today. The other Amish farmers in the community were already in the fields with their harrows, not their plows, but Daett usually managed to be last about everything involving farming.

"Let's go," Robert hollered to his horses. He should have purchased his own farm by now. He was old enough. With his own farm, he could manage things properly, but a bachelor with a farm wasn't well thought of in the community. Sort of like getting the cart before the horse, they said. If a man couldn't snag a wife, what business had he owning a farm? Robert winced. The truth was he could have been dating long ago. At least, he figured he could have. He hadn't exactly asked anyone except Rose. His eye had been on the girl for several years. His attention first drawn by her reputation as a gardener. Maybe his Daett's inefficiency in such matters heightened his sensitivity to the subject. Why Rose was still single, he had no clue. She was a decent looking girl with a dark sort of beauty and a little on the sober side. He didn't want a sad wife, but perhaps efficiency went with sadness. He was ready to assume that to be true, since his Daett could draw a belly laugh at the drop of a hat with his farming tales from the men gathered on the lawn after a Sunday morning meeting. They all knew he told them at his own expense. He had waited with bated breath on many a Sunday evening, expecting Rose to climb into some other man's buggy for her ride home after the hymn singing. She never did. She turned everyone down, as the rumors went. Why would she accept his offer? He had waited long before taking the leap, daring to approach her one evening at a youth gathering. He had been prepared for an instant rebuttal. She had smiled instead.

"Oh—I haven't thought about dating lately."

"I would be willing," he dared say.

"Well, perhaps I should pray about the matter."

Which hadn't exactly been a yah, but a "maybe," at least. He had waited and waited. The whole community was aware of his waiting. If Rose turned him down now, his reputation would be sealed. He would be known as the man who had misjudged a woman. "Just like his father," they would say. "Can't quite get the plow in the ground."

He should never have tried to date Rose. He should have settled for some girl more attainable. Maybe Rose knew of his Daett's farming reputation? If not, surely her family had informed her by now. Daett's failings were no secret, and he was Daett's oldest son. Perhaps Grandpa Beiler's stellar farming reputation back in Lancaster County saved him ... or his own hard work on Daett's farm. He hoped. He hoped Grandpa Beiler's long talked about visit to Nebraska would happen soon. Mamm kept bringing up the subject, longing to see her family again. Knowing Grandpa, there wouldn't be much advance notice. What if Grandpa's presence could turn the tide for him? Impress Rose and her family. Remind them he had successful farmer genes in his blood. A date with Rose and a visit from Grandpa Beiler? What wild thoughts he was having this morning. In the meantime, he must get busy. They were way behind with the plowing again this year, and the whole thing had him on pins and needles.

Robert pulled back the reins and settled the team behind the plow at the end of the field. He snapped on the chains and climbed onto the plow seat.

"Let's go," he hollered. The team leaned into the traces. The soft swish of steel cutting into grassy soil filled his ears. A calmness crept over him. He was a part of the community, as was Rose. They were people of the soil. He had to hope and believe. They would marry and grow old together, as had the generations before them. Everyone must be part of something greater than themselves. The two of them, Rose and Robert, would pass on the great and *wunderbah* heritage placed in their hands by the sacrifices of those who had gone on before them.

"Rose and Robert," he spoke the names out loud. He liked the sound. Rose was the woman he needed, in more ways than one. He was not like his Daett. He had taken after his Grandpa Beiler on Mamm's side of the family. He would marry a decent girl, a worthy girl, who would complement his farming skills.

"Whoa there," Robert called out to the team. They had reached the end of the field. He lifted the plow from the ground and made the turn. He dropped the blade, and the sound of the steel cutting into the ground surrounded him. He settled into the seat. He would have a date with Rose Miller before too many suns crossed the sky. He could feel Rose yielding. She would say yah. Rose Miller would become his wife, and he would have his farm.

CHAPTER 5

The sun had climbed higher into sky since the early morning sunrise, casting shadows into the fields from the fence posts and mailboxes lined along the road. Rose drove Brownie toward Esther's place with the steady beat of his hooves on the dirt road joining the rhythm from Esther's horse. Rose let the sound push the thoughts of Conrad's kind eyes from her mind. She couldn't let her mind go down this road. Not with an English man. Conrad wasn't Wilmer. Conrad didn't even look like Wilmer. Why had a foolish crush afflicted her? This could not be the real thing. Love did not end in ruin, in sorrow, and in soul-crushing sadness. Rose pushed the awful consequences from her mind. How would she explain falling in love with an English man? Moral failings sometimes happened but not in one stunning, unexplainable morning conversation. She would help Esther with her garden today. She would dig her hands in the soil and remember she was a proper Amish woman who didn't notice, let alone feel perturbed by, a young, handsome, English man with haunted eyes.

Ahead of Rose, the farm of Robert's Daett came into view. Robert! She had almost forgotten Robert. Maybe this was her answer? Maybe this morning had been a warning shot? She had best forget Wilmer once and for all and accept the life the Lord had laid out for her. Robert was waiting. Robert was her age. He was willing. Rose caught her breath. Was she willing? Was she ready to let go of the past? She could no longer ignore the plain leading of the Lord. Robert hoped to buy a farm of his own. He had shared the information cautiously with her the evening of Esther's wedding. They could wed by this fall. No more thoughts of a kind English man's sad eyes. No more chance of ruining her reputation beyond repair. Rose caught sight of a team of horses working in the fields near the road. Robert and his Daett would be out this morning. If this was Robert, what a great opportunity to accept his offer and never think of Conrad Wisner again. Maybe this morning had been what she needed to push her over the edge. Seeing the dangers threatening her while she waited—for who knew what. Rose shivered on the buggy seat. Who would have thought her heart would be so weak, so foolish to pound furiously at the sight of an English man. Obviously, she had horrendous hidden flaws. Rose waited until she was sure the man on the plow was Robert before she pulled back on the reins and called to Brownie. "Whoa there."

They bounced into the ditch, and he switched his tail after the stop, as if to remind her they didn't have all day for this unexpected stop. Rose hopped out. Across the field, Robert brought his team to a standstill. He stared at her for a long moment before he dropped the reins and came across the field at a fast walk.

"Goot morning." She called to him, hoping the guilty twitch in her smile didn't show.

He came up to the fence line beaming. "Rose. It's you. I was just—"

She broadened her smile. "I'm not trying to keep you from your work."

"Not a problem." He glanced down the road at Esther's retreating buggy. "Going to help your sister today?"

"Her garden," she said. "Esther needs help."

A pleased look crossed his face. "I hear you're goot with such things—amazing in fact."

"Oh, I'm just helping."

He obviously wasn't convinced. "So, how are things going for Esther and Jesse? Are they settled in with married life?"

"Yah. Certainly! They are very happy. Jesse and Esther."

"Marriage does bring happiness," he said. "The blessing of the Lord. How long since the wedding?"

"Four months or so. Not so long."

"Seems like a long time since I had the privilege of eating supper with you." He shifted on his feet.

Rose ignored the compliment to look across the field. "How's the farm work going?"

His face darkened. "We should finish today, I hope."

"Are you plowing?"

The darkness furrowed his brow. "Yah."

"I didn't mean to imply—"

"It's okay." He winced. "Daett has his ways, and we did have quite a few problems with the equipment this spring."

"Things happen." She offered.

"You might as well know," he said. "They happen quite often around here, but I'm not like Daett. More like Grandpa Beiler."

"Is he a goot farmer?"

"You haven't heard?" Robert looked disappointed.

"I—I mean. I'm sure you're a great farmer, and you're Daett doubtless has his goot and bad days, like everyone else."

"I suppose so." He stared down the empty road. "The new county extension agent was by the other day. A young fellow who moved into the area. Full of new English ideas, he is. I like them though. He thinks we should try a new hybrid corn seed on our farms. He claims the seed companies offer something much better suited for the prairie."

"Conrad Wisner?" She whispered the name.

He appeared startled. "You know the man?"

Rose could feel the heat rush into her face. "He rents from Jesse and Esther." The awful truth must never be told.

His face sitting so close to her at the breakfast table, her heart thumping in her throat.

"He must be a nice neighbor," Robert said.

"I think he is." Rose tried to still the racing of her heart. "Will you be implementing these new English ideas?"

"Perhaps when I have my own place. Daett doesn't think change is goot—at least, not too quickly."

"I'm sorry." She managed.

"Has Conrad been to your place?"

Rose tried to breathe. She couldn't lie. "He stopped by this morning. Edwin spoke with him at length after breakfast."

"Out early, I see. I do like the man."

"Sunday evening will be okay for our date." Rose blurted out the words. "If you still wish."

He was staring. "You're accepting?"

She forced a smile. "We have waited awhile."

He looked choked for a moment. "Of course. I'm more than willing. Sunday night then."

She nodded.

He was staring, saying nothing when Rose bolted toward the buggy and climbed in. She shook the reins and Brownie leaped forward. She leaned out of the buggy for a quick wave. Robert stood by the fence row, his face turned toward her. For a moment Rose saw Conrad's face flicker in the distance and quickly squelched the vision. Conrad was history. She would soon be the proper wife of an Amish man. This foolishness must stop.

Moments later, Rose turned into Esther's driveway and came to halt by the hitching post. She tried to still her breathing before she climbed out of the buggy.

Esther was hurrying out of the barn when Rose reached the ground. "What was that little stop about?"

Rose turned to face her. "I wanted to speak with Robert."

"Speak with Robert?"

"I accepted his offer of a date on Sunday night."

"On the spur of the moment?" Esther didn't sound happy.

"He had asked earlier, and this was a goot chance to respond."

Esther came to stand beside Brownie's head. "What's wrong. You're usually not this impulsive."

"Impulsive! I've been trying to make my mind up for months."

"And this morning lightning struck?" Esther sounded sarcastic.

"You're supposed to be on my side."

"I didn't know there were sides."

Rose waved her hand about. "Conrad Wisner, and—I need to work in your garden. Desperately! Calm myself."

"Why did you accept Robert's date offer this morning?" Esther persisted.

"Because I had to, if I wished to retain my sanity ... and my reputation."

"You're talking in circles."

"Okay. I'll be plain speaking. My face this morning—if you didn't notice, while I was around him."

Esther shrugged. "I noticed, but—"

"There are no ifs, ands, or buts about the matter." Rose jerked a tug off the wooden single tree. "I'm losing my mind. I need to settle down before I seriously offend the Lord."

"How are you offending the Lord?" Esther stayed rooted in place.

"I'm not going to tell you."

"Yah, you are." Esther came closer.

"Okay." Rose hid her blushing face. "I feel something awful for the man."

"This is love?" Esther mused. "I was wondering on the way over, thinking about the way you reacted this morning."

"We will speak no more about this!" Rose ordered.

Esther ignored her. "Falling in love is of the Lord."

Rose faced her sister. "Conrad Wisner isn't love."

"You act like you're in love."

"With an English man!" Rose waved her arms about.

"Listen to yourself!" Esther retorted. "Ranting and raving."

"I know." Rose took several deep breaths. "I'll be okay."
Esther didn't look convinced.

"Are you objecting to me dating Robert?"

Esther wrinkled her face. "You can date whomever you wish, but if someone else has captured your heart? This does present a problem."

"If this is love, you know how the last one went," Rose whispered, feeling the blood leave her face. "This one will be worse. Ruin, not sorrow. Esther, think!"

"I *am* thinking." Esther replied. "Remember the man lives right over there."

Rose refrained from turning her head. She had forgotten Conrad rented from her sister. Thankfully the man was out working and hopefully hundreds of miles away.

"He's thinking of joining the community," Esther said.

The world spun before Rose's eyes. "He told you this?"

"No," Esther said. "I just think so."

"See," Rose said. "I will have no more fantasies. Not in you or in me."

"Seeing Conrad Wisner this morning was the reason you spoke with Robert on the way over." Esther stated more than asked.

"I want nothing to do with an English man." Rose shot back. "Help me here."

"Okay." Esther smile was strained. "Sorry for interfering. My garden awaits us. The Lord knows I need help."

They unhitched Brownie from the buggy while Esther chattered cheerfully away. "Jesse will thank you personally for coming today. When I didn't get the seed in the ground last week, I think the poor man had visions of bare shelves in the basement this winter."

"You exaggerate!" Rose declared. "Jesse sees you and nothing else."

Esther looked troubled. "Sorry. I can't leave the subject. I can't stand to see you throw away love!"

Rose stood firm. "I accepted Robert's offer of a date, and I'll not go back."

"There's time until you say the wedding vows to change your mind." Esther muttered.

Rose could feel her hands grow cold. Esther was right, and she didn't trust herself.

"Give yourself some time," Esther said.

Rose gathered herself together. "Conrad is an English man, and he will always be an English man. You know what the Lord thought about my feelings for Wilmer. My foolishness will not lead me astray again."

"What you had with Wilmer was a beautiful thing," Esther said. "You're making a mistake with Robert."

"I don't think so," Rose said, and silence fell between them. They finished unhitching to take Brownie into the barn and left the horse munching on a bale of hay. On the way out, Esther gathered up her gardening tools, while Rose retrieved the string and stakes from the back of her buggy. With quick steps, they approached the garden site, and surveyed the ground.

"Okay. Where shall we start?" Esther asked no one in particular.

"In which direction do you want the rows laid out? Rose responded.

Esther squinted into the bright sunlight for a moment. "How about running them parallel with the house. Jesse would like that, and I want a huge garden."

"Sound great to me," Rose said. "Off we go."

Working beside her, Esther said nothing more about Conrad or Wilmer or of love.

CHAPTER 6

Several miles away as the crow flies, Robert pushed his hat back on his head when he came to the end of the field and called loudly to his team. "Whoa, there." They paused and stood with heads hung low. He let them rest, while his thoughts raced. Had he just achieved success? The thought took his breath away. Rose had said yah. The risk had been worth taking. He had been right to wait. He was going to take Rose home for a Sunday evening date. He was not like Daett. He was like Grandpa Beiler.

Robert ran his callused hand over his face. A new world was opening right before him. He could feel the certainty with the same strength he felt a few hours ago, knowing Rose would accept his offer of a date. Marriage with Rose lay on the horizon—the not-so-distant horizon.

"Thank you, Lord," he said out loud to the heavens. His team looked over their shoulder, obviously uncertain of his command.

"Let's go," he called out. "We have to get the plowing done before this evening."

CHAPTER 7

Rose and Esther worked side-by-side, running strings from one end of the garden plot to the other, digging the furrows with their hoes, and covering the seeds. By lunch time, half of the area had been seeded, with stakes left at the end of the rows to mark their progress.

Esther straightened her back. "Don't you think it's time we eat."

"Sounds goot to me." Rose studied her sister's figure for a moment.

"What?" Esther asked.

"Are you—?"

This time Esther blushed deeply. "I wondered if you'd notice."

"Does Mamm know?"

Esther shook her head.

"When's the due date?"

"Late October, from my calculations. I haven't met with the midwife yet." Esther hugged herself. "I'm so praying for a boy. Jesse wants a boy, even if he claims otherwise."

"This is wunderbah!" Rose exclaimed. "And I'm the first of the family to know."

Esther reached over to squeeze Rose's arm. "We're sisters. I'm so glad you know—and first, but come, we need food."

Rose made a face. "Desperately, I would say."

Esther laughed. "You can say that again. Let's go."

Rose followed her sister into Esther's small kitchen, where they prepared sandwiches. Sitting across from each other, they ate in silence.

"What are you thinking?" Esther finally asked.

"You and the baby, for one. I can hardly imagine this is happening."

"We should think about you," Esther said.

"There's nothing to think about. I'm seeing Robert on Sunday evening."

"You know what's going to happen."

"What?"

"Robert will want a wedding this fall. You're both older, and he's been itching to buy his own farm."

"So."

Esther made a face. "I wish Conrad had shown up earlier."

"Stop this!" Rose ordered. "Conrad is a temptation. I should have accepted Robert's offer a long time ago. This morning was the Lord's warning to me, showing me the weakness of my own heart."

"I wish you wouldn't settle," Esther said. "Not after waiting so long."

"You know I wasn't waiting for—"

Esther nodded. "I understand, but I was convinced you could fall in love again, even if you weren't."

"I don't think so," Rose said. "Not with an Amish man at least, and Conrad is English. You know I can't go there."

"I want the best for you. Like I have the best." Esther smiled. "I really do."

"I know. You're very kind to me, but on this one thing you're wrong."

Esther reached over to touch Rose's arm "Let's say no more about this for today, okay. To a splendid date on Sunday evening with Robert Schlabach."

"And to a healthy man child this October." Rose returned. Esther would have to accept things the way she had to accept things.

"May the Lord's will be done," Esther said.

"Amen." Rose stood to walk over to the kitchen sink, where she startled, staring silently down the road.

Esther's footsteps rushed to her side. "What?"

Rose pointed with one hand, unable to speak.

"Conrad." Esther sounded quite pleased. "He's home early."

"He's coming into your driveway." Rose croaked.

"Maybe he could see we were working on the garden and wants to help. What an amazing man."

"Wants to help us!" Rose felt dizzy, the walls spinning slowly toward the ceiling. "He can't help us."

"He tilled the ground, but I bought the seeds, Esther said. "He probably thinks he owes me a little more for his share of the produce."

"But, he's—" Rose faltered. "You don't really—I mean—working in the garden with us."

"He's perfectly harmless."

"You know what I mean." Rose retorted.

"You'll be okay. Come." Esther ordered. "The Lord must be working things out in his own way, so let's not complain."

"Complain." The walls were still spinning. "I can't go out there."

Esther took Rose by the arm and headed toward the door. "Follow my lead and you'll be okay.

"I—" Rose tried to protest, but the words died in her mouth.

CHAPTER 8

Conrad paused a moment to look over the garden progress before he hopped out of his pickup truck. There was no one in sight, but he was impressed. Nothing had been done last night, and now half of the garden was filled with furrows and clearly marked stakes. He had stopped back in at the Miller's place an hour ago to drop off a packet of information, and Edwin had volunteered the information. Rose had gone over to help Esther with her garden.

"Sounds like you might have something to eat this winter after all," Edwin had teased with a chuckle.

Conrad had made his mind up on the spot to offer his services but hadn't informed Edwin. The man would hardly have detected an interest—an untoward interest in his sister from the Amish point of view. He didn't want to take chances, but maybe he was pushing the edge again. He couldn't help himself. The woman drew him powerfully. What he would do about her sister Esther, he didn't know. Their relationship had been cordial up to this point. He didn't want to disrupt anything or break any proper norms. He would play things low key. There could be nothing wrong with offering his help with a garden in which he would be the beneficiary of the produce. From what he knew of Esther and Jesse they were logical people who would see his motive, if any questions arose. Rose on the other hand? Would she object to his presence? He didn't know. Leaving would be the easy solution, with one excuse or the other. With a clear rejection from this Amish girl, he could go on with his life and know with certainty this unexpected road held nothing but a dead end.

He looked up when the two women appeared on the front porch. A twinge of doubt filled him again. Where was he taking this situation? This girl was from another world.

"Howdy." Esther called out. "Have you come to help?" Her face was beaming.

His fears dimmed, overcome by the peace which crept into his heart. "If I may," he replied, closing the pickup door. How could his interest in Rose be wrong?

A stab of fear returned when he saw Esther glaring at him.

"You know my garden secrets," Esther hollered, "but you're still a welcome sight."

Relief flooded him. "Are you putting the seeds in without crushing them?" He teased.

"The nerve of the man!" Esther sputtered.

Rose was looking away, he noticed, and appeared quite disturbed. Doubt niggled again. He forced himself to chuckle. "You know I trust Amish women, with or without the green thumb."

Esther placed her hands on her hips. "Are you really going to help us?"

"I think so." He glanced at Rose.

"Then we accept," Esther said. "Right, Rose?"

The sister didn't say anything other than give a quick nod.

He motioned toward the garden with his chin. "Things are going quite well so far from what I can see."

Esther tilted her head. "The seeds haven't sprouted. If that's what you mean."

He laughed. "You have nice, neat rows at least, and you're over half done. I see nothing wrong."

Esther appeared mollified. "Okay, but Rose is the expert in gardening. Remember?"

44

"I know." He tried smiling to Rose. "What shall I do to help?" He wished the girl would respond, but she didn't.

Esther handed him a hoe. "You can put in the rows, after we have run up the strings."

"I think I can handle strings and row." He followed them to the garden, where Rose busied herself driving a stake into the ground. He gathered up a ball of string along with his courage and moved over to wait beside her. If Rose showed any signs of discomfort, he would leave her alone. He promised himself. "Done?" he asked when she looked up.

"I think its deep enough." Rose wiggled the stake with her hand. He was certain a faint blush colored her ears. Was she rejecting or appreciating his presence?

"Can I tie the string?" he asked. She didn't answer but stepped aside. Conrad tied the string securely with a slip knot and glanced up at her. "Approve?"

"It looks goot," she said.

She was definitely blushing but avoiding his gaze. "Good enough to make the garden grow?"

"Strings have nothing to do with a garden growing," she muttered, "but you know they don't."

"Maybe it's a magic string?"

"Do you believe in magic strings?" Alarm filled her face.

He met her gaze. "I was teasing."

"Oh." She looked away, her face flaming.

"Where did you learn your gardening skills?" he asked, trying to distract her.

"I—I guess I—" Her flustered look increased. "Maybe from Grandma?"

"Was your grandma a gardener of great renown?"

"I don't know. They live in Lancaster County, but Mamm said once, in a passing sort of, why I was goot with a garden. Not like Grandma, just sort of like—" Her face had lost some of its color.

"You're a humble people." He observed.

"I don't know," she said. "We try to remember our place under God. He made us from the dust of the ground."

"We're creatures with great failing." He agreed. The memory of gunfire filled his ears.

"You understand then?" She was looking at him.

"I was raised in a Christian home." He looked away.

"Did you fall from the faith?"

"Not really," he said. "I joined the army."

"Your faith approves of such things." The alarm was back.

"They do," he said. "I know things are brutal in war."

"Did you bring peace to their land?"

"A little," he said. "Maybe for a day or two."

"Our people choose to live in peace, with the Lord, and with each other, without war."

"I know." He forced a smile. "Perhaps yours is the better way."

"Perhaps," she said. "Peace with ourselves comes from being at peace with God and our fellow man, even our enemies."

"You may be right." He looked away again. "I should get busy."

"Of course. I'm sorry I distracted you with my questions."

"I think I was the one with the questions," he said, not waiting for an answer before moving off with the string in his hand. He passed Esther and asked out of the corner of his mouth. "How am I doing?"

"Rose approves," Esther said. "That's what counts when it comes to gardening."

He was certain he caught a deeper meaning. Esther must approve of his interest in her sister. A woman would notice what a man might miss. He paused at the end of the garden and waited until Rose caught up with him. "Did I run the string out straight?" he teased.

Her gaze remained fixed on the ground, her discomfort obviously back. "There is nothing about running out strings to approve or disapprove."

"Don't you like teasing?" he asked. She didn't respond, concentrating on pounding the stake. "Let me help." He knelt beside her.

Rose stepped backward and nearly fell.

"Sorry, I didn't mean to scare you."

"Here." She thrust the hammer toward him.

He gripped the stake with both hands. "You pound?"

She hesitated.

"Please." He tried his best begging voice.

"What if I hit your hand?"

"You won't," he said.

"I might."

"Amish women don't miss stakes."

"Are you teasing again?"

"Would I tease with my hands on the stake?"

"I guess not." She raised the hammer and came down hard.

He almost flinched. "Are you trying to scare me?"

"You said I wouldn't miss."

He kept his grip and the hammer fell again. "You're trying to scare me."

There was a hint of a smile on her face. "Maybe?"

"I'm not letting go." He warned.

The hammer fell again. "I think that's deep enough."

He let go with a sense of relief.

"Will you be holding the next one? she asked.

"I think I'll dig the row and let you pound the stakes."

He was certain Rose had a ghost of a smile on her face as she left for the far end of the garden.

Conrad watched her progress for a moment before he busied himself digging down the string line.

"Are things going okay?" Esther asked, when he passed her.

"I think so," he said, though he had not the slightest idea. What was progress in this world of the Amish? When he arrived at the end of the garden, Rose had already secured the next stake and moved on. She was avoiding him, but maybe she wasn't. Amish girls were modest creatures from what he could tell. He couldn't expect them to accept an outsider with open arms, especially one who might have a romantic interest. Was such a thing even possible for them? He pushed the questions from his mind and transferred the string to dig the next row. Rose kept ahead of him with the stake driving. He wished she would wait and speak to him, let him hold the stakes for her, but he had gone far enough for one day. The girl wanted him to leave her alone—now at least. He would respect her, but he would not forget her. He couldn't.

When the plot was full, he leaned on his hoe to catch his breath. Rose had joined her sister, conversing in their own tongue while they dropped the seeds in the last row.

"Worn out are we?" Esther called from halfway across the garden.

"I should have brought my tractor," he called back.

"You can't use a tractor for this." Esther waved toward the first row he had dug. "We are ready to have the seeds covered."

"I can cover them." Rose objected.

The girl did want him to leave.

"It's time for you to go home." Esther intervened. "Conrad will help me finish."

Rose's smile was strained. "Conrad—he surely has other work."

"I'm here for the day." He encouraged Rose's timid smile. "Thanks for the concern, though." She looked away.

"Are you going to help Rose with her horse and buggy?" Esther motioned vaguely toward the barn.

He startled. "As if I know anything about harnessing a horse to a buggy."

"Esther will help me!" Rose pronounced, and marched off without looking back.

Esther grimaced and followed her. Conrad covered two rows of seeds while the women brought the horse out of the barn and hitched him to the buggy. Conrad straightened his back and waved as Rose went out the driveway. She didn't respond, keeping her eyes straight ahead of her. There was his answer, Conrad told himself. Any connection he had felt with the girl was more imagination than reality. He should have known two such radically different worlds could not be combined into one.

"Got two rows done." He grinned sheepishly at Esther when she returned to the garden. "Have I earned my vegetables?"

"You have more than earned them!" Esther declared. "I can't thank you enough. We would not have finished today before Rose had to leave. I would have hated asking Jesse to help me tonight after he came in from the fields."

"Glad to help," he said, and prepared to continue with the work.

"You came for more reasons than helping with the garden." She deadpanned. "How did you know we were working on the garden."

He paused, his hoe halfway in the air. "Your brother. I took some info back for him. Sorry for being so obvious. You can tell your sister I meant no harm."

Esther didn't move. "You think Rose isn't feeling what you're feeling?"

"I don't know," he said. "I mean, I understand the strangeness, shall we say, of the attraction I feel for her. I'm not from your world, but I do have feelings—"

"You don't have to explain." Esther interrupted. "I'm on your side."

"Which means?"

"For now, I am." Esther gave him a bright smile. "All I can say is, don't give up hope. I think the Lord is at work."

"You do." He contemplated the thought.

"You're Christian, religious," she stated more than asked. "God works in our lives."

"I do believe," he said, "but this—"

"Is beyond belief." Esther finished for him.

"Maybe." He nodded quickly. "A fair summary, I think."

"You're a man worthy of my sister." She deadpanned again.

He raised his eyebrows. "What a compliment coming from you—from another world."

"My sister can't leave the community." She was intently gazing at him.

He looked away. "I expected as much, but we aren't even close to such a decision. You saw your sister leave. She—"

"My sister is running away from her feelings for you. She accepted a date this morning from an Amish man she doesn't love."

"Oh," he said. These people's openness and honestly was a little disconcerting.

Esther was looking at him. "What I want to know. Are you wondering if an Amish girl is worth the journey?"

"Not really." He wacked at a clod of dirt with his hoe.

"Well, if you are, you should be thinking instead about whether love is worth the journey."

He looked up. "I hadn't expected to hear such words—"

"From an Amish woman." She finished. "Well, the world is full of surprises."

"Yes, it is." He agreed. "Shall we finish the garden?"

"We shall," she said, and took the row beside him.

CHAPTER 9

On Sunday evening, Robert's buggy took shape in the long line moving toward where Rose waited at the end of Deacon John's sidewalk. Rose clutched her shawl against the cool breeze which had sprung up since the young people had gathered before dusk had fallen for the evening hymn singing.

"Hope you have a good time." The girl standing beside her teased.

Rose pulled her shawl tighter. "I think I will." She forced out the words. How did Jane Mast know about her date with Robert?

"Robert's a decent man," Jane said, smiling. "Considered him myself before I started dating Danny, but Robert clearly had his eyes on you."

"Thanks for the compliment." Rose muttered.

"You'll make a nice couple." Jane was still smiling.

"I'm sure we will." The words sounded strained, as if she were lying.

Jane didn't seem to notice. "There he is now."

Robert's buggy came to a stop in front of Rose, and the door slid open.

"Good night." Rose tossed over her shoulder. She tried to sound cheerful, but a dread had wrapped itself around her heart.

"Goot evening." Robert's voice greeted her from the darkness as she climbed into the buggy seat.

"Goot evening." She managed, her voice a whisper.

"Was Jane Mast talking to you?" Robert sounded worried.

Rose kept her gaze straight ahead. "Yah."

"Did she—?" Robert seemed to search for words.

"I don't mind you telling Jane about our date." She was close to lying again. Something did bother her.

"Sorry, I couldn't help but share the goot news." Robert attempted a laugh.

"I'm okay." Rose settled into the buggy seat. She caught a glimpse of Robert's face as they passed the light from the kitchen window. The troubled look was still there.

"Got a little chilly after supper," she said, trying to put him at ease. "I should have brought my coat."

"Weather changes quickly this time of the year," he said, pulling back on the reins to check for traffic before pulling out on the highway and turning south. "Should we get the buggy blanket out?"

"My teeth aren't chattering." She attempted humor.

He didn't laugh. "The blanket is right under the seat."

"I'm fine. You'll have me home soon."

He shook the reins, as if to hurry his horse onward, but the creature plodded along at a steady trot.

"What's your horse's name?" she asked.

"Danny Boy."

"Is that the name you gave him?"

"Nah. He came with the name from the sale barn."

"Do you like him?" He still looked ill at ease.

"I'm getting a faster horse before long." He appeared to scowl in the darkness. "They're expensive, and a farm comes first."

"They are." Rose agreed. "I don't mind steady horses, and a farm is quite important."

"I thought you would agree." A pleased look crept across his face. "I have great news. We got a confirmation letter on Saturday. Finally! Mamm's parents are coming this week from Lancaster for a visit.

"Oh." Rose caught her breath. "Your Grandpa Beiler."

"The trip has been long talked about." He pulled back the reins for a stop at the intersection and glanced at her. "I'm so happy everything is happening at once. Grandpa will want to meet you."

Rose ignored the compliment.

He seemed to rise a few inches on the buggy seat. "Grandpa is one of the best farmers in Lancaster. You'll like him, and Mamm is having the extended family over for supper on Friday evening. I want you there to meet Grandpa. I want you to come for supper."

"Ah—they can meet me on Sunday," she said. "I mean—I'm—we're just—"

"Please Rose." He begged. "Grandpa is a very important person in our lives. I would like to have you attend the supper."

"I'll have to see." Her head was spinning.

"You mean you'll know after this evening?"

"No, Robert, I didn't mean to say—"

"I'm sure the Lord has opened the way for us." His voice was firm. "We have waited long, and we have prayed."

Rose gave in quickly. "It's not such a big deal, I guess. If you want me to attend, I'll come."

"Thank you." His chin came up, as the buggy bounced into the Miller's driveway.

They came to a stop by the barn, and Robert leaped out. Rose climbed down carefully so her feet didn't slip on the unfamiliar step. Without asking, she found the horse blanket under the seat, while Robert tied Danny Boy to the ring at the hitching post. He seemed lost in his thoughts when she walked forward with the blanket. Matter-of-factly he took one side, and they slipped the blanket over Danny Boy's neck tucking the ends down between the shafts.

"Shall we go into the house?"

He didn't answer, already headed across the lawn toward the dim glow of the kerosene lamp shining in the living room window.

CHAPTER 10

About the same time across the darken fields, Conrad Wisner sat with his legs under the small kitchen table in Esther and Jesse's kitchen. He licked the last of a large piece of strawberry pie from his fork and pushed back the empty plate. "Such food is fit for a king!"

Esther beamed at him. "I may not know how to plant a garden, but I can bake."

Jesse chuckled. "She's great with pies if not with a garden."

Esther slapped him playfully on the shoulder. "Careful now. You didn't ask about my gardening before you married me."

Jesse grinned. "I think your lack of gardening skills is mostly in your head."

"What do you think?" Esther turned toward Conrad.

Conrad made a face. "You expect me to get in the middle of this? Oh, no!"

"You'll learn how to grow a garden," Jesse said, quite confident. "If there is any truth to your claim of a lack. Otherwise, we starve in the winters."

"Now who's being dramatic?" Esther gave Jesse a fake glare.

Conrad lifted his hand. "Let me interrupt. I think from what I could tell the other day, you do know how to garden."

"Really?" Esther didn't look convinced.

"Certainly," he said. "You haven't made gardening your specialty, but rather other things."

"Exactly my point." Jesse put on a triumphant look. "The seeds will grow just fine."

"Because they were planted by Rose." Esther muttered.

"On the other hand, some people do have a green thumb." Conrad admitted.

Esther turned to him. "So, it's not in my head."

"Everyone can learn, that's my theory."

Jesse clapped his hands. "I agree, so let's not spoil a perfectly goot evening with worries about gardens not growing."

Esther scowled. "At least, I can make a decent strawberry pie."

"An excellent strawberry pie!" Conrad corrected her.

"I second Conrad's opinion," Jesse said. "Now enough on the subject. How are things going in the community for you?"

Conrad settled back in his chair before he answered. "The Amish farmers are quite receptive to the new ideas, it appears. The younger ones at least."

"Old people do drag their feet." Jesse shrugged. "Such things go without saying."

"I suppose so." Conrad allowed. "People are people."

"Another piece of pie." Esther pushed the half empty pie pan toward him. "I have another plate in the cupboard if need be."

"Another piece?" Conrad's mouth watered at the thought. "How I wish." He patted his stomach.

"Tonight we splurge!" Jesse declared. "Join me for another piece of Esther's amazing strawberry pie. Tomorrow we work hard in the fields."

"Well—" Conrad gave in. "Who can turn down such an offer, but tomorrow it's the treadmill for me."

"No jogging outdoors?" Jesse asked.

"Gym jogging. Not quite the same."

"You can run around my fields." Jesse offered.

"What a sight he would make." Esther attempted to hide her laugher behind her apron.

Conrad joined in while taking another large piece of pie. "This will be the death of me yet."

"Welcome to life with an Amish woman."

"Didn't say I dislike the idea." Conrad contemplated his plate. "Homemade strawberry pie. What a blessed existence indeed."

"The Lord leads in strange ways, even with strawberry pie." Esther joined in.

Conrad took a bite, savoring the sweet goodness, the vision of Rose's beautiful face dancing in front of his eyes.

CHAPTER 11

Over at the Miller's house, Rose searched the cupboard for the plate of brownies she had prepared on Saturday. Neither of her brother's would have dared devour the plate of goodies without permission from Mamm. Had she misplaced the dessert? Why was her mind not working?

She could hear Robert stirring on the couch, waiting for her return. He had marched into the house and sat down—with her trailing him the whole time. Maybe he had expected her to hurry and catch up with him? She couldn't bring herself to accept the indignity. Maybe he was nervous, but he didn't act nervous. If she had indeed lost the brownies, maybe a blessing in disguise had shown up. Robert would think her entirely incompetent as an Amish housewife and promptly leave. She wanted him to leave, which was a horrible thought to have—considering. What was wrong with her. If Conrad sat in the living room on the couch, she would have nothing but a fluttering happiness in her heart.

Rose steadied herself on the counter. This had to stop. The brownies were somewhere. She had not lost them. Mamm might have moved them to the pantry. Rose began to cross the kitchen floor but paused at the bright display of stars visible through the kitchen window. She hadn't noticed them before, which was strange. Star gazing was an instinct for her. Rose moved closer to the window from where she could see even more of the sky above her. The Milky Way swept across the ridge of the barn. Rose leaned over the sink but pulled back abruptly at the sound of Robert's footsteps behind her.

"What are you doing?" he asked from the kitchen doorway.

"The stars—" She faced him. "I just noticed they were out extra bright tonight. How beautiful they are."

"I guess so," he said, not moving any closer. "We drove home under the stars."

"You noticed?"

"The stars are out every night," he said. "The same way the sun shines even above the clouds."

"But they're so special on a dark night, so visible. Look!" She motioned toward the window. "The Milky Way seems tied to the barn ridge."

"I didn't know you were a dreamer," he said. He didn't sound happy.

"I'm not," Rose protested.

He shrugged. "They're nice tonight, but they're always nice, and they're just stars. I don't believe in making more out of things than the Lord has made of them."

Pain stabbed her, but Rose managed to speak clearly. "I guess being practical is goot."

"I think it is," he said. "Did you come into the kitchen for something."

"Yah!" Rose's head spun. "The brownies. They're somewhere."

He waited, watching her while she opened the pantry door. The plate sat there in plain sight. Maybe she was the one who had placed them in the pantry. She didn't know anymore who had done what or where was where. Rose handed him the plate.

"The whole plate?" he stared at the pile stacked high.

"I didn't mean you had to eat them all, just carry them into the living room. I have to get the milk and glasses."

Robert hesitated before disappearing. Was he opposed to helping in the kitchen? Neither of her brothers would have objected to carrying a plate of brownies to the living room, but maybe there were Amish men who did?

Rose rubbed her forehead. This was his first date—her first date. She wasn't acting normal either.

Rose poured the milk into the glasses, after retrieving the pitcher from the refrigerator, spilling several drops on the table. She tried to calm herself, before grabbing a dishcloth from the drawer and wiping up the mess. Robert was waiting with the plate of brownies beside him when she walked into the living room.

"I, I—" Rose gave up and handed him a glass of milk.

He promptly took a bite of brownie and a large swallow of milk. "Perfect," he said. He seemed pleased.

Rose forced herself to sit beside him. Robert didn't offer her a brownie. Maybe she was supposed to lean across him and grab one. She couldn't make herself move. Robert started on his second brownie.

"When is your Grandpa arriving this week?" she managed to ask. Her throat was so dry, her lips stuck together. A swallow of milk helped while Robert finished his brownie in silence.

"Wednesday," he finally said. "Grandpa Beiler is a great success story. He ran a prosperous cabinet business in Lancaster for many years, but Grandpa is a farmer first. He owned two farms by the time he retired. He's active in the community back home and quite interested in how we're doing out here on the prairie. I hope to make a great impression."

Rose managed to smile. "So, the Schlabach family is about to have their place inspected?"

Robert grimaced. "I think we can pass the test, even if we don't come up to Lancaster standards with the way Daett does things. I plan to fix up the place a little before Wednesday."

"Your grandpa shouldn't compare your product with what the farms produce in Lancaster. There is the soil difference for one. Lancaster's dirt is black and very productive."

"You're right," he agreed, looking cheerfully at her. "You'll make a farmer's wife indeed. I hope Grandpa will know how to make the comparison. If not, maybe you can inform him. He would be impressed."

Rose ignored the compliment. "What do you hope will happen with your Grandpa's approval? More relatives moving in from Lancaster?"

Robert took another brownie. "Maybe? There has been some talk."

"Maybe I should reconsider my decision to show up for Friday evening, with your Grandpa's high standards?"

Robert grinned. "You're the one area in which I have no fears. You'll impress Grandpa."

"May I have a brownie?" Rose changed the subject.

Robert appeared perplexed for a moment, before he passed the plate. "An idea occurred to me yesterday," he said, "but I wasn't planning on bringing this up so soon in the evening."

"I'm not prying." Rose assured him.

"I want to tell you," he said, "since we're now—" He smiled, gazing at his glass of milk. "A wunderbah day has come for me indeed."

Rose waited, an uneaten brownie in her hand.

"While Grandpa is here," Robert continued. "I hope to ask him if he would consider extending me a loan to purchase my own place. Of course, he must be impressed with what I'm doing, which I think he will be. Especially once he meets you."

"I'm sure things will go well." Rose rushed out the words. "Your grandpa sounds like a generous man."

He nodded, his face hopeful. "Grandpa is a goot businessman, but I think I have a fighting chance with you on my side. I can't see how he could think ill of you."

"Another brownie?" She offered.

"I think I will." He took one from the plate. "I think the Lord has set me in a very goot place."

Rose didn't look at him. "Is this really why you want me there on Friday evening? To impress your Grandpa?"

He didn't flinch. "I want you with me for my own reasons, of course. But Grandpa? Yah! You will help my case. I need you, Rose. A wife is there to bless the life of her husband. I hope you are not offended with how the Lord made things."

"I'm not offended, just—I don't know. Disappointed maybe. I had hoped the two of us could have a little more time, to perhaps get adjusted before we became a settled thing."

He seemed not to hear. "Do you think I can come up to Lancaster County standards if I have my own farm?"

Rose clung to the edge of the couch to steady herself. "I'm not personally familiar with Lancaster farming standards, but I think you could run a decent farm on your own."

He nodded. "I suppose you do, or you wouldn't have consented to a future with me."

Rose stood. Did the man already consider them an engaged couple? Had she given him cause to think so. "I'm going to the kitchen. Can I get you something?"

"Maybe a glass of water," he said.

Rose fled and ended up in front of the kitchen window. She lifted her face to the starry heavens and pressed back the tears. Was she a dreamer, an idealist? Had she been one these long years and lived in ignorance? Mamm thought Robert was a decent man. The whole community did, and Robert was named after his very successful Grandpa. Who was she to judge the man? Had not her own imaginations led down a very dangerous path? Attraction to an English man. Rose pulled her gaze away from the heavens, filled a glass with water, and returned to the living room.

Robert took the glass without looking at her. "I'm quite thrilled this is settled. I knew the Lord was answering my prayers even before you stopped by the other day when I was plowing in the field."

She ducked her head. "I'm glad you're happy."

His gaze drifted to the living room window. "Just think, if Grandpa can be persuaded, if he believes farming is profitable on the prairie, what that will mean not only for us but for the community. With Grandpa's blessing everyone will feel a great confidence in our future here."

"I didn't know the community had doubts."

"Grandpa is such a successful businessman," he said.

Rose tried again. "I think you will do very well with a farm purchase. From what I know, none of the farmers in our community are losing money. I don't think your Daett is. I know my Daett isn't."

Robert's brow creased. "We're breaking even, I think, but I imagine the others could also do better. This new county extension agent's help arrived just in time. Grandpa will have another reason to have confidence in us."

Rose forced the words out. "Esther and Jesse think the world of Conrad."

He looked very pleased. "This is the Lord's leading. There is his timing in everything."

She turned away less he see the creeping redness in her face. "Our people do read the Lord's hand in the flow of daily events."

"What a brilliant idea!" He exclaimed. "I could invite Conrad for supper on Friday night. Introduce him to a real Lancaster Amish farmer. Grandpa would be doubly impressed."

Rose caught her breath. "Conrad? At your house for supper? Surely he wouldn't come."

"Of course, he would. Conrad is quite interested in helping the Amish. I could tell him my reasons, and you have met him."

"I have." She managed.

"See," he said. "You must know why everyone thinks so highly of him. Conrad is a blessing from the Lord to the community."

"I'm a gardener," she whispered, "not a farmer."

He laughed. "They're closely related. Why did you think I was certain you would be such a blessing on my farm?"

"Conrad plowed Esther's garden for a share of the garden produce." Rose heard herself say. Her mind wasn't working anymore.

"See." Robert's face lighted up. "Conrad is a man after our own hearts. He fits right into the community."

"He's an English man," Rose said, hearing the fear as if someone else were speaking.

"And a goot friend!" Robert declared. "I'm thankful the Lord has sent him to the community at this time."

"I, I—" Rose's voice gave out. She fled to the kitchen with Robert's empty glass of water and took her time with the refill.

Robert was smiling when Rose returned. "I hope I can fully express to you what this evening means to me. Our relationship has begun in the middle of many weighty matters, but I feel like our relationship was already ongoing during the long years we waited, like the Lord was working in our hearts, preparing us for this time."

Rose looked down at the hardwood floor. "I believe I failed in not giving you a favorable answer sooner."

"I agree," he said, "but you have come around to seeing your mistake, and I'm very happy."

Robert took another brownie, and silence fell between them, broken only by the creaking night sounds of the old house moving in the wind.

"What do you have planned for this week?" Rose finally asked. "Other than Friday evening."

Robert seemed to come out of his reverie with a start. "Cleaning out the barn tomorrow morning and fixing some of the barn siding, if there is time. I have to impress Grandpa, you know."

"Are you painting the boards?" Rose tried to smile.

"If the weather holds."

"Perhaps I should offer to help."

"We have plenty of help," he said and stood to his feet. "If you come on Friday evening, I'm happy, and I'll be seeing you again next Sunday evening?"

"If—yah, of course. I mean—"

His face fell. "I hope you're not hesitating again. Didn't you just admit your mistake?"

"I—yah, certainly—next Sunday evening."

He picked up his coat near the living room stove. "I have greatly enjoyed the evening."

"I—it has been—yah. We had our first date."

"The Lord has blessed us," he said. "I'll pick you up on Friday evening at 5:30."

Rose stood to follow him to the door. She stayed by the window until his buggy lights drove out of the lane, faded out of sight, and headed toward the west. The rising moon had climbed into the sky, obscuring the dimmest stars. Robert hadn't noticed. But why should he? Robert was right. Such things had little to do with real life. Gazing at the moon was a thing from her childhood which had to give way in the full light of womanhood. Look what temptations her silliness had already exposed. Conrad, the English man. How embarrassed she would be if Conrad even imagined that a decent Amish girl would—surely such a thought has not entered his mind in the presence of her blushing face. Rose dug her fingernails into her palms until the pain drew a sharp gasp of breath.

Rose pulled her gaze away from the horizon and walked away from the window. She would redeem herself on Friday evening with Conrad. She would show him how a decent Amish girl acted around an English man, smiling, decent, and distant. She took the stairs two steps at a time, and nearly dove into her bed to bury her face in the pillow while silent sobs racked her body.

CHAPTER 12

Across the fields, Conrad lingered on Esther and Jesse's front porch, where they had moved after the last of the strawberry pie had been eaten. Peace filled him, like he hadn't felt in years—not since he had been a child at home on his parents' ranch. Above him the stars bright enough to outshine the moon twinkled faintly through the fast-moving clouds, blown westward by the brisk wind. Seated across from him, Esther had a shawl drawn over her shoulders with Jesse on a chair pulled close to her.

"Shall I bring you a blanket?" Jesse offered Esther.

"I'm totally comfortable." Esther responded. "What a gorgeous evening this has been, and with such goot company."

"I'm very grateful for the invitation … and for the strawberry pie."

Esther gave Conrad a bright smile. "Next time, we will have you over for supper for a full meal—mashed potatoes, gravy, and a potloaf meat."

Jesse smacked his lips. "You won't want to miss such a meal."

"Couldn't pass up the offer," Conrad agreed, "but I can't become a bother."

"No bother." Esther assured him. "We can't have a bachelor starving next door."

"You cook or do store-bought food?" Jesse asked.

"Do I look like I cook?" Conrad patted his stomach.

"You do tonight." Jesse chuckled.

Conrad joined in their laugher. "After two large pieces of strawberry pie, I certainly do."

"I love this life," Esther said. "Time to sit on the front porch with friends and enjoy the stars. We're so blessed by the Lord."

"I must say, I agree," Conrad said. "You don't have electric conveniences, but you also don't have the negative things of modern life—radio, internet, or television."

"Keeps life simple." Jesse stated.

"It's a beautiful way to live." Esther gushed. "How many people still sit on the front porch with friends at this hour of the night."

"Or any hour," Conrad said. "I couldn't agree more."

"Our faith is an old faith." Jesse continued. "We cling to our faith because we wish to live close to nature and to God."

Conrad nodded soberly. "Do the two go together, you think?"

"We're not philosophical," Jesse replied, "but I suppose they do."

"You have your own schools." Conrad added. "I'm not sure where this enters the equation."

"Teaches us the basics." Esther spoke up. "We aren't the most educated people in the world, but we can read and write, think and work. Which, I think, is enough."

"Seems like the basics should do."

"Makes goot strawberry pie," Jesse said, and they laughed together.

"I like this life." Esther added. "I just do."

"I can't blame you." Conrad stood to his feet. "I have imposed enough on your kindness for one night."

"No rush." Jesse objected.

"Thank you for the evening and the excellent cuisine, Esther."

She made a face. "The pie was easy, now for the garden."

"We will look forward to a bountiful harvest," he said. "Good night."

"Good night," they called after him.

They were still sitting there when he glanced back, two dim forms outlined by the soft glow of the kerosene lamp in the living room window.

"What a life," he said to himself, "but a good life. A very good life. I wish I had gotten here sooner."

CHAPTER 13

On Friday evening, Rose waited at the end of the Miller's driveway for Robert's arrival. She heard his horse coming in the distance, the steady clip clop, sounding clear on the evening air. When Robert's buggy came into view, Danny Boy trotted along with its head held high, as if the horse shared his master's joy.

"You're seeing him again on Friday evening," Mamm had said in astonishment. "My plodding girl is finally laying herself into the traces."

"Do you object?" Rose asked. A momentary hope rising. If only Mamm would.

"Of course not!" Mamm exclaimed. "You should be wed to the man by now."

"I'm working on it," Rose had muttered.

"What's the occasion?"

"Robert's grandpa is visiting to inspect the farms in the area. More people might move in from Lancaster if he thinks well of the area."

"Grandpa Beiler comes to visit, and you're right in the middle of this." Mamm beamed. "I must say I'm impressed."

"I'll just be there," Rose demurred, but Mamm hadn't appeared convinced in the least.

Conrad would be in attendance. She couldn't get the man out of her mind. Esther hadn't helped with the account of their Sunday evening.

"He's such a fine man," Esther had gushed. "We had him over for strawberry pie on Sunday evening."

"The English man?" Mamm had raised her eyebrows.

Esther had rushed on. "He's lonely over there in his little house by himself. Aren't we supposed to be hospitable?"

"Seems like I'm hearing a lot about him," Mamm had said, looking like she wanted to say more.

"Daett had him in for breakfast." Esther declared. "We'll be inviting the man over soon for a full supper meal. Treat him to the best of Amish life."

Rose felt a cold sweat creep over her. She yanked her thoughts back to the present at the sound of Robert's voice.

"Whoa there," he called out, pulling Danny Boy to a stop in front of her.

Rose climbed in without looking at Robert and settled on the seat beside him. "Goot evening." She managed.

"Goot evening," he said, the reins dangling in his hands. "I'm impressed. You were waiting at the end of the lane."

"I thought I'd save you the trouble of driving in." She demurred, which wasn't quite the truth. She had wanted a few moments to prepare herself to face Conrad while standing in the fresh evening air, which obviously hadn't worked. Robert seemed pleased, though, and clucked to Danny Boy. They turned around in the road to head back the way he had come.

"Did you grandparents arrive safely?" she asked, more to make conversation than anything.

"I'm here," he declared.

"You might have come anyway." Rose tried to tease, but her humor was horrible compared to Conrad's light touch, which made the heart sing. She thrust her hand toward the buggy door in a desperate attempt to cast thoughts of Conrad out of her mind.

Robert looked strangely at her. "I was teasing. Did you just throw something out of the buggy?"

A piece of lint, Rose was tempted to say, but she couldn't lie on top of everything else she was doing wrong. "I see you survived the week," she said instead.

His puzzled look vanished into a laugh. "Yah, I did. Grandpa seemed quite impressed. I got a jump on things and had Conrad visit on Tuesday for a chat with Grandpa. They conversed like old friends, and Grandpa fully approves of Conrad's recommendations. Thinks we should follow every one of them to the T."

"Is Conrad still coming tonight?" Rose asked, feeling an awful, unwanted dread he might not be.

"Yep!" Robert said. "I expect the two will wrap up the details of their conversation." He jiggled the reins, but Danny Boy kept his steady plod down the road.

"It's a lovely evening," she said, trying to distract herself. Had she just felt what she did? A disappointment at the thought Conrad might not be coming. She should be feeling the exact opposite.

"A nice evening indeed," Robert agreed.

"We can be thankful," Rose hurried on, hoping her guilt wouldn't show on her face. "The weather could have turned bad, could be raining cats and dogs."

Robert shook his head. "The Lord has his hand on this whole project. He wouldn't bless us with rainy weather the week Grandpa is here."

"Grandpa Beiler is probably used to rainy weather."

"The Lord is blessing us," Robert insisted. "The good weather is a further sign."

Rose devotedly wished the dark clouds would gather and open their flood gates, but she pressed her lips together and said nothing.

Robert seemed lost in his own thoughts until they arrived, and Robert drove up to the barn door. "Grandpa should be out here somewhere," he said, looking around.

As if in response to his words, the barn door opened and Robert's Daett, Mose, came out followed by an elderly, white-bearded man with an exceeding jolly face.

"Grandpa Beiler," Rose whispered.

"He probably doesn't remember you, so make a good impression." Robert ordered. He climbed out of the buggy to make the introductions. "Rose, this is Grandpa Beiler."

Grandpa's smiling face approached the buggy door. "Goot to meet you, Rose. I've heard much about you."

"Don't believe half of what Robert says about me." Rose pretended to scold.

Everyone joined in the laughter, and Grandpa and Robert began to unhitch Danny Boy.

"How are you doing?" Mose asked, looking up at Rose still seated on the buggy seat. "I hope the evening isn't too overwhelming with the whole family here, plus the English man, the county extension agent."

"I'll be okay." Rose tried to smile and climbed out of the buggy. "I had best go into the house. See if there's anything I can do to help with the supper preparations.

"The women should be in the kitchen," Mose said, obviously approving of her decision.

Rose hurried across the yard. More buggies had begun to pull in the driveway with children peering out of the doors. She waved, and everyone waved back.

She entered the house without knocking and peered into the kitchen. "Goot evening." Robert's two youngest sisters, Phyllis and Jane, were working at the counter. They gave her bright smiles. Robert's Mamm, Edna, hurried over from the kitchen sink, followed by an elderly woman, who was obviously Grandma Beiler.

Edna greeted her with a quick hug. "What a joy to have you come tonight. I was so happy when Robert told me."

"Is this Rose?" Grandma Beiler asked.

Edna clucked her tongue. "I'm forgetting my manners. Yah, this is Rose."

"And you're Grandma Beiler." Rose offered her hand.

"Yah." Grandma Beiler was smiling broadly. "It's goot to meet you. I see Robert has done well for himself."

"Thank you," Rose said, wishing she could ignore the compliment. "Can I help with something?"

"We've got everything covered." Phyllis and Jane hollered together.

Grandma Beiler reached for Rose's arm. "Come. Take a chair. You're a visitor like we are. Chat with us."

"You know I'm not sitting." Rose retorted. "There is surely something I can do."

"A real working woman, I see." Grandma Beiler was clearly pleased.

"Rose is one of the hardest workers in the community." Edna assured Grandma. You should see her garden each summer. It's much better than mine, or anyone else's for that matter. She has the touch."

"What a garden this must be," Grandma Beiler said.

"Can we talk about something else?" Rose asked.

They laughed, and Phyllis and Nancy made room for her at the counter. Phyllis leaned toward Rose conspiratorially but whispered loud enough for the whole room to hear. "Robert is so happy."

"I don't think the poor man has slept since Sunday evening." Nancy added. "He's working day and night."

"That's because of his grandpa's arrival." Rose objected.

Nancy went right on, as if Rose hadn't spoken. "I declare the man hums a tune in his sleep. I hear him every time I walk past his bedroom."

"He has it worse than Mark and Lonnie ever did," Phyllis said.

"Stop it, girls," Edna chided.

"We're just teasing," they said together.

"It's okay." Rose collected herself. "I hope to have goot times with Robert on our Sunday evening dates." She wasn't lying. She did hope!

"Is your family from around here?" Grandma Beiler interrupted.

"They came from Lancaster, way back," Rose said. And from the look on Grandma's face, this was the hoped-for answer.

"You can help us with taking the silverware tray into the dining room," Edna offered.

"Thank you." Relieved for something to occupy her hands, Rose followed the two girls out of the kitchen.

CHAPTER 14

Fifteen minutes later, Conrad drove his pickup truck past the parked buggies and pulled into the barnyard ditch. He bounced to a stop and took a moment to look around before he climbed out. There was a group of bearded men with broad rimmed black hats gathered in front of the barn. Over half of them were looking in his direction. Had he done something wrong? Maybe he had parked in a designated buggy spot? The fact was unlikely. There weren't any fence posts in front of him or other fixtures on which to tie a horse, and most of the men had turned back toward the group to resume their conversations. The sight of an English vehicle pulling into an Amish gathering must have caused the consternation. Likely by now, everyone had been informed he was an invited guest or had recognized his truck. He had met most of the Amish farmers in the district, at least in passing.

From the looks of things, this was quite an extended family. A large number of buggies were parked in the yard, and a few were still on the road behind him. Maybe he had bitten off more than he could chew? This might not be the cozy, comfortable family gathering he had enjoyed with Jesse and Esther on Sunday evening.

Conrad pushed open the door of his pickup and stepped out. He had been invited, and the encounter couldn't hurt his relationship with the community. He had interests which reached both into his business and personal life.

A bearded man separated himself from the group as Conrad approached and offered his hand. "Goot evening. I'm Mark Schlabach, Robert's brother. I live at the other end of the community. You must be the new extension agent."

"I am." Conrad shook his hand.

"I heard many goot things about you. Glad to have you."

"Thanks." Conrad replied.

"This is my brother, Lonnie." Mark motioned behind him.

Conrad shook Lonnie's hand. "Good to meet you, sir."

"You're making quite a stir in the community." Lonnie grinned. "Heard you impressed Grandpa."

Conrad chuckled. "Don't know about me impressing your grandpa, but I was impressed with the man. Lancaster County has great farmers, which I knew. I guess they have to be with the price of land out there."

"Grandpa is quite impressive." Mark agreed. "He'd make goot out here on the prairie with our cheap farmland, I think. We're hoping so, at least."

Conrad nodded. "No objection there. The state is trying to stay up-to-date and help where we can."

"You're here for supper, I hear." Mark moved on.

"Yep! I'm not passing up Amish cooking."

Lonnie joined in the laughter. "There will be excellent eating, I'm sure."

The rest of the men came up to offer their handshake in greeting, including the elderly Schlabach. "Goot to see you back, son. Couldn't resist the Amish cooking, hah?"

Conrad slapped his stomach. "The memory of Amish strawberry pie from Sunday evening still rests comfortably in there somewhere."

Grandpa's face broke into a broad smile. "Glad to see you fitting right into the community. Speaks well for the state, having such quality employees."

"They try." Conrad replied.

"How about heading for the house!" Grandpa proclaimed. "This day has worked up quite an appetite."

Everyone joined in the laugher and headed up the sidewalks. A single buggy straggled into the driveway behind them and pulled up to the barn. Conrad almost offered to help unhitch but changed his mind. His actions might be interpreted as intrusive in this close-knit community.

Conrad followed the group instead. The comfort of the gathering crept over him, a feeling of home with a sense of belonging such as he hadn't felt in a long time. He could fit into this crowd without too many adjustments. He'd only have to add a beard, suspenders, and a basic knowledge of the German language. Conrad listened to the sound of their conversation. When they weren't speaking directly to him, their mother tongue flowed freely. The forgotten memories from the German classes he had taken in college, stirred in his mind. Vague phrases began to take shape, but the accent was unfamiliar.

These people stirred another longing in him, his desire for a wife. He had abandoned the search in college, halfhearted though the effort had been. None of the girls he dated seemed serious about marriage. Here, marriage was of the highest priority. You could feel the urgency in the air, the primordial instinct to match male and female, to take your place in the long line of human existence assigned and prepared for you.

Joining what they felt seemed natural to Conrad, like he had always wanted to find this place in life, to sit by hearth and home, to hear the sounds from house and barn rising and falling around him. They were nearing the front door, and the delicious smells of supper wafted over the porch railing, stealing past the closed front door. The crescendo of conversation seemed to increase.

"Can you understand anything we're saying?" Mark half-shouted in his ear.

"I had some German in college," he said, "but nothing matches exactly."

"This is Pennsylvania Dutch." Mark grinned. "A mangled dialect from the old country after the long centuries."

"I figured as much,"

"You're single, I take?" Mark asked. Doing another abrupt conversation change.

This must be a feature of the community, Conrad figured, or of German thought. He smiled and nodded. "I am."

Mark studied him for a moment. "Are you fleeing heartbreak?"

Conrad couldn't help but laugh. "No. I just haven't found the right girl."

"The pickings of decent girls out there are pretty slim, from what I hear." Mark appeared quite sober with his pronouncement, even saddened.

"For what you would be looking for, yes."

"What are you looking for?" Mark shot back.

Conrad shrugged. "I guess I stopped looking."

"Now, now!" Mark slapped him on the shoulder. "I see there is hope for you. The Lord made a man to love one woman, to give his heart to his family."

"I'm not disagreeing," Conrad said.

"Slim pickings out there," Mark said again.

"Maybe the community has one to spare for me." Conrad teased.

"I think all the good ones your age are taken."

Conrad made a face. "My lot in life, a day late and a dollar short."

Mark's hand came down hard on his shoulder again. "You're a good man, don't let anyone tell you otherwise."

They continued up the steps, and the smell of food washed over Conrad, along with the sight of Rose's face among the crowd of women. She wasn't looking at him. She was dating an Amish man, and he had no reason to lay a claim to her attentions. Yet, a smile from her direction would have seemed more precious than anything he had experienced in a long time. But she belonged to another man. The thought of that hurt all the way through him.

CHAPTER 15

Inside the house, Rose busied herself carrying plates of food from the kitchen to the large table set up in the dining room. Along the walls, smaller tables had been prepared for the children. Everyone would fit, Grandma Beiler had been declaring for the last half an hour.

"Some of the younger girls can eat in the kitchen," Robert's Mamm, Edna, had been saying just as often, "but I think everyone will fit."

A feeling of dread kept creeping over Rose, thinking about eating at the long dining room table with Conrad somewhere within sight. Likely close, as the unmarried young people usually ate together. She would not be included on the list of young girls potentially eating in the kitchen. Robert was eating at the dining room table, and she would have to sit beside him.

Would have to, Rose heard her own thoughts. Why was she thinking about *have to*, with her boyfriend? Maybe the meal would bring this awful dilemma to a head? Maybe Robert would notice her obvious attraction to Conrad and would terminate the relationship? Not in public, of course, but quietly before she left for home. What a relief she would feel. What freedom would come at first, but what awful condemnation would surely follow. Already her face was growing red at the thought of seeing the handsome Conrad seated so near to her. Her steadfast resolutions to forget the man had obviously come to naught.

Rose scurried back into the kitchen and forced herself to smile down at the little faces gathered around the table while the women worked. They smiled back but didn't speak. They didn't know her. This wasn't her usual family gathering. She was in unfamiliar waters in more ways than one, feeling like she didn't know herself since Conrad had appeared and Daett had invited him in for breakfast.

"Here's the silverware," someone said, and shoved the tray into her hands.

Sweat popped out on Rose's forehead. There was nothing she could do but return to the dining room. Keeping her gaze down, Rose exited the kitchen and laid out the silverware, distracting herself by leaning down to tousle a young boy's hair. "How are you this evening."

He peered up as if his hunger was self-evident.

"We'll have food soon," she told him, and forced her feet to move on down the dining room table.

"Goot evening," several of the men greeted her.

She had to look up to answer. "Goot evening." She forced a smile.

They knew she was Robert's girlfriend, and a sulking female was no credit to Robert. She couldn't hide in the kitchen for the entire evening or avoid the men. She had to get over her horrible crush for this English man.

With her head up, Rose couldn't help but see Conrad sitting in the far corner of the living room. He sent her a wave and a shy smile. Her face responded on its own. She smiled back and nearly dropped the last few pieces of silverware. With a great effort, Rose collected herself, laid out the last pieces, and dashed back to the kitchen.

"This isn't real." Rose muttered under her breath. "It just isn't real."

"There you are!" Phyllis exclaimed, right in Rose's face.

Rose flinched "I can take something."

Phyllis appeared puzzled but handed over the mashed potato bowl. The house had grown quite warm and might provide the justification for her burning face. Enough, at least, until she could control herself and avoid Phyllis for a moment, who had to have noticed. Pretty soon she would have to leave this family gathering in total disgrace.

Rose kept her gaze on the bowl, as she passed through the living room again. If she hit some man's shoulder and went flying across the hardwood floor, she would never live down the embarrassment, but a worse shame would occur if anyone found out about her feelings for Conrad.

Rose set down her bowl of mashed potatoes with a loud whack, the noise muffled in the crescendo of conversation filling the dining room. She retreated and caught her breath standing behind the hot stove. At least, here she was hidden from Conrad and Phyllis's view. There was more food to transfer, but there was no way she could run the gauntlet again. Rose circled the stove, pretending to tend the wood in the firebox. Phyllis and Nancy went past her repeatedly, but with the number of women in the house, no one asked for her help.

"The food is ready." Rose finally heard Edna announce in the kitchen doorway. The heat from the stove was about to overcome her, but at least her bright red face had a natural explanation.

"You're sitting beside Robert," Phyllis said in her ear, on the way to the dining room.

"Of course!" This she had expected.

"Right there." Phyllis motioned.

Rose moved in the direction Phyllis pointed. She was having problems staying on her feet, but she made it to the empty chair beside Robert.

"Howdy," he said. "Looks like you've been overworking yourself." He looked pleased.

"The hot stove," she muttered, and seated herself.

Out of the corner of her eye, Rose saw Conrad sit across the table from her on the right, with Robert's shoulder partially blocking the view. She pulled her head back.

"Things are going quite well with Grandpa," Robert whispered.

"I'm glad," she whispered back.

"Let's pray and give thanks for the food," Mose announced. "Would Grandpa please ask the blessing."

"Certainly!" Grandpa declared and began to pray as they bowed their heads. "Now unto our most gracious heavenly Father, we give thanks tonight, first for our safe trip out to Nebraska, and for the wunderbah days we have spent here. And for this evening with family and friends, we are most grateful. Bless the food prepared for us. Bless Mose's and Edna's home, and those who have gathered here. We give you thanks and praise your worthy name. Amen."

"Amen," several of the men echoed.

The food was passed—mashed potatoes and gravy, fried chicken in the pan, corn, green beans, and a tossed salad. The pies were still on the kitchen countertop and would be brought out later.

Robert piled his plate high and gave Rose a sideways grin. "I've worked hard this week."

"I'm glad everything has turned out okay." She kept her head hidden behind Robert's arm.

He heaved his shoulders back, as if a great load had been lifted from them. "Grandpa is going to help me."

Conrad was in full view. "With buying the farm?" she managed, growing lightheaded at the sight of Conrad's face.

"I'm encouraging myself." Robert muttered. "The conversation about the farm will come tomorrow, but Grandpa is quite impressed with you tonight. I can tell."

Rose ducked her head behind Robert and remained quiet. The effort wasn't fully rewarded. She still could see Conrad out of the corner of her eye. He wasn't paying her any attention, which was exactly how things should be. This was not Conrad's problem. He would be as horrified to find out her feelings for him. Doubtless the man had a girlfriend somewhere, maybe even marriage plans, as she did. They were ships passing in the night, and there was nothing anyone could do to change the situation. Conrad didn't want things to change. She didn't either. Not in her heart, or was it the other way around? Rose felt a prickle creep up her arms at the thought. Her heart would not betray her. The problem was her emotions and their unreliability.

"How are things in Lancaster?" Someone hollered across the table to Grandpa, and Rose jumped.

"Weather's nice." Grandpa replied. "Spring arrived early this year."

"There has been no rain." Robert bent close to say.

"I—yah—rain would have been—"

"Grandpa likes nice weather," Robert said. "Most old people do."

The effort to reply died away in Rose's mouth. Conrad had given her a kind smile. She was going to pass out right here in Robert's presence.

"What's your opinion of Nebraska by now?" Another man asked.

Grandpa paused with his spoon half lifted. "The country seems nice enough," he said. "I'm favorably impressed. Robert has been giving me the walk through since I arrived."

Rose tried to focus and to smile. They were speaking about Robert, her brain vaguely told her, and she must react positively.

"You can't trust Robert." Mark laughed. "He's highly prejudiced at the moment."

"You don't think I could fool Grandpa." Robert shot back.

"You could try." Mark retorted, to loud laughter.

"Robert hasn't pulled the wool pulled over my eyes." Grandpa replied. "You men have a hard row to hoe out here. I was expecting as much, but it looks like the Lord is providing. I got to speak with Conrad here on Tuesday, your local county extension agent. He has great ideas. I would encourage everyone to listen well and follow his advice."

"That's quite an endorsement," Lonnie said.

"Thank you." Conrad grinned, bobbing his head. "Thank you very much."

"It's a great endorsement." Robert agreed. "I hope everyone follows Grandpa's wisdom. I certainly plan to."

Grandpa laughed along with them. "Let me say, I wish you the best out here on the prairie. On my part, I will have a goot word to speak for the community once I get back to Lancaster."

"Could that mean more families moving into the area?" Mose asked.

"Perhaps. That's up to them," Grandpa said. "Maybe I'll come myself when I'm ready to retire."

This produced another round of laughter and more back slapping.

"You should be happy you're here to see this," Robert whispered into Rose's ear. "Everything is working out very well."

"I'm glad for you," Rose whispered back, thankfully she could speak in a clear voice.

Robert appeared happier than she had ever seen him.

CHAPTER 16

Conrad mingled in the crowd after the supper time concluded, and another prayer of thanks was offered. These people prayed a lot. Not that he objected, but the extent of his former spiritual life had been largely delegated to a Sunday morning church service. He didn't always attend even then and had been doing less and less since his tours in Iraq. He blamed his busyness, but the matter went deeper. The Amish had their spiritual and natural existence deeply entwined and were at peace with both. Life didn't seem to interfere with their devotion to God.

He heard footsteps and turned to see Grandpa Beiler approaching him.

"How're things going?" the older man asked. "You get plenty to eat?"

"Enough for the rest of the week, I think." Conrad slapped his stomach.

"I take it you're living a bachelor's life?"

"I am." Conrad admitted.

Grandpa looked very disapproving. "The Lord didn't make a man to live alone."

"Any suggestions?"

Grandpa chuckled. "The mysteries of the heart? I will leave them to the Lord, but you're doing the Lord's work out here on the prairie. No questions there."

"I'm trying, while pursuing my career."

"You never know where the Lord's hand appears." Grandpa said, quite soberly. "Don't keep any road off limits, regardless how strange the turn."

"I'll keep your advice in mind."

"We'll heading back to Lancaster next week. I'll keep you in our thoughts and prayers."

"I would be honored."

"The Lord cares for us, son. Always remember." Grandpa paused, looking off toward the darkened horizon.

"Thank you." Conrad offered.

"How long are you assigned to this county?"

"I think for a few years at least. We haven't discussed details."

"I hope to see you here when I visit again." Grandpa smiled up at him.

"I'll look forward to your return."

"You'll have to stay around for the cooking, if nothing else."

They laughed together, and Grandpa drifted into the crowd.

Conrad stepped outside. There was something strange about the old man's words, but he couldn't place the feeling. Almost as if an invitation had been given. But to what? Had the old man noticed his interest in Rose? Such an observation should have invoked a negative reaction, since the girl was obviously claimed by one of the community men. Conrad looked over his shoulder, pondering the situation. He caught a glimpse of Rose's face through the living room window standing underneath the gas lantern, with a small child in her arms. The distance and the low light brought out her beauty in ways he hadn't noticed before. She appeared angelic, with a haze of glory lingering around her face. He pulled his gaze away. Rose was dating an Amish man, and he didn't belong here except for an evening of food and conversation. He couldn't make his feet move, though. He felt a deep desire to linger, to stretch out this moment. Conrad studied Rose's face through the window. He could gaze unabashed at her since she couldn't see him standing outside in the shadows. As if Rose perceived his watchful gaze, she looked straight at him. There was a wistfulness in her eyes, a sadness even. Rose looked down at the child she was holding, and a smile crept across her face. The sadness didn't leave, though. Her sorrow was part of her beauty, he realized.

Conrad turned away. Rose couldn't see him, but he felt like an intruder. He shouldn't be where he was or see what he had seen. He had no right to think of an Amish woman other than as a friend. Appreciating her beauty might be appropriate for a moment, but he was crossing the boundaries of propriety. Yet no other girl had ever stirred this much hesitation in him, or interest at the same time. He felt like an alien, a product of the modern world who felt at home in the sixteenth century.

"Here you are!" Mark called out, and Conrad pulled his gaze away from the window. "I wondered if you had left."

"Just taking a few steps to settle the awesome food I've eaten." Conrad tried to chuckle. He stole a quick glance at the living room window where Rose's face was still visible.

Mark didn't appear to notice his interest. "Happy to have you here. What did you think of the evening?"

"Food was excellent, obviously. Who do I thank, by the way?"

Mark shrugged. "Mamm, I suppose, though she won't be expecting a special thanks. Food-making is a joint venture at a family gathering."

"I thought so." Conrad agreed. "If you would, pass on my thanks to the appropriate women."

"I will, and thanks for coming."

"A good night to you." Conrad nodded, and slipped into the darkness.

He climbed into his pickup truck and closed the door. His dome light blinked out. He was sure Rose's face was still framed in the living room window, but at this distance, there was only a blur.

"Stop it," he told himself. "You're not Amish, and even if you were, she's taken."

He turned the key to start the truck and drove off into the night.

CHAPTER 17

On Monday morning, the sky on the horizon was an explosion of red and orange. Robert noticed the colors through the barn window as the dozen cows the family milked mooed softly behind him. With his milk pail in hand, he walked over for a peek.

"Looks like the rain's finally coming," he muttered. "Grandpa isn't going to like this."

A foreboding gathered over his spirit, but he shook off the emotion. He was a practical man and not under the control of his feelings. What did a little rain matter? Grandpa was used to rain. The man had grown up with rain and had likely worked often in the rain. This moody feeling came from his time spent with Rose. He had known the girl could be sober, but not so—Robert searched for words. Dark maybe? More like impractical, with silly notions running through in her head about stars and moonlight.

He would have to guard himself against Rose's negative influence. He was a simple man, and Rose would have to learn to step down from her lofty, daydreaming heights. Opposites attract, he had often heard. Obviously, they did. Clearly, a beautiful girl like Rose could come with some not so beautiful problems. He should have settled for a more practical woman. He hadn't, though, caught up in his vision of Rose's loveliness. He hadn't been completely honest with himself. He was drawn to Rose for reasons other than her excellent reputation as a gardener. Maybe he should yet change course? Could he, though, with Grandpa here and his farm purchase nearly in hand? The practical girls in the community had married long ago, and he wasn't young anymore. He couldn't change course and wait years before he purchased his farm. He would have to finish what he had started. Rose was worth a little trouble. She was a lovely and dreamy woman but would have to change. Not the lovely part but the dreamy part.

Robert frowned and turned away from the window. Milk sloshed in his bucket as he dumped the contents into the strainer. No sense in getting caught up in an endless analysis of his state of being. Rose made him happy. He needed to think no more on the subject. Grandpa was here, and things were going well. Grandpa was looking at a farm with him today, and he was happy, rain or no rain.

The milk bucket clattered in Robert's hand. He was happy. He really was. Rose had served him cherry pie and homemade vanilla ice cream last night. The woman could cook, even if she was a dreamer. A man couldn't complain about a woman who was an excellent cook on top of being an excellent gardener. Life would take care of Rose's dreaminess.

"Where do you get ice cream on a Sunday evening," he had asked.

Rose had ducked her head. "We made some for the family yesterday evening, and I kept a little for you. Do you like ice cream?"

He had not answered, taking a big bite. "Is this a family tradition? Making ice cream on Saturday evening?"

"You wish," she had said, seeing right through him. What else did Rose know about him?

Visions of cherry pie topped with ice cream danced in Robert's head as he returned to his milking. Daett usually helped with the morning chores, but with company to entertain in the house, Phyllis was filling in for Daett, while Jane helped Mamm prepare breakfast.

"How are things going with you and Rose?" Phyllis asked, peering at him from her perch on a three-legged stool set beside a cow's udder.

"Okay," he said.

"I can tell you had a goot time last night."

"She served ice cream." He admitted. "Rose knows things are sealed up for us."

Phyllis laughed. "The bishop will be getting a visit from another blushing couple this fall, no doubt."

"Are you jealous?" he attempted to tease.

"I'm happy for you," Phyllis assured him.

"There are a few thorns," he muttered.

"With Rose?" she asked. Her puzzlement vanished before he could answer. "You mean with your farm purchase?"

He accepted the escape hatch. "Grandpa will help me, I'm sure."

"The Lord is certainly blessing you," she said, returning to her milking.

"There is a boy who would take you right now if you gave him encouragement," he said.

"Really." She feigned surprise.

"Take him, is my advice to you."

"My, are we being practical this morning." She scowled at him. "This from a boy who just snagged his dream girl."

"I feel practical." He shot back. "There's nothing wrong with being practical."

He situated himself on a three-legged stool, to stroke the cow's side gently, before setting down with the pail. The steady stroke of milk filling metal buckets echoed in the stillness of the barn. Robert's mind filled with visions of Rose's loveliness, all mixed up with ice cream and cheery pie.

"Where are you and Grandpa going today?" Phyllis interrupted his thoughts, standing in front of him with her bucket filled.

"How do you know we are going anywhere?" he asked, looking up.

"It's not a big secret," she said. "Grandpa talks."

"Then you know the answer," he grumbled.

"Do you have a farm in mind?" She sounded quite cheerful.

"I do. The place near Pawnee City, right off Route 50. The sign has been up for several months."

"How lovely," she said. "I've seen the place when I made trips into town for Mamm—the big house on the hill. Isn't the house a little much for a young couple?"

"Big houses can be filled quickly."

"Does Rose know of your plans?" Her eyes twinkled down at him.

"I told her we were looking at farms, but Grandpa and I can decide," he said.

He didn't want Rose involved with her dreamy thoughts. Not until he had heard and acted on Grandpa's practical ones.

"Did you tell Rose on Sunday evening, at least?" Phyllis insisted.

"I was eating ice cream," he snapped.

"I think Rose should be involved." She shifted her bucket to the other hand. "Just my two cents' worth."

"She won't care," he said. "Rose can fix up the house as she wants after the wedding."

"You're already promised to each other?" Phyllis gave a little gasp. "I thought things were going well, but so quickly?"

Robert said nothing, leaving the assumption unanswered. They were promised to each other in a way, even though the exact words hadn't been spoken.

"You should certainly show Rose the place then!" Phyllis declared.

"I will." He agreed.

"How did you get Rose to commit so quickly? Phyllis still hadn't moved.

"Perhaps with my charms?" He sent her a crooked grin.

Phyllis gave him a skeptical look. "You do have your charms."

"I could have gotten a girl much sooner," he said.

"I know." She gave him a smile. "You held out for the best girl."

"Thanks," he said, and bent his back to the milking.

She disappeared again behind the cow, and they finished the last of the milking before Phyllis left for the house. Robert opened the stanchions and shooed the mooing animals outside. Dawn had broken on the horizon with the darker red and orange replaced with flaming tentacles of light leaping skyward, as if they reached for the far horizon. He looked away. He was not going to let Rose's influence affect him. A glorious sunrise was just part of another day which the Lord had made.

He would have a farm soon with Rose as his wife by the fall. What man wouldn't be happy? Rose knew how to grow a garden and could stir up an awesome ice cream mix on Saturday night. Her dreaminess would be a minor problem.

CHAPTER 18

As dawn broke over at the Miller's house, Rose gathered the plate of eggs in her hands in the dim light of the kerosene lamp to carry them to the table. She returned to the stove and stirred the bowl of gravy warming on the burner. Breakfast preparations were almost complete, and the men would be in from the barn soon.

"So how was last night?" Mamm asked from across the kitchen.

"Okay, I guess." Rose tried to smile.

"I hope you're seeing him again." Mamm's tone was sharp.

Rose's head came up quickly. "Of course!"

Mamm appeared satisfied. "When is Robert's Grandpa leaving? I forgot to ask on Sunday."

"Later this week, I think."

"Robert didn't say last night?"

"He didn't say anything about his Grandpa other than their plans for this week," she managed.

"He must have forgotten." Mamm shrugged. "Men do forget."

"He liked the ice cream." Rose tried to sound cheerful.

She hoped Mamm didn't ask about Robert's plans. They were looking at farms, for a place where she was supposed to live. If the words were spoken out loud, she would break down in tears, and who knew what else would be said.

"Did something go wrong?" Mamm asked, appeared worried.

"Not really."

Mamm studied Rose for a moment. "I hope not. You finally settled on a man, so don't let doubts spring to your mind."

"I'm planning to hold course," Rose kept her voice resolute. "Robert's a decent man."

"I agree." Mamm moved over to the stove. "Another daughter settled down and raising her family will make me very happy."

A vision of Conrad's gentle eyes drifted through Rose's mind. She quickly changed the subject. "Esther said yesterday her garden things are up."

"What did you expect?" Mamm asked.

"I'm not great at everything," Rose muttered.

"I'm very happy you're settling down." Mamm's face glowed, seeming not to hear.

Rose took a deep breath. "I—I'm struggling sometimes, but—"

"There's nothing to fear," Mamm assured her. "Robert's a very decent man."

"Do you think he—?" Rose couldn't get the words out. Robert must love her, and Conrad wasn't available to her.

"Just take the man." Mamm gave Rose a sharp look. "Now we must get busy."

"I'll do the right thing," Rose said, setting the plates on the table.

"I know you will," Mamm comforted, "and thank you."

CHAPTER 19

Working in the Schlabach's barn, Robert took the empty milk buckets into the washroom and cleaned them with soap and cold water. He checked the temperature in the cooling vat before leaving the room. Taking a broom from the wall, he swept the floor from the dirt the cows had tracked in. Once he finished, Robert turned off the gas lanterns and exited the barn. Robert made his way up the walk to open the washroom door. The smells of breakfast poured in from the kitchen. He entered, cleaned up, and found Daett and Grandpa seated at the table, waiting.

"We were about ready to come looking for you," Grandpa teased.

"Just doing the last of the chores." Robert pulled out a chair and sat down.

"Did you see the sunrise?" Grandpa asked.

"I did," Robert replied.

"Gazing at it and thinking of Rose, no doubt?"

Robert grinned sheepishly. "Not really. I'm a practical person, though I was thinking of the ice cream she served on Sunday night."

Grandpa grinned. "Can't blame you for liking ice cream. I'm not surprised Rose makes amazing ice cream in addition to being an excellent gardener."

"She does," Robert agreed.

Grandpa reached over to slap him on the back. "Don't lose her now."

"I won't," Robert assured him.

Grandpa settled back in his chair. "Breakfast is ready, I believe."

"Certainly." Mamm set a large plate of pancakes on the table. "We have a special treat this morning."

"How about this?" Grandpa chuckled. "Pancakes."

"Let's eat then!" Daett declared, turning to Grandpa. "Would you ask the blessing?"

Grandpa bowed his head and began to pray, "Our gracious heavenly Father, we give you thanks again for the food prepared before us. Bless what we are about to eat and bless this house. Give us guidance as we venture forth to our day's duties. Give Robert wisdom as he thinks about buying a farm and of taking on the responsibilities of a new home and family. Bless Rose, grant them a happy courtship, and a goot life together—if this is your will."

Something in the sound of Grandpa's words made Robert start—*if this is your will*. Those were familiar words attached to petitions asked of the Lord for life's many choices but rarely associated with a dating couple. Marriage was a given, always in the Lord's will. Was there doubt in Grandpa's mind? Something Grandpa saw in his relationship with Rose?

"Amen." Grandpa concluded the prayer

Robert sat there, frozen, wondering what Grandpa could mean.

"Eggs?" Mamm asked in his ear.

Robert forced himself to move, taking several of the eggs before he passed the plate. He cleared his throat, "Grandpa."

"Yah." Grandpa's fork stopped halfway to his mouth.

"Do you doubt the Lord's will for Rose and myself?"

Grandpa finished his bite and chewed slowly. "One must always allow for the Lord's will, son."

"I agree," Robert said, though he didn't.

"Do you have worries?" Grandpa asked.

"I don't," Robert said, wishing he hadn't asked.

Grandpa looked ready to say more but joined in the light table conversation instead. Robert decided he was asking no further question on the subject. Surely, Grandpa had no objections to his marriage with Rose.

With the food eaten, the final prayer of thanks was offered. Everyone filed into the living room for a short time of devotions. Grandpa read from Daett's old German Bible, choosing a passage in the Old Testament, Micah chapter six. Roberts listened intently to the words, "He hath shewed thee, O man, what is good; and what doth the LORD require of thee, but to do justly, and to love mercy, and to walk humbly with thy God?"

"What convicting verses," Daett said, when Grandpa closed the book.

"Those are indeed words of wisdom." Grandpa agreed. "Men and women must seek to live right and do so with mercy toward others and humility before God."

"Amen." Daett echoed and they knelt for the final prayer.

The women left for the kitchen, and Robert headed for the barn, where he threw the harness on Danny Boy. Grandpa was waiting for him when he came out with the shafts lifted high while Robert swung Danny Boy underneath them.

"Remind me again," Grandpa said when they finished hitching up. "What time is the real estate agent meeting us?"

"At nine." Robert checked his watch fob. "In an hour or so."

Grandpa climbed into the buggy without answering.

"Do you want to go somewhere else first?" Robert asked, the worry from the kitchen table returning.

"Maybe a little sightseeing." Grandpa smiled. "Before or after the meeting with the realtor. Makes no difference to me."

Robert did the calculations in his head. "We have time before the meeting."

"Sounds great to me." Grandpa settled back into the buggy seat with a groan.

Robert climbed in and shook the reins. Danny Boy trotted out of the lane with his head up, as if he knew the importance of this day.

Grandpa motioned with his white beard toward the dark clouds that had begun to gather on the far horizon. "Hopefully we can beat the rain."

"I know." Robert's worry increased. "Either way, I do appreciate you coming along with me today. Even if we can't walk the entire farm, your advice will be greatly valued."

Grandpa chuckled. "Glad to, son. I'll tell you what I know, but I must say, you're doing fine from what I have observed. I'm encouraged to see such a fine new community develop and grow out here on the prairie. It would be nice if everyone could stay in Lancaster, but the Lord has his ways."

"Thanks," Robert muttered, some of his doubts disappearing. Grandpa wasn't saying anything further about their breakfast table conversation.

Danny Boy trotted along, the wind stirring in the trees as the buggy passed. Robert turned north, pointing out different farms and naming their Amish owners. Deacon John's place, Bishop Bontrager, Ezra Mullet, Henry Yoder, Emmett Stoll, and Jonas King.

Grandpa asked questions about the families who hadn't moved in from Lancaster. He soon made the connection to someone he knew and nodded as they drove along. Grandpa clearly approved of everything he saw. They crossed the rickety bridge near Table Rock and headed south. When they pulled into the driveway with the bright 'For Sale Sign', the realtor's car was waiting for them.

"Sorry I'm late." Robert offered in greeting.

The realtor checked his wristwatch. "Five minutes. Not bad for horse and buggy timing."

"I was showing Grandpa the community." Robert told him, climbing down to tie Danny Boy to the tree in the yard.

He made the introductions. There was no hitching post, but the problem would be remedied once he purchased the place.

"You from around here?" The realtor offered Grandpa his hand.

"Lancaster County," Grandpa said. "Most of the Amish fellows around here are from there."

"Nice farming country, I hear. Glad to have them and you."

"Just visiting." Grandpa told him, nodding toward the horizon. "Perhaps we had best see this land before the rains arrive."

"Certainly! Hop in the truck, and I'll take you around."

"You have a shovel on you?"

The realtor laughed. "I do. The first time an Amish man asked me the question, I was caught shorthanded. Now I know better."

Grandpa chuckled. "Not everyone checks the soil so closely, I suppose."

"They do not." The realtor assured them.

Robert climbed into the back of the truck for the bouncy ride into the first field. He liked the view from the road, but from here, the ground appeared even better. They halted, and Grandpa climbed out. Robert hopped down to dig in the dirt with the shovel.

Grandpa bent down to run his fingers through the ground. "Prairie dirt. There's no question, but the color is dark enough. With the help of your extension agent, you should be able to make the land produce."

The verdict was the same for the other three fields they checked. Robert knew he wanted the place, long before they got back to the house. The first drops of rain stung his face when he climbed down from the truck.

"Like it?" The realtor asked.

Robert nodded.

"You want to see the house?"

"The girl I'm marrying will like the house, and certainly we do."

"You sure?" the realtor asked. "I can give you a tour now and another one with her later."

"I'm—we're fine."

"Come on, let's see the inside," Grandpa said. "There's no harm in looking."

They laughed, and Robert followed the two toward the house. Before they arrived, the clouds opened. They ran the last few steps and huddled under the porch while the realtor unlocked the door. The house could be a shambles, but Robert wanted the place. Desperately! Deep down in his bones, he wanted to work the fields of this farm with a wife keeping the house. Any one girl would do, at the moment. He wished he had known this truth about himself sooner.

CHAPTER 20

In the meantime, Rose stepped out on the front porch of the Miller's home as the rain blew in from the north. She stretched out her hands past the roofline, and the cool drops ran down her fingertips. Rose soaked in the moment—the patter of rain on her skin, the feel of the dampness spreading up her arms, and the lash of the wind on her face. A moment later, Rose brought her hands back and wiped them dry on her apron. What was she doing? Daydreaming again! She had to stop. Robert didn't share her appreciation for these moments in life when the Lord seemed so close. When she wed the man, Robert wouldn't be pleased if he found her out on the front porch on a rainy day with wet hands and a moist face.

She should be thinking about sensible things today, like Robert's likely visit with his Grandpa to tour a farm he hoped to purchase, instead of reaching for raindrops falling on her fingertips. Rose gave her hands another quick wipe on her apron. Pain gripped her as she remembered those moments when she waited on the couch for Robert to invite her to tour at least one of the farms with them. Wasn't she proper in expecting an invitation? Robert clearly had plans to wed her, even if the words of promise had never been spoken. Grandpa Beiler would not have objected to her being in attendance and expressing her opinion about the house. She had only to remember Grandpa's kind eyes to know the answer.

Robert hadn't wanted her to go with him or thought to ask. Either way, the omission hurt. When did Robert plan to involve her? After he made the purchase of the farm? Maybe this was another way her dreaminess must go? Mamm probably never went to see a farm with Daett before their wedding day. She didn't dare ask Mamm, less she break down in tears. Robert and his grandpa were sensible men. They could make the right decision without her input. Once wed, her domain would be the house and the garden. She would keep the place spotless for Robert, fix his meals, and grow a garden unlike any she had yet grown. She wanted this life—a decent husband, a prosperous farm, and the hopes of a family as the Lord gave grace.

The tears finally came, a small trickle at first, until they poured down Rose's face. Memories of Wilmer came back. Those eyes, with such joy in his face, such life bubbling out of him. They were gone. Forever gone, which was another reason she had to move on. This dreaming must stop. Look where dreaming had gotten her—Conrad, a trap set from the past. Reasons she didn't wish to explain if Mamm caught her crying in the rain. If Mamm wouldn't be so horrified, she would make a full confession, speak the truth about these horrible thoughts which kept going through her mind, this wishing she could see Conrad on Sunday instead of Robert. Mamm's faith in her would be shattered if Mamm knew she wished Conrad was standing beside her this very moment, stretching out his hands to reach for the rain, as Wilmer certainly would have. Conrad's kind eyes would fill with laughter at the feel of water falling straight from heaven on his hands. She was certain Conrad would. Robert on the other hand planned to rip such things from her heart.

"He needs to," Rose whispered.

Robert didn't think life had any sorrows, except the ones her foolish dreaming brought him. The thought made the ache inside of her grow even worse. She wasn't in love with Robert. She was in love with the past. The thought felt like ice in her veins. This explained how she had fallen in love with Conrad. The man was a myth, as Wilmer had been a myth, a brief glimpse of a life which would never be hers. What had she done to bring such an awful banishment down on her head?

"I'll be better soon," she whispered into the lashing rain. "These feelings will soon go away."

Rose reentered the house to continue with the household work.

"Raining hard?" Mamm called from the bedroom.

"Pouring down," Rose croaked back.

Mamm said nothing, but Mamm knew her well enough to know things weren't right. She had to make them right ... and quickly.

CHAPTER 21

Later in the week, Conrad Wisner drove north out of Pawnee City on Highway 50 with no designation in mind. He had the liberty to move at random when the appointments grew slack. He liked this job. Joining his father on the family's huge spread in central Nebraska's Sand Hills, near Mullen, had been his intentions as a young boy, but he had changed his mind after Iraq. There was a restlessness left in his heart, which his former home could not calm down.

He called home once a month or so and spoke with his mother. He visited occasionally on weekends. His brief appearances usually left his father with a wistful look in his eyes. He had let the old man down, though they never had harsh words. Conrad's decision not to return and work on the family farm were his own to make. There was only silence from his parents, amid the sound lingering of gunfire and blowing sand.

He had doubts at times about his choice. His memories from childhood were sweet, as he supposed they were for most children. He held no bitterness against his parents, just a deadness when he thought of what was expected of him should he return—the relentless flow of the farming season, the endless open prairies, and the pressure of the Wisner family heritage. He had wanted those things once but didn't want them anymore. He wanted enough work to keep himself occupied, something new, something which wasn't what he had left behind. Here in Pawnee county, he had found peace in a corner of the Amish world which touched him deeply. Perhaps his zest for life would return? He had only to look into Rose's eyes to feel hope growing inside of him. He had been looking for the answer in all the wrong places, only to run into another dead end. Rose was taken, regardless of what Esther claimed. He couldn't interfere with a girl's dating relationship.

Conrad slowed his Ford pickup and made a right-hand turn onto a county road. In spite of Rose's status, he had told Esther the truth. The Amish soothed him in a way he couldn't explain. He did have thoughts of joining them. Not often, but the feeling was there. As if to demonstrate the point, a buggy appeared in front of him. Conrad slowed to pass, but once the man's bearded face came into view, he pulled to a stop.

"Conrad!" Amos Byler greeted him enthusiastically. "What a pleasant surprise. You seem to pop up everywhere."

"Just passing through," he said. "How are your cows doing?"

"You a veterinarian now?" Amos teased.

Conrad laughed. "I have my hands full."

"You are indeed a blessing to the community with your new ideas."

"The community has accepted me well, thank you."

Amos shrugged. "You're the county extension agent. You bring goot ideas which we agree with—soil conservation, seed types which fit the area, and a general knowledge of Nebraska which we Lancaster folks don't really have. Nothing like a man born in his own country."

"I do come from Mullen." Conrad reminded the man.

Amos only beamed. "From one of them big grain farms, I hear. You must have attained much of your knowledge growing up on your Daett's farm."

"I also went to the university."

"The university!" Amos scoffed. "That's book learning. You have something else, not unlike us. You grew up with your hands in the soil. No university can teach a man how to handle the ground."

Conrad grinned. "I suppose not. Are you off to town?"

Amos grimaced. "Broke both tips on my plow. Thought I had spares but can't find the things anywhere."

"You think Pawnee has the tips?"

"I was hoping and praying," Amos said.

"Praying won't help much at this point."

Amos chuckled. "I expect I was figuring too much for the Lord to manufacture them for me, but maybe I was praying for patience."

"Why don't I drive you into Beatrice." Conrad told him. "You may have to go as far as Lincoln for two tips."

"You would do this?" The surprise showed on Amos's face.

"What's an extension agent for, if not to help farmers."

"You are indeed sent from the Lord!" Amos proclaimed. "Let me drive old Maud back to my hitching post, and we will be on our way."

Conrad retreated to his truck while Amos turned his buggy around on the road. This wasn't exactly part of his job description, but he couldn't imagine his boss would object to a minor Amish public relation's outreach when the appointments were slack. The Amish were a closed community, and he had been fortunate to penetrate their reserve this far.

CHAPTER 22

At the Miller's house, Rose pressed the freshly made dough into the pie pan until every crevice was filled. With practiced ease she formed the creases on the rim of the plates. Across from her, a large bowl of pecan pie filling sat on the counter.

"Getting ready for Sunday?" Mamm stuck her head into the kitchen doorway to ask in a teasing tone.

"There'll be plenty for the family." Rose answered with a strained smile.

Concern flickered on Mamm's face. "Are you feeling better about your relationship with Robert?"

"I'm making pecan pie for him."

"You'll be okay," Mamm assured her. "A few more dates, and your feelings for him will grow by leaps and bounds."

"I'm hoping,"

She wasn't lying. She did hope.

Not daring to look at Mamm, Rose poured the gooey pecan goodness into the line of pie plates. Mamm was gone from the kitchen doorway when she finished and lifted her gaze.

With the oven door open, Rose centered the pie plates on the steel rack and closed the door. She walked over to the kitchen window to stare out at the lashing rain. Had there been time for Robert and his Grandpa to tour a farm? She should be happy they hadn't invited her along in this downpour. She would have been nothing but a bother for the men. Robert would tell her on Sunday if any choice had been made.

Rose turned away from the window as tears slipped down her cheeks. She was to blame for this situation. Her long wait before she had given Robert an answer had worked against her. If she had been dating the man since Robert had first made his request for a date, Robert would have been comfortable asking her to tour a farm with his grandpa. Rose had moved toward the stove when she heard a rattling of buggy wheels rising above the soft patter of the rain. Someone had pulled in the driveway. A quick glance through the kitchen window revealed Esther climbing out of the parked buggy.

Rose returned to the stove and checked the temperature before making a dash to the washroom for her coat. She was out the door and reached Esther's buggy before her sister had her horse out of the shafts.

"You shouldn't have come out in the rain!" Esther scolded, her raincoat tied under her chin.

"Neither should you," Rose shot back.

They looked at each other, breaking into laughter.

"Quack, quack, what a mess." Esther joked.

"Here. Let me take the horse into the barn." Rose reached for the bridle. "You're the one who shouldn't be out in this weather in your condition."

"I'm coming with you," Esther said stubbornly.

"You'll have Mamm worried when she sees the buggy." Rose warned. "You had best go inside while I put up the horse."

"I guess so." Esther gave in reluctantly.

Rose paused. "There isn't anything wrong? Like with the baby?"

"No, just morning sickness, which is dragging into the afternoon—at least, I think. Maybe I did come to check in with Mamm?"

"Here. Let me take the horse into the barn." Rose reached for the bridle.

"I'm coming with you," Esther said stubbornly.

"I'll be right behind you." Rose tugged on the horse's bridle. "Though I don't know what to do about morning sickness."

Esther didn't answer as she hurried toward the house, her head down in the rain. Who could blame Esther for wanting the familiar comforts of home in uncertain times?

Rose pushed open the barn door and led Esther's horse inside. If she had done her duty with Robert—Rose pressed her hand against her forehead. She couldn't blame herself for everything. These were the normal problems everyone had. Things like morning sickness, and husbands, or boyfriends in this case, forgetting to involve their women in major life decisions.

Esther was sitting on the couch when Rose returned to the house, with Mamm fussing over her. "Have you seen the midwife yet?"

"I have an appointment next week." Esther justified herself. "Maybe the reminder scared me, thinking about what could be wrong."

"We will pray the Lord protects you," Mamm said. "We will trust him. In the meantime, you're welcome to stay however long you wish. Relax. You'll feel better by tonight."

Esther lay her head back on the couch. "Thank you. I knew you would have answers for me."

"I had best get back to my pies," Rose said.

Esther perked up. "I thought I smelled pecan pies."

Rose gave her sister a smile. "You can have one to take home in an hour."

Esther grimaced. "Jesse would be so pleased. I had planned to make pies this morning, but then—"

"Babies come first," Mamm comforted.

"And morning sickness," Esther groaned.

Mamm patted Esther's shoulder. "You can't have the good without the bad."

"Maybe I can bring a pie back the next time I come," Esther suggested.

"Stop it," Mamm ordered. "You'll always be our daughter, and daughters don't bring back food when they take something home with them. Now relax, while I finish cleaning the bedroom."

"I'll sit with Rose in the kitchen." Esther stood to her feet. "Knowing for certain what is wrong takes the stress away."

"Suit yourself." Mamm shrugged and left.

Esther followed Rose into the kitchen.

"You don't have to help. Why don't you sit down and visit with me instead?" Rose told her. "You can't have gotten better already."

"Maybe I will." Esther made a face. "Truth is, I feel bad about taking your pie, and it looks like I will need help with my garden for the rest of the year."

"There isn't much to do but pull weeds. Your neighbor can help when I can't be there. He's getting vegetables."

"You mean Conrad."

Rose looked away. She hadn't been able to say his name, and her face was turning red. Esther would surely notice.

"The good part is," Esther whispered conspiratorially, "this could be your chance to see him from time to time."

"Esther." Rose also lowered her voice. "You're not helping. Remember! He's an English man."

"Well!" Esther was smiling. "What if he wasn't?"

"But he is."

"I spoke with him in passing this week. He's thinking about joining the community. I told him your relationship with Robert wasn't solid."

Rose felt the blood leave her face. "Esther! Why?"

"Because this is the truth, and he is thinking of joining."

"Conrad told you this?"

Esther wrinkled her brow. "He has had the thought, he said."

"Esther!" Rose warned. "Stop trying to get me in trouble! The man jokes a lot."

Esther looked very unrepentant. "Conrad was serious."

"You don't know. You're leading me into temptation."

"I want what's best for you, Rose. Conrad Wisner would be the best."

"He's not Amish, and you don't know if he will be Amish. Like ever, and I'm not English. I'll never be English!"

Esther tilted her head. "I know you wouldn't leave the community. I don't think ill of you."

Rose set her chin. "I'm dating Robert. I'm practically—so let's drop this foolish subject."

Esther looked horrified. "You're not really—I mean, already promised. This soon."

"Not exactly." Rose admitted. "But the same as."

"You're the one who's in a dream world," Esther said.

"Which is exactly what I'm not." Rose snapped.

Esther sighed. "You're not happy. I know you're not. I want you happy."

"I'm very happy, or I'll soon be," Rose retorted. Where did this anger toward Esther come from? Her sister truly was trying to help.

"What have you planned for supper?" Esther asked, apparently thinking a change of subject was in order.

"Vegetable soup." Rose replied.

"Then I'll help for a few moments." Esther stood to her feet. "I'm better now."

Rose didn't object. As they worked, Rose knew she was saying the right words, but she couldn't hear herself speak. If she didn't sit down soon, she was going to pass out. Which was exactly what she couldn't do. Sit down or pass out? Life had become an impossible choice.

CHAPTER 23

Conrad followed Amos toward his home, a distance which turned into a half mile trot, during which Conrad kept his eye on his truck speedometer. Amos was averaging fifteen miles an hour, even with Amos's obvious attempts at getting the maximum speed out of his horse. What would traveling through life be like at these speeds? Conrad grimaced. There were positives strewn among the negatives. This, at least, decreased the destruction of the modern world down to manageable speeds.

Ahead of Conrad, Amos slowed to swing into his driveway. Conrad followed with his truck. Once parked, Amos leaped out to hastily tie his horse. He hauled a bag out of the back of the buggy, to toss the item into the back of the pickup.

"This is so goot of you!" Amos exclaimed, as he scrambled in. "Thanks so much. I would have wasted an hour or more lining up a driver, so I can certainly pay you the regular mileage rates."

Conrad shook his head. "This one's on the house."

"Thanks," Amos said again.

They pulled out of the driveway and headed up the road.

Amos settled into the seat. "I must say I'm impressed with you. Not just for this favor, but for the good report Grandpa Beiler gave you last week."

"Oh!" Conrad glanced over. "Is he a relation of yours?"

Amos airily waved his hand. "Back somewhere, I suppose, but not close. Everyone calls him Grandpa. He's well known even by Lancaster farming standards, which are high, I assure you."

"I'm sure they are."

"A bad word from Grandpa Beiler about your new methods would not have been goot."

"I see."

Amos nodded wisely. "We respect our old people, especially successful ones like Grandpa Beiler. He likes your ideas, which makes it much easier for the rest of us to accept them. This is very goot. Believe me."

"Thank you."

Did the Amish always go out of their way to make an outsider feel welcome? Was this the Lord's doing perhaps, adding to the feelings he had for Rose—who was dating someone else, regardless of what Esther claimed.

He pulled to a stop at Highway 50 before heading north.

They drove in silence for a few moments before Amos asked. "What were your experiences like growing up on your Daett's farm?"

Conrad brought his thoughts back to the present. "I had a happy childhood. We worked hard. Seems like there was always something which needed doing."

"Which is goot," Amos said. "You have the looks of a man who knows how to work."

"Wouldn't have it any other way."

"How did you end up in Pawnee County?"

Conrad winced. "I decided take another route after college, and there was an opening here, so I applied. The rest is history, as they say." He couldn't bring himself to say anything about the war.

Amos appeared concerned. "Your Daett didn't want you to work for him on the farm?"

"He did and still does, but this is home to me now."

"Are you on goot terms with your Daett?" Amos asked. The doubt lingered in his voice.

"I came for personal reasons." Conrad attempted a smile.

"I see," Amos said, although he obviously didn't.

They turned west on Highway 4, and Conrad accelerated the pickup truck. He had better speak the truth with this man. Denial would serve no one well.

In the meantime, Amos took another stab at the obvious question. "Trouble with a girl back home?"

Conrad laughed. "No. I had a few girlfriends in college, but no broken hearts there or at home."

"We must all except the Lord's will in such matters," Amos said, clearly not convinced. "I once thought a young woman was right for me, but things turned out differently. I have no regrets over the Lord's choice."

"There was the war in Iraq." Conrad forced out the words. "I served three years, and they paid for my college."

Amos's brow furrowed. "A war. I heard there was one. You were there?"

"I was." Conrad admitted.

"The Lord is against killing," Amos said. "I thought from the sound of things your father brought you up with faith in the Lord."

"He did." Conrad kept his gaze on the road. "They have a different understanding on war than the community does."

"I see," Amos said, sounding again as if he didn't. "Killing must be an awful thing."

"You're right, killing is awful, even when they say the actions are lawful." Conrad heard his own voice tremble. He wished he could have avoided the subject with this Amish man. With anyone, in fact.

The flashback came quickly. The road strewn with broken objects. The gunner above him firing at the larger ones, moving them slightly before he drove past. Just as quickly he was back, driving on a US highway with an Amish man seated beside him.

"Maybe the Lord has brought you to the community for a purpose?" Amos was saying.

"Perhaps." Conrad allowed.

The thought had already crossed his mind, but Amos didn't know about his feelings for Rose or the resulting conflict the situation presented. Stealing a community girl couldn't be on Amos's list of actions sanctioned by the Lord.

"Perhaps you will find healing among us," Amos said.

"I thought I was almost a member," Conrad tried for levity.

Amos didn't seem amused. "We do not joke about these things."

"I'm sorry. I meant no offense."

Amos nodded soberly. "I know, but being one of us—living as we do is not a light matter."

"I admire your people." Conrad assured him.

"I know you do." Amos wasn't smiling. "Joining us is a serious matter, but you would be welcomed."

Conrad forced a laugh. "Who would be the county extension agent?"

"The Lord can overcome any obstacle." Amos assured him.

"Driving a horse and buggy all over Pawnee county each day? I don't know."

Amos made a wry face. "We live a peaceful life, but I can see how our way would appear difficult to those who did not grow up as we did."

Silence settled again, the hum of the truck tires on the pavement steady beneath them. Conrad slowed as they passed through another small town. "Do any of your young people ever stray from the prescribed path?"

"You mean fight in a war?" Amos guessed.

"Yes, fight in a war."

"They have not in my memory, but there are stories from the great war, when Amish men left the community to fight Hitler."

"Fighting Hitler does seem like a worthy cause."

"He was an evil man, and the Lord judged him," Amos said. "What more can I say?"

"But you would not have gone to war?"

"I would have loved my God more than my country," Amos said. "I would have been willing to risk my life trying to heal the wounds of war. Many of our people walked such a path."

"You mean something like the Peace Corp?"

Amos nodded. "There were ships lost at sea with conscientious objectors on board."

"Maybe I should have been born Amish and spared some of my choices in life." Conrad tried for a light tone.

"The Lord makes those choices for us," Amos said.

"I'm sorry, I shouldn't be teasing."

"We all have questions about life." Amos stroked his beard, his smile carrying an understanding look.

Conrad slowed for the outskirts of Beatrice, navigating quickly through the streets to arrive at the hardware store.

"There we are," he said, pulling into a parking spot.

Amos hopped out without further ado and rushed into the store. Conrad followed at a more leisurely pace. He found Amos flourishing about a pair of plow tips, a triumphant look on his face. "I found them."

"What good news, indeed." Conrad agreed.

With the items paid in cash, they exited the store and were soon on the road again.

"I want to say thanks again," Amos said, once they were parked near Amos's horse, still tied to the hitching post. "You sure I can't pay you?"

"The trip didn't take long," Conrad assured him, "no pay necessary."

Amos lingered by the pickup door. "Would you come in for a piece of pie and a glass of milk perhaps? I saw my frau was busy this morning."

"You have the time?"

"You had time to drive me into town." Amos shot back.

"Why not," Conrad said, and climbed out of the truck.

Amos led the way into the house. They entered without warning to walk past several small children to the kitchen.

"This is Mary," Amos introduced his wife, "and this is Conrad."

Mary greeted him with an unflustered smile. "Goot afternoon, Conrad. I have heard things about you."

"Good afternoon," he returned the greeting. "Hopefully, good things?"

Mary chuckled. "You don't expect me to repeat the bad things when I see you've been hauling Amos around on the road."

Conrad joined in the laughter. "I sure hope you're teasing."

"We don't have much time." Amos interrupted. "Can you get us a piece of pie and milk. I would feed Conrad something before he goes."

"Certainly." Mary didn't hesitate and quickly produced the requested items.

Amos waited until Conrad began to eat before he took a bite.

"I assume you found the plow tips?" Mary asked.

"We certainly did," Amos said. "Conrad took me there and back quickly. The Lord was with us."

"You also have my thanks." Mary told him, while Conrad ate.

He soon finished and stood to his feet. "What a wonderful pie, but I must be going."

Mary accepted his praise with a nod. "You're very welcome. I hope you have a goot rest of the day."

"The same to you." Conrad followed Amos back out of the front door and climbed back into his pickup truck. He waved, as he drove away.

Cherry pie in the middle of the afternoon, the event planned on the spur of the moment. Who said the slow ways were not the best ways?

"I think I could be an Amish man." Conrad told himself.

CHAPTER 24

Around the same time, Rose followed Esther out to her buggy, and stowed a warm pecan pie under the back seat. "You take care now."

Esther climbed in, but hesitated. "Thanks for the pie, but I was serious about Conrad."

"I know, but you're not helping. I'm not interested."

"But your heart is." Esther insisted. "Be serious. I grew up with you. Think how happy Conrad could make you."

Rose's voice trembled. "If you keep this up, Mamm will hear us, and then—"

"Mamm is not going to object if you marry an Amish man."

"Conrad is not Amish. You know better."

"He could be Amish. I know he could if you—"

"If I—"

"Smile at him. Encourage him."

"You ask for awful things," Rose whispered.

"For your own good," Esther said. "I can't stand seeing you tortured by Robert."

"I'm dating him," Rose hissed.

"You're in pain," Esther said. "Don't disagree with me."

Rose said nothing. What was there to say? Esther spoke the truth.

"See. Something must be done."

"But an English man? Listen to yourself, Esther."

Esther took the reins. "Keep your heart open. I ask nothing more, for both our sanities. I see this is why I came over today, to encourage you."

Rose clung to the buggy wheel for support. "Robert is buying a farm with me in mind as his wife. The matter is already decided."

Esther gave her a fierce look. "Nothing is decided until the wedding vows are said."

"Why are doing this to me?" Rose pled.

"Because I know I'm right, and you've been such a great sister to me."

"Conrad will not become Amish."

"Just don't commit to Robert. Please! Dating is to find out whether you're right for each other, so don't settle. I know how you are. You like to get things over with, especially unpleasant ones."

"I've been waiting a long time, and the wait wasn't unpleasant."

"Thank the Lord," Esther said. "If you hadn't waited, you could be wed already. Now, you have an option."

"Esther!" Rose tried again, but her sister clucked to her horse and drove out of the lane.

Rose was left standing there, staring at the back of the departing buggy.

CHAPTER 25

The sun was high in the sky the following week when Rose came out of the Millers' basement door with her straw hat pulled tight on her head. The first heat of summer simmered in the morning air, pushed away at the moment by the stirring breeze. She had been busy the entire morning, but there were a few hours left before lunch to give the garden some much needed attention. She paused to look down the road in either direction. There was no sign of buggies or of English vehicles. Which wouldn't have mattered if there had been any. She was beginning to fear phantoms. Conrad's pickup was not going to appear out of thin air.

Esther's words last week had stung more than she wished to admit, but she couldn't give in to dreams. Not again! Conrad was a dream, an absolutely unreachable and unreasonable one. Nothing but an addled brain explained her sister's fixation with setting her up with Conrad Wisner. Everyone knew how difficult the transition was into the community if you were not born into the faith. She would think no more about Conrad Wisner—in the present and in the future. Esther's confused brain must not affect her own dreamy inclinations.

On one thing Rose was clear. Her date with Robert on Sunday evening had gone much better. He hadn't said anything about visiting a farm he was interested in buying, but Robert would do so when the time was proper. She couldn't allow a hurt to fester in her heart in the meantime. Robert was being appropriate. Their relationship was on solid ground. Slow and steady was the best Amish model. No rash decisions, and especially no emotional ones.

Rose hurried across the yard to enter the barn and retrieve her gardening tools. She returned outside to survey the garden plot for a moment before kneeling down and inspecting the ground. The young plants had begun to push skyward, as if consumed with eagerness to produce their bounty. Rose hovered over them. Plants weren't alive, and yet they were. The Lord had made them to glorify himself and bless the world with their abundance.

Rose ran the hoe along the edges of the young, sweet corn plants. They shimmered in the sunlight as the dirt stirred around them. They were doing well, even if she had chosen a different variety from the one Conrad Wisner had purchased for Esther's garden. Maybe next year she would try his suggestions, if Conrad still rented the place across from Esther and Jesse's. English people came and went quickly. They were from a different world. Esther's brain must have been really addled to think such strange thoughts—Conrad Wisner as an Amish man. To think of Rose Miller saying the wedding vows—of placing her hand in the man's hand. Rose grew dizzy at the thought. She would never be Mrs. Wisner.

Rose gathered herself together and whacked her hoe into the ground.

"Stop it." She ordered herself.

Rose pushed the memory of Conrad's handsome face out of her mind and focused on the young plants near her feet. They seemed so familiar and so comforting. Unlike the horrid thoughts she had been having of late. She had to gain control of her mind. She was Rose Miller, the Amish woman whose gardening skills were well known and praised by many in the community. She was obedient, a girl not given to strange actions. She was free, but not free to enter a world of dreams.

Rose bent low, loosening the dirt around the tender plants. With her hands she gave the budding sprouts an environment in which to expand their roots, to experience the fastest growth possible. In the same way love should be freeing, pulling one closer to the Lord. Robert freed her from her dreams. She would be happy soon. She would be his wife and thank him for being her husband.

"Rose," Mamm called from the house, interrupting Rose's concentration.

"Yah." Rose turned to see Mamm hurrying across the yard.

"I'm so embarrassed!" Mamm exclaimed when she arrived, her face flushed. "I opened the oatmeal bin in the basement to refill our jar upstairs, and—I must have left the lid open too long the last time I was down there." Mamm's hands flew to her face.

"What's wrong?" Rose asked.

"The oatmeal's wormy," Mamm whispered. "I couldn't believe my eyes, but there they were, not an inch beneath the surface when I dipped in the bowl."

"I'll drive into town and get more." Rose offered at once. "What were you baking?"

"Cookies, but it'll be too late for cookies when you get back. It's breakfast tomorrow morning which concerns me. I need to make a fresh batch of baked oatmeal."

"Well, the mistake can't be helped." Rose comforted Mamm. "I'll go right away."

"Do you have the time?" Mamm's glance took in the garden. "I had thought I could go myself."

"My garden can wait."

"You're such an angel!" Mamm gave Rose a grateful hug.

Rose grimaced. "I don't know about an angel, but I can help you dispose of the ruined oatmeal."

Mamm nodded and the two hurried back toward the basement door.

"Do you think I have early Alzheimer's?" Mamm asked on the way down the steps.

Rose gave Mamm a quick smile. "Your mind seems quite sharp to me."

"Thank you," Mamm whispered, as they entered the basement.

Together they lifted the tub of oatmeal from the shelf and carried it outside to the garden.

Mamm took a brief glance toward the barn and the field beyond. "I'll have to tell Daett sometime about this accident."

"He doesn't have to see us disposing the oatmeal," Rose said. "You can tell him later."

Mamm nodded, and they tipped the tub over. The wiggling worms appeared among the dry flakes of oatmeal. Rose looked the other way, and so did Mamm. They quickly spread the contents evenly along the edge of the garden. When the tub was empty, Rose took her hoe, and scrapped the oatmeal into the dirt, until the two blended together. "There! Fertilizer for my garden!"

Mamm rung her hands watching, with frequent glances toward the fields behind the barn.

"Daett will understand," Rose said. "Now, I'll be on my way to town. Can I get anything else?"

"I'll make the list for you," Mamm said, still looking distracted. "Can I help you hitch Brownie to the buggy first?"

"I'm okay." Rose left Mamm standing in the garden. She whistled at the back-barn door until Brownie trotted up. "Ready for a quick trip into town?"

The horse neighed, as if she understood every word.

Rose led Brownie into the barn, where she swung the harness over the horse's back. With the straps tightened, Rose took Brownie outside where Mamm had the buggy shafts lifted high in the air.

"I told you I'm okay." Rose told her.

"I want to help." Mamm protested, and Rose swung Brownie underneath.

They silently fastened the straps and the tugs.

"Here's the check book," Mamm produced the brown folded tablet from her apron pocket, "and the list I made while you were in the barn."

"See. No Alzheimer's." Rose encouraged.

Mamm managed a smile, and Rose climbed into the buggy. With the reins firmly in hand, Brownie trotted forward to turn right at the end of the lane. Rose waved out of the open door before she settled into the buggy seat for the ride into town. Her garden work could wait until this afternoon. She was ahead of schedule and had time to spare. This felt goot, being of use to Mamm, being in the flow of life on the farm, and helping out in emergencies. She was Amish and would never be anything else. This was not a dream world.

CHAPTER 26

While Rose drove toward town, Conrad Wisner was on the sidewalk in front of the Pawnee courtyard talking to a local farmer. Mr. Oswald had his hat pushed back on his head and a stick of straw in his mouth. "So how are things, young man?"

Conrad smiled. "I like my job."

"Seems the state only hires the young fellows fresh out of college anymore." Mr. Oswald commented. "You do have a degree, I take."

"University of Nebraska. Agriculture."

"All those fancy names." Mr. Oswald grumbled. "The state taking our money and instructing us, people who have lived and worked here most of our lives."

Conrad's smile vanished. "The state is here to help, I can assure you, and no offense meant."

"I guess so." Mr. Oswald peered out from under his straw hat. "You do have a good head on you from what I've been hearing. Maybe you should stop by my place and impart some college wisdom to an old man."

"If you wish," Conrad said. "You're located south of town?"

"That's right."

"I've been studying the farms, so I think I can find yours."

Mr. Oswald frowned. "Don't know if I like the state studying us. Makes a man nervous, I say."

"We're here to help." Conrad tried again.

"You're not mandating things, are you?"

"Not yet."

Mr. Oswald glared at him.

"I was teasing, sir."

"It's no joking matter out here on the prairie," Mr. Oswald said. "The government's got their fingers in everything and up to no good anywhere, I say."

"I'm a local boy of sorts." Conrad told him. "Maybe we can work on changing your feelings."

"So I heard." Mr. Oswald grunted. "You're from up in big grass country. Give me a call sometime next week."

"I will."

Mr. Oswald continued down the street, and Conrad turned to walk back to his pickup when another farmer he didn't know approached him.

"I'm Mr. Helmps." The man offered. "You're the new county extension agent?"

"I am." Conrad extended his hand.

Mr. Helmp's handshake was firm. "What do you know about fungus on young corn plants?"

CHAPTER 27

Rose pulled Brownie to a stop at the intersection, and when the traffic cleared, turned the horse south toward Pawnee City. There was a farm with a *For Sale* sign on the left. Rose didn't slow but scrutinized the white house as she passed. This must be one of the homesteads Robert had visited with his Grandpa. The place looked ideal and bigger than she remembered. The house wasn't too fancy, at least from the outside. Which was how things should be for an Amish house—plain looking. There were electric wires running from the road to the house, but such things could be remedied in no time. Once the power was cut, wire holders could be turned into the ceilings for lanterns, and gas lines could be run for the stove and refrigerator. The house could easily be converted to the Amish way of life.

Rose studied the barn with Brownie's hooves beating on the black top under her. The building was huge, which was exactly what Robert needed to run a successful farming operation. There was a plot for a garden beside the house, a little overgrown with weeds at present, but a site which had obviously yielded its abundance in years gone by. Brownie picked up her ears, as they trotted past, seeming to know there might be something special about this place.

Rose took a quick glance backward before they reached the edge of town. She was dreaming and must stop this. She couldn't be certain of anything until Robert chose to share the information. She concentrated on driving through the stop lights and finding a parking spot at the IGA supermarket.

Rose climbed out of the buggy and tied Brownie securely to the light pole. When she looked up, Rose immediately ducked her head. Conrad Wisner's truck was sitting in one of the parking spots near the courthouse, and worse, Conrad Wisner's lengthy form was standing with his back turned toward her, chatting with an English man.

Rose froze in place. Conrad had to have noticed her drive in, but surely, he wouldn't come over to speak with her. Rose's throat went dry at the thought. This was an English town and Conrad was an English man. Conrad would come over to speak with her. She need ask no further questions about the matter. Maybe if she hurried by before Conrad ended his conversation, a horribly embarrassing situation could be avoided.

Rose tried to move her feet, but she couldn't get them into motion. She held on to Brownie's bridle, drawing strength from the familiar feel. She still hadn't moved when Conrad finished talking with the English man and headed across the street toward her.

"Rose." He sounded surprised.

"Yah." Her face must be blazing red and her voice croaking. She was still clutching the straps of Brownie's bridle.

Conrad appeared not to notice. "Nice day to shop in town."

"Yah. Mamm needed some things."

"How's your garden doing?" Conrad was smiling. "Esther assured me hers has sprouted, due to your green thumb."

"My sister exaggerates." Rose tried to pry her fingers from the leather straps.

"Perhaps," he said. "You're an impressive gardener."

"Thanks." Rose dared sneak a look at his face. His words were so healing.

"Grocery shopping, I take." He grinned. "Do you need help with the list?"

"I—oh, of course not. I mean."

His grin grew. "I was teasing, though the experience would be great. Helping an Amish girl fill her grocery cart."

Rose clutched at Brownie's bridle again. "I don't know," she said.

"Are you okay?" Conrad appeared concerned. "I'm sorry if my teasing disturbed you."

"I'm okay." Rose stood straighter and let go of the bridle. "I should get right back to the house."

"Of course. A busy Amish girl. I'm detaining you." Conrad took a step backward.

Rose waited a moment for her dizziness to clear. Now she had made Conrad feel bad, and he wasn't to blame in the least. "I—" She tried to speak evenly. "I'm glad I got to see you today. I wasn't expecting—" Horror swept over her. What was she saying?

Conrad looked confused. "I had to come and say hello. I hope—"

"No. I'm fine. I really am."

"Happy shopping then." Conrad was smiling again.

Rose didn't move. "What are you doing today?"

Conrad shrugged. "Nothing much. Headed to the office for some paperwork, then out to the field. Not all the farmers are open to our new ideas."

"Are the Amish giving you trouble?" Rose couldn't imagine they were, but the question burst out.

"No." His smile grew. "I'm being treated quite royally by your people."

"How goot to hear." Rose took a quick breath. "But I'm sorry. Now I'm keeping you."

Conrad appeared not to hear. "Will you be helping with your sister's garden this summer? I can't imagine her doing all the work by herself, and she seems to think you make plants grow with your very presence."

"Maybe. I don't know. Esther works hard like every Amish woman does, but she has a baby on the way."

"Oh," he said. "I didn't know."

Now she was spilling family secrets.

He smiled again. "I took Amos Troyer into the Beatrice hardware the other week for some plow tips he couldn't find in Pawnee City."

Rose forced herself to focus. "You drive the Amish?"

He laughed. "A courtesy haul, let's say. Amos did offer to pay, but I declined."

"I see." Rose's head was spinning. "I really should—"

He nodded. "Have a nice day. I look forward to seeing more of you over at Esther's garden, if nowhere else. My presence won't scare you away, I hope, since I couldn't accept produce from your sister's garden without pitching in with more of the labor."

Rose didn't dare look at him. "I'll have to see what Mamm says, but Esther does have a large garden, and the baby—" She stopped.

"Don't miss me when you come over," he said. "I'll tell Esther and she can keep me informed of the work schedule."

Rose choked. Now was the time to object, but no words would come out of her mouth.

"I work across the street," he said. "Stop by when you have spare time, and if I'm in, I'll show you around."

Rose ducked her head and hurried away. Conrad was still standing on the edge of the street when she looked back at the big double doors. Rose hurled herself into the store, right past the shopping carts, and went down the long aisle so fast her skirt flowed out behind her.

CHAPTER 28

Conrad stared at the grocery store for a long time after the double doors had closed behind Rose. He liked the girl, there was no question there. Perhaps more than he had ever liked a girl before, but she was Amish, obviously committed to the faith, and he was an outsider. These were people who played by the rules. He had always played by the rules, but here there were even stronger rules, rooted in history and a commitment to family.

"Are you really willing?" he muttered and shook his head. "And is she really available?"

"How you doing, Mr. Wisner?" A farmer he knew came hurrying down the sidewalk. "You're exactly the person I need to see this morning."

"Yes." Conrad waited, the vision of Rose's face stuck in his mind.

"I need you to look at the condition of my soil and suggest a seed choice. Could you—"

"Yes." Conrad said, but the man's words had seemed to vanish into thin air. "Excuse me, Mr. Chester, but could you repeat what you just said?"

The man looked at him strangely, glancing down the street before he spoke again. Rose had gotten to him. No question about it, which wasn't something Mr. Chester would be concerned with.

"I can be out whenever your schedule allows," he said. He still hadn't heard any further information Mr. Chester might have been trying to convey.

"How about tomorrow around ten?"

"Perfect." Conrad responded, his gaze still drawn toward the double doors of the grocery store. Perhaps he should hang around and help Rose load her groceries into the buggy.

He should not, Conrad decided, and resolutely turned to follow Mr. Chester down the street.

CHAPTER 29

On Sunday evening, Rose clung to the side of Robert's buggy, as his horse trotted along in the stillness of the late evening darkness. Their greetings had been a quick "Hi," when Rose had climbed into the buggy.

"Nice evening isn't it," Robert finally said.

"Yah. I agree." Rose replied, not turning to look at him. Why did she feel like leaping out of the buggy and running home on foot?

The steady clip clop of the horse's hooves filled the silence.

"What have you been up to this week?" Robert asked.

Rose stared into the darkness. "The usual. Working in the garden, washing, and a trip into town."

He glanced at her. "What for?"

Rose's gaze didn't move. "Shopping at the grocery store for Mamm."

"You're frugal, aren't you? With money and things?"

Rose forced a laugh. "I think so."

"I couldn't have a frau who didn't know how to pinch pennies," he said.

"I know how to grow a garden." Rose offered.

He seemed to ponder the point. "Which is goot," he finally said, "but money can be quickly wasted in English grocery stores. Mamm only goes once a month and buys in bulk when she can."

The words burst out of Rose's mouth. "Which can have its downside, when you have accidents."

"Accidents?" He looked worried.

Rose wished she could undo what she had said, but the words had been spoken. "Okay." She admitted. "Mamm found our oatmeal wormy. We're a careful family, but things do happen. Someone—Mamm thinks it was her—left the lid off the tub."

"The whole barrel became wormy?"

"What was left in the tub because we do buy in bulk. We needed some for the next morning, so I went to Pawnee City, which I assume you know, doesn't have a bulk food store."

"Are you sure you didn't leave off the lid?" he asked.

"Would this make a difference with—?"

He held up his hand. "No. I know old people have trouble with their minds."

"Mamm isn't old." Rose protested.

He jiggled the reins, and his horse sped up.

"Is this a big problem with you?" Rose insisted. "I try not to be careless, but things can happen, and Mamm isn't losing her mind."

"I'm not trying to argue," he said, "just saying."

Rose tried to breathe evenly. Were they quarreling? She had never heard of couples quarreling over wormy oatmeal— their parents' wormy oatmeal. She wasn't wasteful, and Robert would surely see this once they were wed.

"Grandpa and I went to see a farm—like I told you, back when he was here," Robert said, obviously wanting to change the subject. "I've been waiting to tell you until they accepted my offer. They did so on Friday, at a decent price."

Rose tried to clear her head. So, this was the reason Robert had been saying nothing. She should have known he had a goot reason.

"You do care about the farm?" He was looking at her.

"Of course." She spoke much too loudly. "You should have told me sooner."

"I didn't want you worrying," he said.

"Of course," Rose calmed herself, "but I wouldn't have worried. I would have liked to be involved."

"There was nothing you could have done," he said. "Grandpa and I loved the place."

"I'm sure you did, but I—"

"You'll like the house," he said, "and Grandpa told me he is willing to finance the place if they accept my offer, and they did. Took them awhile, but they didn't even counter."

"I'm glad for you." Rose managed. "Would the property be right outside Pawnee, there on the main road with the *For Sale* sign."

"How did you know?" He looked suspicious. "Did someone from my family tell you? I told them I wanted to break the news."

"No one told me." Rose assured him. "I drove by there this week, like I said, going to the grocery store, and I couldn't help wondering. A likely guess, I suppose."

"You've been dreaming," he said. "At least this time you were right. I think we're quite set with Grandpa's help."

"Things seem to be really working well." Rose tried to encourage.

"The Lord is smiling." He agreed. "Many things have come together for me lately, and quite quickly I must say."

"I'm glad for you." She smiled up at him.

He seemed not to notice. "You'll like the place. Grandpa said the soil is excellent, and there is a large garden spot behind the house."

The words slipped out. "I noticed."

He didn't look pleased. "You did?"

"I mean, when I was driving past the place."

"You should have waited to imagine things until you knew for certain." He chided.

"I wasn't imagining." Rose protested. "I noticed there was a garden spot. I know we're not—I mean, we're just dating, but I can give an opinion."

"What do you mean, we're not—?"

She ignored the question. "I should have waited to think anything until I knew for certain." She gave him a pained smile.

He appeared mollified. "We shouldn't quarrel, and I do want you involved when there is a question. In this case, the road was clear and open with Grandpa's advice."

"I understand. My opinions wouldn't have changed a thing."

"I don't think you would have disagreed with our decisions," he said, happiness returning to his voice. "Get this. Not only is Grandpa offering me the loan on the farm, but enough money for the implements, and the horses."

Rose took a deep breath. "Sounds like you're all set. What great news."

His smile was broad. "I'm very happy."

"We should celebrate."

"No need for dramatics," he said, his smile fading. "This is the Lord's blessing."

"Can't we celebrate the Lord's blessings?"

"We should be thankful, but not make a big fuss. It's not right to make a fuss about the Lord's things."

She fell silent, the beat of Danny Boy's hooves steady under the buggy.

"There was a bit of bad news," he said. "Mamm got a letter this week. Grandma had a fall after they came back from the trip. Exhaustion from sitting on the train those long hours, Grandpa thought."

"How is she?" Rose turned to face him.

"They have a maid in to help, so it's serious. A broken hip, I think."

Rose couldn't keep the alarm out of her voice. "Any broken bones are serious at your grandma's age. I'm sorry to hear the news."

"Grandpa thinks she'll be well in a few weeks, but they do have a full-time maid. Everything will be okay."

He pulled back on the reins and guided Danny Boy into the Miller's driveway. They came to a halt by the hitching post, and Rose climbed down. Robert followed with the tie rope in his hand to secure his horse to the rail.

Rose waited until he finished. She felt numb inside. Everything seemed upside down and inside out.

Robert, though, was smiling when he approached her. "Ready?"

Rose turned without answering and led the way to the house. She opened the front door and left him seated on the couch while she retrieved the brownies and milk from the kitchen.

Robert peered into the plate when she came back. "These look goot."

"Maybe this can be our celebration," she said. "A little celebration."

He seemed not to hear, reaching for a brownie. "I was remembering something from this week."

"Oh." Rose sat down beside him. "Something about the farm you're buying."

"No," he said, chuckling. "Phyllis had a run in with a skunk."

"A skunk! A skunk isn't necessarily funny."

"This one was." He dismissively waved his hand. "The thing got into the chicken coop, and Phyllis nearly stepped on him, but she didn't get sprayed. I think the skunk was more scared than Phyllis was."

"Skunks spray when they're scared."

"Not this one," he said. "There was no spray. Just the normal stench set off by a skunk and the loud yelling from Phyllis with chickens running everywhere."

"I'm glad Phyllis didn't get sprayed."

"Have you ever been sprayed?" He was looking at her contemplatively.

"No, but I can imagine."

He furrowed his brow. "You shouldn't imagine so much. Phyllis escaped harm, and I was able to keep our dog, Shep, out of the ruckus. Everything turned out as things should. Daett fixed the hole in the wire, and we shouldn't be having any more trouble."

Rose took a brownie and bit down on the gooey goodness. She chewed but couldn't swallow.

CHAPTER 30

Across the fields from the Miller's place, Conrad sat on Jesse's and Esther's porch with a bowl of ice cream in his hands. He had come over for a visit on Esther's invitation. The ice cream was a surprise, and from the looks on the young couple's faces, a further surprise was coming. Esther was watching the darkened horizon intently. Jesse, seated beside her, was holding Esther's hand.

"She likes these kinds of things," Jesse said, with a quick smile, not explaining anything further.

"It's going to be so special tonight." Esther gushed.

Conrad took a bite of ice cream, waiting in silence until a soft glow began to bubble on the horizon. He quickly guessed what the main attraction of the evening was.

"A full summer moon." Esther confirmed. "Thanks so much for agreeing to share this special evening with us."

"Summer moons are special." He agreed, his gaze fixed on the unfolding drama.

How many of these had he seen from his father's fields while growing up. A round blaze of glory, which filled the sky on the horizon. Even the cattle had seemed to notice the closeness of the heavens. These were precious moments he had buried somewhere inside of him, only to have them resurrected on the front porch of an Amish home.

Conrad swallowed hard, his spoon held limp in his hand. He had expected pain to appear when memories of the past returned like ghosts to haunt him. Instead, he felt strangely and deeply at peace. As if this was a moment to treasure above all moments. As if time had paused and was waiting with them to see what would be revealed.

CHAPTER 31

With the brownie in her mouth, Rose finally managed to swallow not once, but three times. Her head felt light. Across from her on the couch, Robert had finished his food. Rose glanced around the living room, trying to clear her head. Outside the window, the bubble of light on the horizon brought back the memory in a rush.

"We could go outside and watch the moon rise." She blurted out.

Robert's head turned. "A moon is rising." The words more statement than question.

Rose ignored the cut in his voice. "The rising is special tonight. This will be the first full summer moon. Esther told me, Jesse and she plan to watch from their front porch."

"I've seen moons rising a hundred times." Robert muttered. "We will have none of this."

"You want to take a peek?" She tried to smile.

"I don't look at moons," he said. "I mean, I see them all the time. There's nothing special about moons. Don't the English give names to moon risings?"

"I suppose," Rose allowed, "but the English also named the days of the week."

"Do you have any more brownies?" Robert asked, obviously wanting to move on from the conversation.

"I think so." Rose retreated to the kitchen and tried to collect her emotions.

Robert would see how upset she was, but on the other hand maybe he wouldn't. He didn't seem to notice much about her.

"There you are." Rose brought back two more brownies on the plate.

Robert held out his empty glass of milk.

"Of course." Rose swallowed hard.

He had a patient look on his face.

Rose bolted back to the kitchen and returned with the glass filled.

Robert took a big swallow and set down the glass. "No more talking about moons and the English ways." He ordered. "We need to get back to the issues dealing with real life. At home, we're struggling with mastitis in our cows—again. Those are real concerns. We had the vet come out. He left medicine but couldn't find anything unusual going on. Expensive those vets are."

"I'm sorry," Rose said.

"Farms have plenty of trouble in them." Robert continued. "I hope you learn to leave your dreaminess behind you before we wed. I need your full attention keeping the farm running, and the garden of course, during the summer. There will be no time for moon watching. Not if we wish to pay our bills. I couldn't bear the shame of admitting to Grandpa Beiler I couldn't make my payments."

"Of course not." Her throat was clogged again. "I will—I mean—I think I can be helpful when things go wrong."

He gave a little nod of his head. "You may have noticed our family's large amount of farm problems, or rather my father's large number of problems. I hope to cut down on such things once I have my own place. I can't have any silliness going on, or time being wasted."

"I—of course. I won't—I never dreamed you would think I would bring harm to you."

Robert seemed not hear. "People think things," he said, "but they don't always really know. I'm going to improve on Daett's way of running a farm, especially with the help of our new English extension agent. What's his name?"

Rose couldn't get a sound out.

"You're supposed to help me," he said.

"Conrad," she whispered.

He looked pleased. "Thank you. You did remember."

Rose's heart was pounding in her throat, the vision of Conrad's kind eyes floating in front of her eyes. "Tell me more about the house." She choked out.

"You saw the place, driving by." He looked accusingly at her.

"I didn't see the inside." Rose protested.

"The house will suit you," he said. "My big concern was whether I could get the loan. I lay awake nights worrying, thinking of the shame I would experience if the bank turned me down. A problem which Grandpa solved. Now the only concern is making the farm work and paying back the loan."

"I'm sure you're up to the task."

He frowned. "You'll be helping me, or are you having doubts about the hard work?"

"Of course not, but I would like to see the house."

"I can't imagine you being unhappy with the house."

"Can I see the place?" Rose couldn't believe she was begging.

"Okay." He gave in with a sigh. "I have another appointment with the realtor on Tuesday morning. I'll pick you up around ten."

"Thank you," Rose whispered.

He was already on his feet. "I should be going. Tomorrow will be a full day. We have the hay field to cut and manure to haul from the winter pile."

"The moon is rising." Rose couldn't believe she dared say the words.

He must not have heard. "I'll see you on Tuesday morning, then."

Rose stayed seated while the front door slammed behind Robert. Her head throbbed. She heard his buggy drive out of the lane. Slowly she rose to her feet and walked out on the porch. Robert's buggy lights were out of sight, but the sound of Danny Boy's hoof beats rose and fell in the distance. The moon hung heavy above the horizon, a soft glow resting on the tree line below. The wind stirred a few lose strains of hair across Rose's face, and the tears came. What had she expected? She knew Robert was a practical man. Where the road led, she hadn't envisioned. What harm could Robert see in a few moments shared with her on the front porch enjoying the Lord's beautiful handiwork in the sky?

Rose retreated to the washroom to wash her face. She was wide awake with the ache in her heart filling her entire body. The clock ticking in the living room read a little after ten. Robert had left early. Rose lifted her light work coat from the hook on the washroom wall and slipped her arms into the sleeves, to step out into the night. She left her shoes on the front porch along with her stockings near the chairs where she had wanted Robert to sit with her. She walked barefoot into the garden. The coat warmed her shoulders, and the ground held the heat of the day, oozing upward like a balm through the soles of her feet. The leaves of the small corn plants rustled against her dress as she passed. The moon was brighter here, away from the glow of the gas lantern in the living room. She felt protected, sheltered. This was her garden, her refuge. Robert would think her mad if she told him. He saw her garden simply as a way to feed his family. Nothing more.

Yet she was about more than just practical considerations. So much more. Surely this place would always be hers, to walk alone while Robert and her household slept. The Lord would never take this from her, or would he? The question brought on a fresh burst of agony. Why was she being asked to walk this valley, this deep dark place which would last, not a day or a week, but a lifetime as Robert's wife. Must she die this deeply? Must the cut of the Lord's knife be so sharp? Had her sin been this great?

She had met Conrad Wisner near her garden but through no fault of her own. Was Robert right? Was she being punished for imagining things, feeling impossible hopes, holding dreams which had no meaning? Wilmer had been taken from her. There was no question about that, and look where her hopes had led her—to Conrad Wisner, the English man. She had experienced a flood of emotion for an English man and had dared to think this love. Robert was right. He must be right. She could not go on with any other thought. Yet the pain was no less, nor the terror which rose inside her diminished. Living with Robert each day would be a reminder of her former life which she had lived so wrongly.

The tears came again. She had best lose her love for gardens. Robert would be horrified if she slipped out like this at night, if he awoke and found her wandering through the loose soil barefoot with a thin coat over her shoulders. He would think her mad if she spoke of the earth's heat rising through her feet, of feeling the touch and strength of the eternal God himself filling her.

Rose turned and rushed back to the house, to leave her coat in the washroom. She raced upstairs and dove under the bed quilt fully dressed. She huddled there for a long time before she dared move again.

CHAPTER 32

In the meantime, Conrad stood outside the front door of his small rental home. There wasn't room for a chair, let alone two, and the moon had risen too high to view from under his roof line. He took the few steps away from the house and looked upward. The moon had turned white and grown considerably smaller since its birth on the horizon. He had seen the moon for the first time tonight through new eyes, through Amish eyes. They had the ability to draw wonder from the natural world in a way which modern society had long lost. Even his own childhood had not rivaled this.

In slow motion, the glory had settled deep into the soul. The homemade ice cream had helped, but here things definitely moved at a crawl. The Amish had the strength to slow down and wait, to savor what was simple and plain, yet deeply profound.

A memory stirred from his days in college, and Conrad pulled out his smart phone. He chuckled in the dark. He wasn't quite Amish yet. His finger punched in "Poe's poem on the moon."

The screen flashed black and white, clearly readable under the moonlight. He read slowly.

"I saw thee once-once only-years ago:
I must not say how many-but not many.

It was a July midnight; and from out a full-orbed moon,
that like thine own soul soaring.
Sought a precipitate pathway up through heaven,
there fell a silvery silken veil of light, with quietude,
and sultriness and slumber,
Upon the upturn'd faces of a thousand roses that grew in an enchanted garden,
where no wind dare to stir, unless on tiptoe-"

He stopped and looked up at the moon again. The sense had become unmistakable, a stirring from within him which finally burst to the surface. Rose had probably never heard such words, let alone read them, but she *was* those words, as if Poe had captured her spirit, her warmth, and her beauty.

"I have gone mad," he said out loud. "Totally mad. She's an Amish woman and dating someone. You can't think of her in this way."

A silvery silken veil of light, with quietude, and sultriness and slumber.

CHAPTER 33

On Tuesday morning, Rose walked out to her garden with her bonnet tied tight under her chin. There had been no thoughts of Conrad flittering in her brain since Sunday. She had made sure by an extreme exercise of her will, banishing any vision of him, burying the mere breathing of his name in any conversation with the men folk.

Rose caught her breath. The effort had been exhausting, but a measure of peace had settled in. She had kept busy with the garden, being practical, refusing to think about the moonlit night she had walked among her plants. The last rows had been weeded yesterday, but the wind from last night had blown over several of the plants. She straightened them, waiting for Robert to pick her up for their appointment with the realtor. Robert need never know the tears she had cried on Sunday evening after he had left or the thoughts which had raced through her head. Those had been horrible thoughts which she was determined not to repeat. Maybe she should never watch another moon rise in her life.

"Rose!" Mamm's voice from behind made her jump. "Why are you out here?"

She pasted on a smile. "Remember? I told you Robert would pick me up this morning."

Mamm's worried look didn't fade. "I know, but you're walking the garden, doing nothing."

"I should pull some weeds." Rose bent over, searching among the green stalks and finding nothing.

Mamm came closer. "What's wrong? Don't you like Robert's farm?"

Rose stood up and brushed the dirt from her hands. "I liked what I saw from the road."

Mamm's worried look remained. "Did Robert say something about the condition of the house? Is it a dump?"

Rose forced a laugh. "He didn't say, but I think the house is fine."

"So—" Mamm let the words hang. "Something is troubling you. Has Robert asked you yet? To marry him?"

Rose looked away. "No."

Mamm clucked her tongue in understanding. "You like to have things in order, and he's showing you the house, buying the farm, and hasn't asked yet."

"I'm fine." Rose glanced down at her garden plants. "We did take our time beginning our relationship. I guess we're a slow couple."

"Robert isn't moving slowly," Mamm said. "He must be assuming. Is he right?"

Rose kept her gaze on the ground. "I would say, yah, if he asked."

"Why so unhappy?"

"We're practical. The Lord has brought us together."

Mamm wrinkled her brow. "You must not grieve your lack of feelings. Those will come. They always do. Once you know Robert better. Once you are wed to him."

"I know." Rose agreed.

"I hope you don't state your opinions too freely about the house," Mamm said. "I think this is what niggles at you. You're afraid the place is insufficient."

"Maybe?" Rose allowed. "I don't know anymore. I'm tired of thinking."

Mamm tilted her head. "I knew it. Every young bride worries about her house, especially if her boyfriend buys the place without getting her opinion. Robert should have known better."

"It's okay." Rose assured Mamm.

She wasn't lying, and Mamm wouldn't believe her if she put forth a correction. Not without telling the truth about Conrad. Something she couldn't do.

"Do you want to wait inside?" Mamm asked.

"I'd rather stay out here."

"I'm in the house if you need me." Mamm's footsteps faded away.

Rose slowly moved down the row of carrots, finally finding a few fresh weeds which had begun to burst out of the ground. Rose comforted herself while her fingers were in the soil digging deep for the roots of the weeds. Gardens grew what was planted, and what wasn't planted.

The tears came again. She would have to pull out of her heart the things she had not planted. Rose dabbed her eyes quickly with her handkerchief at the distant sound of horse hooves beating on the road. She turned her face into the sun and closed her eyes. A breeze stirred, cooling her skin. She pinched herself to stop further tears and thrust her handkerchief deeply into her dress pocket.

"Enough of this!" She declared out loud.

Robert's buggy came into sight, and Rose walked out to the end of the lane. Robert brought Danny Boy to a halt in front of her, and Rose hopped into the buggy.

"Waiting for me?" He was clearly pleased.

"How are you this morning?" She smiled up at him.

"A little nervous I guess. I'm sure you will like the house, but—"

Rose forced a laugh. "Surely, you don't expect me to object? It's a little late now."

"I know. You'll like the house a lot, even the changes I want to make."

"Changes?"

"You'll see," he said. His confidence appeared to have returned.

"I promise to keep my comments to a minimum." Rose offered.

Robert glanced into the lane. "Your garden's looking good this morning."

"Thank you."

"You're a great gardener," he said, and turned Danny Boy around to head back toward town.

Rose settled into the buggy seat.

"Were you out weeding the garden when I came?" he asked.

"I pulled a few weeds in the carrot row."

"I like a woman working while she's waiting," he said. He seemed pleased with himself.

Rose squelched the pain rising in her heart and changed the subject. "How's the closing coming on the place?"

"We'll have a date soon," he said. "Perhaps after today's meeting."

"You're moving fast."

"I guess so. I'm ready to get out on my own and try some of the new farming methods Conrad Wisner is introducing."

"Conrad," she whispered, and a cold chill crept through her body.

He was looking at her with a questioning gaze. "You don't object to the man helping the community? Why would you? Especially after you saw him at our place and how well he fits into the community's ways?"

"Of course not." Rose tried to breathe evenly.

"Conrad Wisner is a great blessing to the community." He lectured.

"I'm sure he has goot farming ideas." Rose allowed.

"Oh, he does," Robert said, his attention drifting to the horizon. "What a beautiful morning to see our future farm and take another step in our new life. The Lord must be pleased with my plans."

"I'm sure he is." Rose swallowed hard. She wasn't lying. The Lord surely wasn't pleased with her thoughts.

Robert turned south at Highway 50, and the realtor's car was waiting for them in the driveway. Rose waited until Robert had tied Danny Boy to a tree, before she climbed down from the buggy.

"Rose, this is Albert Hansen, the realtor." Robert made the introductions.

Rose extended her hand. "It's goot of you to show us the house."

The realtor smiled. "That's what I do, ma'am. I hope you like the place."

"I already do," Rose said. "I drove past earlier in the week on my way to town."

"That's what I like to hear." The realtor grinned from ear to ear. "Young Robert had me nervous, signing the papers without his fiancée having seen the house, but I see he had his bases covered."

Rose joined in their laugher, as the realtor led the way to the house. Had she heard right? Robert had told the realtor they were engaged.

"This way." Mr. Hanson opened the front door and motioned them to the left.

A stairwell opened in front of the entrance, turning halfway at a landing with shiny oak steps and handrails. There was no door at the bottom of the stairs like the familiar farmhouse had at home. To the right was the obvious door to the master bedroom. Hardwood floors were everywhere—fancy hardwood floors with glittering new varnish, so unlike the scratched floors at home.

Mr. Hanson paused in front of the counter separating the kitchen from the large dining room. "Brand new cabinets installed last year. Maple, the best of the line, with granite countertops."

Rose stared. The fancy cabinets. "Did you say your grandpa saw this house?" Rose whispered to Robert.

"Yah," he whispered back, obviously annoyed.

"The remodeling job was done by one of the best carpenters in Pawnee City," Mr. Hanson was saying. "Cleaver Contractors. They do excellent work. Perhaps not on par with Amish carpenters, but close."

"They look great to me," Robert said.

Rose forced herself to nod. Her head was spinning. The house was way too fancy for an Amish home, and she was certain the community's church *ordnung* forbad these kinds of cabinets. This was the kind of house Conrad Wisner might live in.

Robert seemed to read her mind. "Grandpa liked them."

"But—" she objected.

Robert must have known what she meant, because he said, "They're allowed by Grandpa's church ordnung, or he would have said something."

Which avoided the point, but Rose shut her mouth. Arguing with Robert in front of the realtor was not an option.

Mr. Hanson continued the tour of the house. Robert was smiling and laughing. He looked very pleased with everything. There was a washroom in the back of the kitchen which opened onto a covered porch.

"The washer and dryer go with the place." Mr. Hanson waved his hand dismissively. "I know the Amish don't use electric, but they'll sell easily at a garage sale."

"Would be nice to use them for a while," Robert said.

Rose couldn't believe what she was hearing.

Mr. Hanson grinned. "I'm not the one making the rules. Make's me no difference."

Rose felt her face growing red. What was wrong with Robert? He knew better than to crowd the church ordnung, and right in front of an English man.

"I guess we could use a little extra cash." Robert laughed. "Don't want to have the deacon visit us the first week we're married."

Rose felt her face burn even hotter. Robert had no shame, joking about the deacon's visit. She had never had a visit from Deacon John, but Robert apparently—

"Just joking," he said, when the realtor moved out of earshot for a moment.

Rose didn't answer. She was not sure Robert was joking. Was he intimately familiar with Deacon John's Saturday afternoon visits?

CHAPTER 34

While the house was being shown to Robert and Rose, Conrad was driving south out of Pawnee on his way to an appointment with Mr. Helmps. He passed a buggy going the opposite direction and waved. The lady inside waved back with a big smile on her face. He didn't know her, but she must have heard of him. His truck was clearly marked. A warm glow filled him. Being liked had its distinct advantages. Perhaps before long there might be more invitations into Amish homes. Deep down, he knew he couldn't wait.

Conrad pulled through a stop sign and accelerated again. He shook his head to clear his brain. Was this real—this budding relationship with the Amish people? His attraction to Rose was increasing at the same time. Two trains headed for a head-on collision unless he missed something. Yet, he couldn't stop thinking about Rose. He had feelings for the woman which went well beyond the simple friendship he had fostered with the other Amish in the community. Somewhere he wasn't thinking clearly. Somewhere between Esther's homemade ice cream, the moonlight, and Poe's poetry ballad. What did one do with something like this?

He should speak with Rose. Give voice to what existed between them. She had to know, but she was also dating someone else. Maybe if she gave him a stinging rebuke for his impropriety, he would come to his senses. Yet, why would Esther so obviously encourage him in his interest by opening her home to him and saying the things she did? What was he missing? What moved and shaped the Amish mind to produce such obvious contradictions, such clear mixed signals?

On one hand, a door had opened for him. On the other, the door was closed. Rose and any consideration of joining the Amish community was undeniably linked. Maybe they shouldn't be, but they were. Life had been confusing since Iraq. The Amish community had seemed a way forward, until the confusion appeared again. Not a nasty confusion caused by the fog of war, but a warm and gentle mixing of hearth and home. Rose was dating. He kept returning to the facts, which didn't seem to make much difference to his heart.

Conrad slowed and waited for the correct address marker to appear alongside the road. He turned on his blinker and made a sharp left into the driveway.

Mr. Helmps appeared at once in the barn door.

"Prompt man," Mr. Helmps greeted him, when Conrad hopped out.

"I try."

Mr. Helmps extended his hand. "For the most part, the younger generation has forgotten the common courtesies. Glad to make your acquaintance."

"And yours, sir."

"So, what do you know about corn fungus."

"Let's take a look." Conrad responded.

Mr. Helmp motioned with his hand. "We'll take my pickup."

Ten minutes later, they drove up to the field which spread into the distance with growing young corn stalks. Conrad climbed out and walked several rows, inspecting the cobs with his hands.

"Any ideas?" Mr. Helmp's asked.

"White mold, I think."

"I agree, but what's the cure?"

Conrad rubbed his neck. "There's fungicides, of course, but you know about them."

"I do. Tell me what I don't know."

"Are you open to organic remedies?"

"They teach natural remedies at the university?"

"Made us aware of them," Conrad said. "Organic farming has made a big splash on the scene, enough to merit mention."

"I see. Is this progress?"

Conrad grinned. "Depends on your point of view."

"So hit me."

"Milk, 1 to 9 parts with water. You spray weekly. Eco friendly."

Mr. Helmp's chuckled. "Sounds like something my grandpa would say."

"You asked."

"Anything else?"

"There's a remedy from around 1933 using baking soda and soap."

Mr. Helmps laughed. "I think we'll stick with the fungicides."

"Have your pick. They all have their claims."

"You have any more advice."

"The Amish are thinking about organic farming. Are you sure you want them to beat you at the game?"

Mr. Helmps raised his eyebrows. "Really?"

"Big city folks pay big prices for produce grown close to nature."

"Maybe I do need to educate myself."

"I'm here to help any day."

"Thanks for now. Hop in. I'll get you back to your truck."

They bumped across the field, and Conrad shook Mr. Helmps's hand. "You let me know."

"We'll see," Mr. Helmps said, and Conrad drove out of the lane.

CHAPTER 35

Back at the house showing, Rose's head throbbed by the time the tour of the upstairs was concluded. The rooms were huge, as they should be, with plenty of space for two beds in most of them, which was what *kinner* would need—if the Lord granted them. Rose tried to imagine kinner sleeping in the bedrooms but felt nothing. Her whole body had grown numb and cold.

"There's excellent remodel work done up here." Mr. Hanson declared.

They went downstairs, and the tour proceeded through the master bedroom and bath. There was a tile floor and a fancy whirlpool with a large mirror hung on an entire sidewall.

"Just the thing for aching muscles after a long day in the fields." Mr. Hanson joked.

"I couldn't agree more," Robert said.

Rose felt her neck grow red. How could Robert like these fancy English things?

They went through the rest of the downstairs and stepped outside.

"I know you showed me the other day, but can we see the barn again?" Robert asked Mr. Hanson.

"Certainly." Mr. Hanson responded.

"I think I'll look at the garden spot while you recheck the barn." Rose told them.

"She likes her garden." Robert piped up. "She's the best gardener in the whole community." There was obvious admiration in his voice.

"I could use a gardener at my place," Mr. Hanson said.

Their voices faded into the distance while Rose walked the weed-choked rows of the garden plot. This was where her joy would abide, not in the house with fancy English things. Robert clearly meant to keep them. How he would clear the matter with Deacon John was a big question, but he obviously planned to try. She would not object further. This was Robert's decision. She was not a fancy woman, but if Robert and his grandfather approved of the house, she would be happy. A few years of normal living would wear off the newness. With kinner running in and out of doors, sparkling floors became dull. In the meantime, she would throw rugs over a few things, and hang a wall quilt over both large mirrors in the master bedroom. If Robert wanted this farm, she would support him. Rose was determined she would be a submissive and proper wife for the man.

Rose knelt to run her fingers through a spot of loosened soil. Conrad would doubtless visit the place before long since Robert planned to seek Conrad's advice on the farm. She would ask Conrad if the garden soil needed anything more than the usual cattle and horse manure she used from the barns. Since Conrad was apparently a permanent fixture in the life of the community, she would have to face the man. She would have to banish her horrible feelings for him. Conrad meant no harm with his friendliness toward them or toward her. He came from a world where men and women conversed freely with each other. She would have to remember their differences and never think Conrad meant anything serious by his.

"Like the spot?" Robert's voice made Rose jump.

"Looks goot," she said, attempting a smile.

"Didn't mean to startle you," Robert said. "Mr. Hanson and I were in a discussion about barn design. I thought you would hear us."

"I was telling Robert." Mr. Hanson chimed in. "Your Amish people have skills the world in general has long lost."

Rose smiled up at him. "You'll have to come to our next barn raising."

"I would consider the invitation a great honor." Mr. Hanson rubbed his hands together. "Anything else you want to see, Miss?"

"I'm done." Rose replied. "The garden spot is perfect."

"And the rest of the house?"

"We can make the place livable," she said.

He appeared puzzled, but still smiled.

"Let's go to closing at the earliest possible date." Robert spoke up. "You'll need to coordinate with my grandpa in Lancaster for the funds, and you already have his information."

"Certainly!" Mr. Hanson shook hands with Robert and was gone with a wave over his shoulder.

With the car gone, Robert led the way back to the buggy. Rose hopped up and held the reins he tossed up to her until Robert climbed in. They trotted out of the driveway and turned north.

"So," Robert said. "What do you think?"

"You seem to like the place," she said.

"I like the place very much." He gazed over his shoulder for one last look. "The barn and the lands couldn't be better, and the house is quite a house."

"We can cover a few of the fancy things," she said, "and living will take care of the rest."

He straightened his back. "I would like to keep things as they are. There is nothing wrong with the place."

"The fancy things—" she tried to stop talking but couldn't. "Are those things within the ordnung rules?"

"I'll handle the ordnung rules," he said, "and Deacon John. Don't you worry about a thing."

"I'm not worrying," she said.

He didn't seem to hear. "Just think Rose. I've never done this before, purchasing a farm. I'll have my own place—a wunderbah place which has things I've never dreamed of having."

"Like the whirlpool?" she deadpanned.

His back went straight again. "There is nothing wrong with a few nice things."

"But the ordnung—" she managed.

He ignored her and rattled on. "I'll be moving into the place, once I close, but a man shouldn't live alone for any length of time, not without a Mamm or a sister, or—you know what I mean."

Rose tried to breathe, but her chest felt held in a vise.

"Things have been moving along so nicely." Robert gave her a tense smile.

Rose finally found her voice. "I guess my family and yours could bring food over occasionally. Maybe a dish of meatballs or a casserole. Perhaps a dessert?"

Robert cleared his throat. "You know what I mean."

She didn't dare look at him. "I'll have to think about this. I've just seen the house today."

His voice was sharp. "After all of this waiting. You can't do this to me, Rose. I'm moving into the house, and I'm through waiting."

"You'll have to have patience, Robert. I can't talk about marriage right now."

"And when can you speak of a wedding date?" he asked.

"I don't know. We've only had a few dates, and—"

"We've waited a long time," he said, "and the community expects a wedding this fall. I want the date set."

"Fall is not yet," she said, "and I can't think at the moment. You'll have to wait."

"Rose, don't be like this." He looked pleadingly at her. "I can't move into the house without a wedding date set. I couldn't stand the thought, or if someone were to find out."

"Weddings are a great secret in the community," she said. "No one will suspect anything, and we will be dating."

"To what end?" he asked. "Dating is to find out what the Lord's will is, and we knew what the Lord's will was long before we began dating."

"I—Robert, please. I can't commit at the moment. If I had known this conversation would occur, or even had some indication."

"We—I mean, we're buying a place."

"I know. I'll live with the place as it is."

"So why the fuss about the date?"

"I can't—you have to give me breathing room."

He sighed deeply. "I can't say how disappointed I am in how you're acting, Rose. We can't go through our lives like this. With you always—"

"You think, then—" Rose didn't finish as joy rushed through her.

"I think," he said. "I will have to keep working on this problem of yours which goes right back to your dreaminess. In the meantime, the Lord will give me the strength to move into the house without a wedding date to comfort me. Once we are wed, things will be different, I'm telling you."

Rose leaned back into her seat, as an icy coldness crept through her. Robert hadn't picked up on her suggestion, and he wasn't going to pick up.

"I'm glad to see you're trying to be submissive," he said. "Maybe goot can come of this delay, as goot came the last time. I doubt if I would have the courage to buy this farm without the suffering you put me through waiting those long months."

"I'm glad I'm a blessing to you." Rose muttered under her breath.

Robert seemed lost in his thoughts, as he slowed for the Miller's lane.

"Don't drive me in," Rose said. "Drop me off, and I'll walk in."

"I can drive in easily enough," he said.

"You picked me up at the end of the lane, and you can drop me off at the end of the lane."

"This is very strange," Robert said.

Rose was already out of the door before he came to a full stop.

"See you later." He called after her.

Rose gave a little wave with her hand but she didn't look back.

Mamm met her inside the front door. "Did you have a goot time?"

"The house is nice," she said.

Mamm studied Rose for a moment. "What was wrong with the house?"

"It's fancy," she said, "quite fancy, but Robert likes the place."

"There you go," Mamm said. "Stop worrying about fancy. Having my daughter live in a better place than this old farmhouse is not a bad thing."

"But what about the ordnung?" Rose asked.

"Robert is goot for you," Mamm said with a smile. "Let Robert take care of the ordnung. You just enjoy what the man gives you."

"I like the garden spot," Rose said.

"Of course you do." Mamm was already moving on. "Can you start supper for me? I have some outside work."

"I'll change right away." Rose dashed up the stairs to the familiar safety of her room.

She sat on the edge of the bed to catch her breath. Had what happened just happened? She had refused to set a wedding date with Robert? Where had the resistance come from? Marriage to Robert was inevitable, so why postpone the naming of the day? Nothing goot would come of this stubbornness.

She had to accept and to submit, even if life with Robert loomed dark in front of her like a distant summer thunderstorm. She had never imagined marriage could look so foreboding. Maybe the problem was her perspective, her feelings of what married life would be like with Wilmer, and now worse—with Conrad. Horrible thoughts from the past were what made the present moment seem so intolerable. She shouldn't blame Robert for his lack of sensitivity. He was a man, and who knew what men were like—really like. She had never lived with one as her husband. If life with Robert was a disappointment, life with Conrad would be a disaster. They were different, so different. She would have to go English, lose her life in the community, experience the awful fissure which would occur in her family. She would have to set a wedding date with Robert. Soon! Very soon.

"Help me, Lord," she whispered toward the ceiling of the bedroom.

CHAPTER 36

Later in the evening, Conrad slipped across the fields and knocked on the Jesse and Esther's front door.

"Howdy." Jesse greeted him when he opened the door. "What have we here?"

"I'm not inviting myself for supper." Conrad assured him.

Jesse laughed. "Nothing wrong if you would. Our door is always open to visitors."

"Would you have a moment? I won't stay long."

"Sure." Jesse stepped outside. "Is the question farming related or personal?"

"Personal, but Esther is involved."

"Serious then." Jesse stepped back into the house and motioned for Conrad to follow. "Esther, Conrad is here. Do you have a moment?"

There was quick flurry of footsteps and Esther appeared. She gave her apron a quick shake. "Conrad. I've just set the supper table."

"I can't stay," he replied, "but thanks for the invitation."

"Shall we sit?" Jesse offered.

"Outside, outside." Esther waved her hands. "The evening is too nice to stay cooped up in the house."

Conrad grinned and followed the couple out to the porch. They seated themselves as they had a few nights before, but tonight the sky in front of them was dark, the horizon beginning to twinkle with a thousand stars.

"It's beautiful even without the moon." Esther pronounced and gave her apron another shake. "Tell us the goot news."

Conrad cleared his throat. "I have a question. In fact, kind of a continuation of things we have alluded to. Do people really join your community from my world?"

"Conrad!" Esther's face glowed. "Of course they do. I knew you were one of us for a long time."

Conrad grinned. "Thanks, but joining can't be easy."

"Perhaps not." Jesse joined in. "Yet, there are people who have. Not here, in this community, but back in Lancaster."

"How difficult would the transition be?" he asked.

"If you're Protestant Christian, there's not much change in biblical belief," Jesse said. "Largely, just our simple lifestyle, which everyone submits to, and our German language. Did you learn German from school, by any chance?"

"I did indeed have a German class in high school," he said, "lessons I've long forgotten."

"Then you're halfway there," Esther gushed. "I can't say how happy this makes me. You must stay for supper to celebrate."

"I'm only asking questions," he insisted.

"They're well thought out questions," Esther told him. "I know you're on the journey, and you must remain for supper. I won't take no for an answer."

"I can't." Conrad demurred. "I already have supper in the oven—well, the microwave oven. Not quite Amish, but nourishing."

Esther joined in their laughter. "If you won't stay for supper, you must listen to my next great idea. Why don't Jesse and I invite the young people over next week for a garden hoeing, and you can get to know everyone. The community would be helping me with my weeds, and we would be helping you decide whether our life is what you want. If you decide against joining, no one need be the wiser."

Conrad thought for a moment. "Why not, but what are the basics? How do I dress when the time comes? I'll stand out in my regular clothing."

"Wear old denim pants and a work shirt." Esther told him. "You'll blend right in."

"With no suspenders?"

Esther laughed. "You can borrow a set from Jesse, but you might be letting the cat out of the bag."

"I guess so." Conrad allowed. "We don't want to go there at the moment."

"Settled then." Esther beamed. "I'll tell everyone you're our neighbor. You did plow the garden and help plant the seeds. There's a perfectly natural explanation."

"I agree." Jesse chimed in. "Most of them have heard of you as the county's extension agent."

"Makes sense." Conrad stood to his feet. "Thanks both of you for your time."

They waved to him as he left and were still sitting on the front porch when he paused at the door of his small house to look back. He would see Rose at the gathering, but he must be discrete. No one must know what he felt in his heart toward an Amish woman. How this would work out, he had no idea, but the road in front of him appeared open.

"Rose." He whispered, before stepping inside his house. "Beautiful Rose."

CHAPTER 37

The youth hoedown for Esther's garden was in full swing the following week when Rose arrived riding in Edwin's buggy. Esther had told the youth coordinator of the planned event after the last Sunday services. Robert hadn't mentioned anything on Sunday evening about looking forward to working on Esther's garden or anything further on locking down a wedding date. He had been engrossed in the details of what he planned for the farm once the closing occurred.

Why Esther had planned the hoedown was the question.

"I could have come over if you needed help." Rose had told Esther, which was the truth. She had to face Conrad sometime—better at Esther's place than seeing him on Robert's farm.

"I want a youth gathering," Esther had said without further explanation, "and Conrad is joining in with the fun."

Rose had ignored the reference to Conrad. Esther couldn't still be harboring hopes she would leave Robert. Not with the purchase of Robert's farm. Maybe Esther and Jesse were lonesome for their former youth activities? This would be a great way for the couple to reconnect. For her part, this was an easy way of seeing Conrad again during a youth gathering—an unintended consequence which Esther probably didn't think about.

She glanced at Edwin who was seated beside her on the buggy seat, peering about. "Mary is over by the barn," she teased, trying not to think of facing Conrad sometime this evening. Maybe the man would ignore her, and their paths would never cross.

"How did I miss Mary when you saw her right away?" Edwin grumbled.

"You're too nervous." She suggested.

Edwin grunted and climbed down to tie his horse at a fence post along the road.

Rose caught her breath at the sight of Conrad's pickup truck parked in the distance near his house. The man was home, perhaps already at the gathering, but none of this would affect her. She would ignore him, and no one would notice among so many young people.

Rose noticed Robert walking toward Edwin's buggy at a rapid pace. He must have been keeping an eye out for their arrival.

"Wish Mary was as eager to see me." Edwin muttered.

Pain stabbed through Rose, but she didn't answer.

"Howdy there, you two." Robert hollered at them.

Rose ducked her head behind her bonnet, as Robert helped Edwin unhitch.

"I think I'll go see someone." Edwin proclaimed and headed for the barn with his horse.

"What a lovely evening," Robert addressed Rose when Edwin was gone.

"It is," she agreed, not looking at him.

"Perfect for a hoedown," he added.

"I was hoping so." Rose stole a glance at him.

"Like I said, perfect for a hoedown." Robert grinned. "I expected you would be one of the first here, so I came early."

Rose made a face. "Sorry to disappoint you. Edwin was delayed with the chores, and Charles decided to stay home."

He stepped closer. "I didn't tell you on Sunday night because I didn't know for sure, but Grandpa's money will be wired in for the closing in three weeks. The lawyers couldn't get the paperwork lined up any sooner."

She forced a smile. "I'm happy for you."

"I was hoping tonight we could set—" Robert let the words dangle.

"Robert, please," she begged. "There are people around. Let's speak on the matter later."

His grin was gone. "All you have to say is, yah. How difficult is the word? No one knows what you mean, even if they heard. We can set the date next Sunday evening."

"Robert, I can't. Not tonight."

"I have waited a long time, Rose," he warned. "You can't do this to me."

She moved past him. "Let's go help them work in the garden."

He said something she couldn't hear.

A few steps later, he had caught up and led the way into the garden. Rose stopped short at the sight of Conrad among the gathered young people. He was dressed in a ragged pair of denim pants and an ugly old work shirt. He had been talking with the others but noticed her and turned to wave. His rugged handsomeness took her breath away. He looked so happy, even happy to see her, but he couldn't be. He just was being friendly.

"Looks like our county extension agent is here," Robert said in her ear.

"Oh," she said, not wanting him to know she had noticed.

Robert gave a short laugh. "The more weeds he pulls, the less I have to remove."

Several of the young people also noticed them and paused in their work. Rose gave them a wave to cover her flustered spirits.

"Might as well get going," Robert complained and knelt down to grab at the weeds with his bare hands.

Careful for the plants, Rose almost said, but bit back the words in time. Robert would not take kindly to instructions from her on gardening.

While Robert was occupied, Rose tried not to glance at Conrad, but she couldn't resist. She ended up staring at him. At least no one appeared to notice. Conrad had his back turned, chatting with the others working in his vicinity, and from all appearances had forgotten about her.

Rose knelt to work beside Robert. As they pulled weeds, they drifted in opposite directions. So much like their life together, but this did make things easier. Before he was out of her line of vision, Rose was certain Robert had pulled several young carrot plants along with the weeds. She couldn't protest, as the distance between them increased.

"Good evening." Conrad's cheerful voice sounded beside her.

Rose's head came up so sharply, her neck hurt. One hand flew instinctively to press the injured muscle.

"Didn't mean to startle you." Conrad apologized.

"No. I'm—" Rose forgot what she wanted to say.

"Everything is growing very well," he said.

Rose rubbed her neck, giving up on any pretense. "I'm not usually this jumpy."

He smiled. "A strange voice at your ear. I understand."

"You're not a stranger." Rose objected and wished she could put the words back in her mouth. Familiarity with Conrad was the last thing she needed.

He knelt down beside her, gently reaching for a weed with one hand, and shielding the plant with the other.

She stared.

"There," he said, lifting his gaze to her. "One down, but many to go."

The blueness of his eyes made her dizzy, and Rose ducked her head. She couldn't see clearly enough to find the weeds, so she groped among the plants, hoping her movements passed for work.

"Are you over here often?" he asked.

"No." Rose tried to breathe evenly.

"I didn't think you had been." His blue eyes met hers. "I think I would have seen you or signs of you."

Rose's lips moved, but no sound came out. He must think her a babbling infant.

Conrad's face moved closer. "Are you okay?"

"Yah!" Rose pulled back sharply, and her neck hurt again.

"I don't seem to be hitting the right notes tonight," he said. "Shall I leave?"

"Oh, no, please. Everything is fine." Rose clung to her neck with one hand. "I'll be steady in a minute."

He didn't look convinced.

She wanted him close. She didn't want him to leave, at the same time knowing she should want him to leave. This was an awful mess. Rose bent her head and lifted the leaves of a young lettuce plant. Somehow her eyesight worked again. A tiny weed appeared, and she carefully plucked the blade out of the ground. Out of the corner of her eye, Rose could see Conrad doing the same thing.

Conrad glanced up and smiled. "We should get done early with so many young people involved."

"I think so. A community effort," she said. "What is the saying, many hands make light work."

"I like this." He mused. "Working with a group of young people. I never had the opportunity before."

Rose was dizzy again.

"In case you wonder why I'm here." Conrad looked worriedly down at his denim pants. "Esther said I could come and could wear this thing, and this shirt. Try to blend in, but I may have overdone things."

"Oh! You look perfect." Rose heard her own voice speaking. "Quite goot in fact. I thought so the moment I saw you tonight."

"You did?" Conrad appeared skeptical.

Rose wished she could shut her mouth, but the words kept coming. "The outfit goes with you. Quite well in fact."

He grinned. "The Tom Sawyer look, hah?"

Rose heard herself laugh. "Maybe? I hadn't quite pinned down the effect."

He flexed his chest muscles. "All we need is a river and a raft floating down the Mississippi."

Rose didn't answer. She had to stop talking. Someone would notice how well they were getting along. If Robert did—she looked for him among the bent backs but couldn't find him.

"Esther said they have you over quite often for supper." She had to say something. Silence was worse than talking with him.

"They do." He pushed the dirt back in place with his hand after having pulled a weed. "Jesse and Esther are very hospitable."

"Do you enjoy your time with them?"

"Very much," he said. "There is something about your lifestyle which greatly appeals to me."

"Really!" Rose grew dizzy again.

"Here you are!" Robert's voice broke into Rose's fog.

All the cobwebs were gone at once.

"Good evening, Robert." Conrad greeted him.

"Good evening," Robert replied. "I see you know how to work like an Amish man, down on your hands and knees."

Conrad chuckled. "In my Tom Sawyer outfit. Don't you think my selection of clothing makes for the Tom Sawyer affect?"

"Who is Tom Sawyer?" Robert asked.

Rose ducked her head, but not before she saw the astonished look on Conrad's face. "You've never read Tom Sawyer."

"I don't read much," Robert said. "Mostly I work on the farm."

"You do know how to read." Conrad laughed and Robert joined in.

"With college educated people like you around, who needs to read Tom Sawyer."

Their light banter continued, and Rose focused on Jesse and Esther who worked at the other end of the garden, laughing and whispering to each other. She stooped low to pull a weed close to a corn stalk. Anything to keep her mind away from Conrad and the comparisons which flooded her mind. With the two men working side-by-side, she couldn't believe how vastly different they were. Why had the Lord not seen fit to have the community populated with men like Conrad? She would have agreed to a date with him before the question was out of his mouth.

"What do you think of my seed selections for your father's farm?" Conrad was asking Robert. He had moved into the row across from her. His nearness wrapped itself around her.

"Great, and I'll have my own farm in three weeks, Lord willing." Robert announced. "I'll be using all of your suggestions come next spring planting season."

"You like them?"

"I do," Robert said. "I couldn't talk Daett into trying all of them, but like I said, I'm ready next year."

"I'm not trying to cause trouble with my suggestions." Conrad looked worried.

"You aren't." Robert assured him.

"How is the garden going at the Miller household?" Conrad directed his question toward Rose. "I forgot to ask earlier."

Rose straightened her back before she answered. "Goot, I think."

"I'll have to stop by and see for myself sometime."

"You should," Rose said, with a quick glance toward Robert. He didn't seem to even hear.

A moment later, Robert stood up. "I think I'll leave you two and head over to Cousin Fred. I haven't told him the goot news about my farm."

When Robert was gone, they pulled weeds together, two bent figures on opposite rows, the silence like tension between them surrounded by the close proximity of the others.

"So the boyfriend bought a farm." Conrad broke the tension between them.

Rose didn't answer. She didn't want to think about Robert. She didn't care at the moment what the rules were. If Robert left them together, he was partly to blame for this mess.

"Do you like the farm?" Conrad asked.

"Yah! Robert picked a goot farm!" Rose didn't look at him.

"Is there a nice house?" he asked.

"Very fancy." She looked up. "Much too fancy for an Amish person, but with some wear and tear, the problem will be fixed."

"Too fancy?" he asked. "What does *too fancy* mean?"

"Too English," she said. "The cabinets are dolled up with arches on the doors. There's shiny hardwood floors, and there's a whirlpool tub."

"I see," Conrad said.

Rose's face flamed. "I mean—I shouldn't have mentioned the whirlpool tub, but how do you—a whirlpool tub can't run without electricity."

"I guess you're right." Conrad appeared amused. "An Amish home doesn't have electricity."

"Exactly!"

"And what does the boyfriend say about this problem?"

"Robert—" Rose caught herself. "I'm sorry. I shouldn't be talking about this."

"Gardens are much safer subjects." He agreed.

"I'm not—" Rose faltered.

"Have you been dating long? You and Robert?" he asked.

"Two months—there about." She wasn't certain. "We've known each other for a long time. We've been waiting. I mean, sometimes things work out in such a fashion."

"People do wait," he said. "When they are uncertain or when circumstances don't allow them to proceed."

"I don't know why I was waiting," she said, which wasn't exactly true, "but we're not waiting anymore. Which, I guess, is—but really I shouldn't be saying these things."

"I'm not prying," he said. "I'm just curious how things work in the Amish community."

"Don't take us as the ordinary." Rose hastened to say. "Most couples have dated for two or three years before they buy a farm, not two months."

He raised his eyebrows. "Is there a wedding date?"

Rose felt the heat rise into her face. Why was she talking with this man about her wedding, which she wouldn't agree to? She grabbed at a weed and nearly took out a potato plant when she yanked upward.

"I shouldn't be—" he said.

"There isn't one." She didn't look up at him. She desperately wanted him to know, to understand somehow, but how did one understand such a thing?

"Isn't buying a farm without a wedding date unusual for a dating couple, or are the Amish different?"

"We're waiting," she said, "or I am, but the house is nice."

He clearly could make no sense out of her statement. "Even though the house is fancy," he said.

Rose yanked at another weed and didn't answer.

"Your sister and her husband are being very hospitable to me," Rose heard Conrad say, "as are the rest of the Amish. I'm also grateful for this opportunity to associate with the Amish young people."

"We're supposed to be hospitable." Rose managed. He had to know she was being more than hospitable.

"You are indeed," he said. "Esther had me over the other Sunday night for ice cream and to watch the moon rise."

"You watched the moon rising?" Rose stared again.

"Yes." His gaze was fixed on the horizon. "The first summer's full moon."

"Ah—you really did watch the moon rise with Esther and—" Rose closed her mouth to stop the sounds from coming out.

"Aren't you into moon watching?" He appeared puzzled. "I would have thought you would be."

"I love watching the moon." Rose felt the tears sting. "Much more than Esther does."

"You were watching the other night?" He tilted his head.

"I saw the moon from our front porch. Yah!"

"Are you familiar with Poe's poem on the moon?" he asked.

"Edgar Allen?" She was staring again, transfixed this time.

"The very one," he said.

"He wrote quite a few poems on the moon." Rose pressed her eyes shut and quoted, "At midnight, in the month of June, I stand beneath the mystic moon."

"You know the poem." He looked very pleased.

Before Rose could answer, Robert appeared in the edge of her vision.

"I hear you're a moon watcher." Conrad deadpanned.

Robert gave a snort. "Don't tell me you're into this silliness. I see the moon every time I walk from the house to the barn—when it's in the sky, of course. Rose is the one who sits on the front porch and gazes into the light beams for pleasure. A dream world which isn't goot for anyone."

Now Conrad was staring. "So you're not into the wonders of nature even though Rose is?"

Robert dismissively waved his hand. "I'm a practical person, and I'm teaching Rose about practicableness. She's an excellent gardener, and her family is from steady Amish blood. Where her dreamy nonsense comes from, I don't know."

"I see," Conrad said. "I would have thought you a little more romantic."

"A man works hard and supplies for his family," Robert declared. "That's about as romantic as it gets for me."

"There is a romance in gardening," Conrad said. "Would you disagree?"

"Gardening has nothing to do with romance," Robert said. "Neither does the moon. It's up there in the sky to give us light by nighttime, as the sun does during the day. You would not gaze at the sun for hours on end, would you?"

Conrad grinned. "I doubt if you'd see much afterward— at least not without a sun shield."

"There you go," Robert. "Point made."

"You ever hear of Edgar Allen Poe?" Conrad asked.

He had to know Robert didn't know about Poe.

"Is this a corn seed type?" Robert asked.

Conrad chuckled. "I gather you haven't."

"The other night displayed a beautiful moon," Rose whispered. She had to say something.

Robert didn't hear, but Conrad obviously heard, from his quick glance in her direction.

The next few minutes passed in a daze with Robert and Conrad chatting about farming methods and seed types. Rose searched the ground for weeds, but they kept disappearing behind her tears. She felt relief and a deep sadness at the same time when the conversation died out. Conrad moved to the other end of the garden without speaking with her.

CHAPTER 38

Conrad stood off to the side of Esther's garden with his hoe in his hand. He had chosen the spot on purpose for its distance from where Rose and Robert worked. He was treading on thin ice with Rose, but he hadn't been able to help himself with his questions. The girl fascinated him beyond anything he had every experienced with a woman. She was dating, which was obviously a problem, but at the same time something was wrong with the relationship. He couldn't imagine a woman like Rose choosing a man like Robert. What was he missing? He felt a daring, a dashing impulse to interfere—to speak with her, to touch her heart, to draw her close, forbidden though she was to him.

"Howdy, there." One of the young men greeted him. "Been meaning to speak with you."

"Conrad Wisner." Conrad extended his hand.

"Ezra Yoder."

"Good to meet you."

"Enjoying yourself with the youth gathering?"

"I am."

"Are you used to this kind of thing?"

"Not really. I grew up north of here on a prairie farm."

"One of those big spreads."

"Have you seen one?"

Ezra grinned from ear to ear. "Worked on a few last fall during harvest time. We started on the east side of the state and worked our way west."

"Obviously you enjoyed yourself," Conrad said. "Are you doing this again?"

"Probably not. That was my splurge for *rumspringa*."

"Rumspringa?" He wrinkled his brow.

Ezra laughed. "You've never heard of the Amish rumspringa?"

"Not really."

"I thought the whole world knew. Aren't there TV shows—not that I've seen them, but you're English."

"I must have missed them growing up." Conrad joined the laughter. "Tell me. What is rumspringa?"

"Well." Ezra pursed his lips. "We do a little sampling of the world, before we settle down."

"A little sampling. Nothing too bad, though?"

Ezra shook his head.

"How was the sampling?"

"Goot, but I like it back here better. Been dating a girl all year. Naomi Stoll." Ezra beat his chest. "Can't beat Naomi."

"I suppose not." Conrad allowed.

"You have a girl out there?" Ezra asked.

"No. I'm sampling Amish life."

They laughed together. "How's the taste so far?"

"Different. No question there."

"Not thinking of joining us, are you?"

Conrad drew a deep breath. "The thought has crossed my mind. What would you suggest?"

"I don't know," Ezra said. "I was born in the faith, which makes my viewpoint different, I suppose."

"True." Conrad agreed.

"Well, you're welcome to join." Ezra slapped Conrad on the back. "Goot meeting you."

When Ezra left, Conrad's gaze drifted over to where Rose and Robert had been working. They were still exactly where he had left them before his conversation with Ezra.

CHAPTER 39

Rose stood up and forced a smile when Jesse and Esther approached them.

"How are you two doing?" Esther asked.

"Okay," Rose answered. "I think everyone is getting close to done."

"I'm tired of pulling weeds," Robert grumbled. "Seems like woman's work to me."

Jesse laughed. "My sympathies there. At least, we're almost finished. Take a break and come with me. There're a few stanchions I have to move in the barn, which could use an extra hand."

"You don't have to ask the second time," Robert said, and the two walked away, heading across the garden.

"Now, how are things *really* going?" Esther asked, once the men were out of ear shot.

"I can't stop talking with the man." Rose whispered, the horror heavy in her voice.

"Robert?" Esther raised her eyebrows.

"No. Conrad."

Esther looked way too pleased. "I asked him to come with the hopes this would happen."

"You shouldn't have." Rose raised her voice. "You know my weakness."

"I told you he likes the community. We made this gathering especially for him. I didn't tell you because I was afraid you'd stay home."

"You're right there." Rose caught her breath. "Did you say this gathering was specially made for Conrad?"

Esther leaned closer. "Yah, but don't get upset. He's a decent man. I'm glad you're falling for him."

Rose was beside herself. "Esther, I'm a dating woman, whose boyfriend has just purchased a farm."

Esther looked troubled. "Please don't tell me you've set a wedding date?"

Rose looked away. "No."

"There's hope, then." Esther clasped her hands heavenward. "Thank the dear Lord, I thought I was too late."

"Shhh." Rose warned. "Someone will hear you saying these awful things. I'll never live my reputation down if I jilt Robert for an English man."

"An English man who might become Amish." Esther was smiling from ear to ear. "I knew there was still a chance. Robert isn't the man for you. Which is why you couldn't commit to dating him, and why you hesitate about a wedding date."

"We've only been dating for—" Rose's hand waved in the air.

"Exactly," Esther said.

"You have to stop this," Rose warned.

"Stop what?" Esther feigned innocence.

"Trying to get me and Conrad together."

"You're not wed to Robert. I only want what's best for you."

"What's best for me is to live the life I love."

"But you should be in love."

"I am in love."

Esther made a face. "If you're in love with Robert, I can jump over the moon."

"What I have for the man is the same thing." Rose justified herself.

"Listen to yourself." Esther leaned closer. "You're not in love, and you know it."

"We have to stop talking," Rose said, kneeling down to search for weeds again.

"Come with me." Esther grabbed her arm and pulled Rose up.

"What are you doing?" Rose protested.

"Come." Esther headed across the yard and Rose followed obediently.

"Why are we going into the house?" Rose tried to protest again going up the front steps.

Esther didn't answer until they were in the kitchen. "There." Esther pointed. "I have the ice cream mix cooling on the stove. Go downstairs and start making the first batch. No one can make ice cream like you can."

"You're making ice cream?"

"Yah. Why are you surprised? Conrad likes ice cream."

Rose tried to clear her mind. "Ice cream for the entire youth group." She didn't want to think about Esther's mention of Conrad. Everyone liked ice cream.

"Two batches should be enough." Esther grabbed the bowl of ice cream mix. "Get the ice cube trays and follow me. Jesse is bringing another mixer one of his cousins brought along into the basement."

Rose collected as much ice from Esther's refrigerator she could carry and followed her sister downstairs. Esther had half of the ice cream mix poured in her drum and the mixer set up when Rose arrived.

"Dump in the ice." Esther ordered. "I'll go get the salt."

Rose did so, and Esther soon reappeared with a bag of salt and a chair.

"What a wunderbah evening this is." Esther proclaimed. "Now if Jesse hurries in with the other mixer ... He told me he was coming right away."

"You can't make Conrad one of us." Rose interrupted her sister's chattering.

"You should give him a chance," Esther shot back.

"You can, but I'm dating." Rose bent over and carefully poured in the salt, taking care not to spill any on the floor or the top of the drum.

"I have to tell you something," Esther's voice spoke from above her.

Rose stopped working. "Now what?"

"I didn't want to tell you, but I think I should."

Rose straightened her back.

"We had Conrad over the other Sunday evening."

"I know about the moon watching." Rose looked away, determined not to relive the disappointment and comparisons she had experienced earlier in the garden.

"He told you, and you're not convinced?" Esther appeared beside herself.

"I'm dating Robert." Rose bent over to give the handle a firm twirl. "Can't you face reality?"

"This is confirmation my feelings are correct."

"I can't go English, Esther."

"But you have to feel something for Robert to marry him."

Rose didn't respond, remembering. How did Esther always get through to her?

"You poor dear," Esther comforted. "Don't cry. Just dump Robert and trust the Lord."

The basement door burst open behind them, and Rose sat down to seize the ice cream handle. She didn't have to look up to know who had entered. Conrad's voice was clearly mixed in with Jesse's. The evening was only getting worse.

"There you are." Esther turned around to greet the arriving men.

"Conrad had to come in and experience homemade ice cream making for himself." Jesse declared, setting the borrowed mixer down with a thump. "Find out where this wunderbah goodness is coming from."

"I couldn't miss the experience for the world!" Conrad exclaimed. "Once I heard the ice cream making was being done in the basement, I had to come down."

"Perfect!" Esther sounded way too pleased with herself. "I couldn't have imagined a better plan. Here, help Rose with the work, while we set up the other mixer."

"I'm fine." Rose muttered twirling away on the handle of the ice cream canister.

Jesse appeared not to hear. "Sit down and take a spin." Jesse motioned for Rose to vacate the chair and for Conrad to take her place.

Rose did, stepping back, as Conrad sat down. "How exactly is this done?"

"Just turn," Jesse said. "The task is easy."

Conrad gingerly gripped the handle, as if he expected something to explode.

Jesse laughed. "The thing won't bite. Turn a little faster and we'll soon have homemade ice cream."

Conrad took a few turns glancing up at Rose. "There must be more to it than this."

"Ice cream," she said, which made no sense. Her mind wasn't working again.

Conrad didn't appear to mind her confusion, twirling away on the handle while Jesse and Esther set up the other mixer.

Esther pulled on Jesse's arm when they finished. "Let's go up and check on our guests. These two can finish the ice cream."

"We should help," Jesse protested.

"I know nothing about ice cream making." Conrad chimed in.

"Rose does." Esther was already halfway up the steps with Jesse on her arm. "You two are very capable and Jesse is needed for other things tonight."

The two disappeared up the stairs, and Rose tried to breathe. Conrad's presence filled the basement. She found another chair and took a seat beside the mixer.

Conrad smiled over at her. "Well, here we are, making Amish ice cream. Who would have thought?"

Only my sister. Rose almost said out loud. Her heart pounded so loud that Conrad had to hear the thumps.

He spoke gently, "This is very special for me Rose, but I know your sister put you up to this."

"You do." Her words came in a gasp.

"I do," he said. "If you're uncomfortable, I can stick my head outside and call for help. I'm sure someone is more than willing."

"I'm—I'm—" Here was her chance but the words wouldn't come.

He waited in the silence filled only with the turning of their handles.

"What is your sadness, Rose?" he finally asked. "I'm not trying to intrude. Tell me to shut up if you want to, and I will, but there's a sadness in your eyes. There always has been, I think. Since I first saw you in your garden the morning I stopped by your father's place."

No sound would come, even if she had wanted to speak. She couldn't believe he had asked, had seen, had noticed.

"My trouble was the war," He mused. "I didn't do anything I wasn't ordered to. Didn't do anything wrong, really. There was simply the tension, the tanks, the armored vehicles, the guns, and the dying. I'm tired of seeing things die."

Rose knew she was staring again. She simply couldn't speak.

"I'm sorry," he said. "I'll quit if I have disturbed you."

"No, tell me." She bent her head finding her voice, and twirled the handle for a few moments, concentrating, before slowing down again.

"Are you sure?"

Rose nodded without looking up. The sound of his voice soothed her shattered nerves and touched the depth of her pain. His eyes made the memory of Wilmer whole again. Alive? Like the sorrow was finally finished.

"The Humvee ahead of me hit a landmine. Turned the vehicle over. I was the gunner who covered while the injured were pulled out. I shot a few of the enemy—well, quite a few, but I stopped counting. I was saving lives, yes, yet I was also taking lives. The one canceling out the other. Things became—I don't know. There was no dishonor done, just wondering if there wasn't a better way. A longing for peace, not just for myself but for the tortured land we were in, for the people we were fighting against."

"I—I can't even imagine," Rose managed. This was a world she knew nothing about.

"I'm sorry, I shouldn't have." He paused to rub his eyes.

"I lost him in the sixth grade," Rose blurted out. "The boy I loved. He drowned. They came and told me, but the whole thing never seemed real. Even when I saw him in the casket. He was still Wilmer. He was dead, but I couldn't let go."

"I'm sorry," he said. "I had no idea."

"I should have gotten over him a long time ago," Rose rushed on. "I should have stopped dreaming about him. I know I should have. Therefore, I have these troubles. My mistakes are many. I know they are."

He reached across the space between them and touched her arm. "It's okay, Rose. It's always been okay."

"Oh." Her voice came in a gasp. She could almost believe he was right, and yet so much was wrong. There was—she didn't want to even think about Robert in a moment like this.

"Time doesn't heal anything," he said. "Not really. Only the Lord can touch the heart."

"I—you understand." Rose turned before Conrad answered, to focus on turning the handle. She had to keep working or everything would turn into madness. Why was she telling Conrad these things?

"I'm not saying I understand," his voice came from a distance, "but I want to understand. I really do."

Rose bent her back over the ice cream mixer, not looking at him. They were almost finished. The handle had begun to turn harder. She had to get away from the man before something worse happened. Something—she knew what the something was. There had been the moment, alone in woods on a Saturday afternoon with Wilmer. A rare occasion when they had run into each other doing their weekend errands. Their hands had touched among the trees of their small woods. She had wanted—wanted so badly. Had come close, but the distance between them had seemed too great. Her courage had failed her. Wilmer had fidgeted, his hand in hers, suddenly uncomfortable, and the moment had faded. Lost forever. She was losing the forever again. Watching a repeat of her greatest regret from a distance. She should have kissed Wilmer. Even a little peck on the cheek. She should have, but she hadn't.

"Is this handle supposed to be turning harder?" he asked, his words pulling her back.

Rose took a moment to answer, clearing her head. "Yah. We go until we almost can't turn. Should come soon, now."

"I see," he said.

Rose looked away. Did he know? Like Wilmer had known? How could he? He was English, and yet—he was a man. The thought took the strength from her arm, and Rose grabbed the handle with both hands.

"Should I turn both?" He looked worried.

Rose forced a laugh. "You can't, and we're almost done."

"Rose," his voice was gentle. "Did I say something wrong?"

She shook her head, her gaze fixed on the concrete floor. She looked up and couldn't breathe. The desire to capture the moment he had revived gripped her.

"We have something special, Rose," he said. "You have to feel what I feel."

"You're English," she turned her face away, "and I'm Amish."

He didn't say anything, bending his shoulder into turning the handle. She could hardly complete the strokes anymore, even with both hands. They were finished, and the moment was slipping away.

Rose paused and stood slowly.

"Done?" he asked.

She nodded. They were, but they weren't. She couldn't believe she was doing this. Daring to walk here, but she couldn't let this happen again. Tomorrow there would be no Conrad, just the memory of Wilmer, just Robert, and she would walk alone again. Tonight, there was this, and she was insane, but she was going to ask.

"Rose," he said, looking up from his chair.

She stepped closer. "Would you? Please? I have no right to ask, but would you?"

"Would I what?" He stood to his feet.

She lifted her face to him. "Kiss me, Conrad."

The puzzled look vanished, replaced by an intensity in his eyes. "Rose. Are you sure?"

She nodded. She couldn't speak. She could barely stand.

His hands came up, touching her face, enveloping her. His face came even closer, and she moved to meet him. The world went white, the basement walls faded, leaving only him, his lips, and the fire which burned between them.

How long they stood there, Rose never knew. She jerked back with a gasp, clutching both of his hands in hers.

"Rose," he said, his voice low. "You—"

"We can't do this again. Never!" The words burst out. "I'm sorry. I know I asked, but this was so wrong."

"Did I—"

"No, no." Rose rubbed her burning cheeks with both hands. "I had to. I was caught up—Oh—"

"We did nothing wrong." His voice reached her.

"Oh, we did." She met his intense gaze. "We did something very wrong, and we must never do this again. I'm Amish, and you're English."

"Was I a memory?" he asked, the pain flickering in his eyes.

"No, of course not," Rose denied and pain exploded in her chest.

She could not hurt him. She could see he wasn't convinced, and she could not lie.

She took his hands again. "Yah, you speak the truth, and I lied. You were a memory. I'm so sorry."

"I—I had hoped for more," he said, "but I understand."

Now she was making things worse. "You're—I shouldn't have used you. I know I shouldn't have."

"Didn't you like—" He left the question hang.

Rose's mind whirled. She was not going to lie again. "You just gave me the sweetest, most wunderbah kiss I have ever had."

Through his pain, his eyes showed a twinkle. "How many times have you been kissed?"

"Just by you," she said.

"Not by him?"

"If you mean Robert, no."

"I meant the other."

"No, but I wanted to. We almost did, but I couldn't."

"Now you've kissed him."

"I'm sorry." Rose rung her hands.

"You really kissed me," he said. "Can't you see this? We should not let our moment get away."

"We can't." Rose fanned herself as footsteps sounded on the stairs.

"Please?" His eyes begged.

"I can't," she whispered, busying herself moving about the ice cream mixer to no particular purpose.

"Are we done?" Esther's cheerful voice asked. Esther glanced between them, obviously knowing something had happened from her pleased look.

"I got to make Amish ice cream." Conrad squared his shoulders as if nothing had happened.

Esther clearly wasn't changing her opinion. "I'm glad you two got along so well. Let me take a peek at the ice cream."

Rose bolted from the basement and raced up the outside steps. She paused at the top to calm herself, as the tears stung. Darkness had begun to fall, and Rose hurried behind the woodshed. She couldn't stay here forever, but perhaps long enough to collect herself. How could she ever face Robert knowing what secrets she had revealed to Conrad, the English man. Robert wouldn't understand. No one would understand. Esther was partly to blame, but she was the one who had kissed Conrad. She had never kissed Robert, had never wanted to.

"Oh, dear Lord, help me." Rose moaned. She rubbed her face with her apron and forced herself to march out from behind the woodshed.

Robert found her in the fallen dusk. "There you are. I was about ready to come down and help with the ice cream making."

"The ice cream is finished," her voice squeaked.

"Plenty of people willing to help, I'm sure." Robert chuckled.

He couldn't see her face, and she couldn't lie anymore, so Rose said nothing.

CHAPTER 40

Conrad returned to the basement for the second mixer of ice cream after having transferred the first one upstairs under Esther's watchful eye. Rose's sister was brimming with questions, none of which he felt inclined to answer. The encounter with Rose had gone well beyond anything he had anticipated. Explosive and unexpected as her kiss had been, he was not feeling very hopeful. The girl was honest, at least, which didn't remove the pain of having discovered he had been taken for a memory.

"Was Rose—?" Esther asked, clearly probing.

"Your sister is very sweet," Conrad replied, which provoked raised eyebrows from Esther. He was confused himself. He couldn't be expected to explain to Esther even if he had wanted to.

"I hope you enjoy the rest of the evening," Esther said, glancing at him

"I will, and I have enjoyed the evening so far, thank you."

Esther smiled, looking pleased.

He hadn't said much and hadn't meant to imply anything. He had enjoyed the time with Rose, even with the unexpected revelations. He comforted himself with the thought. He had always known his romantic ideas about Rose were out of bounds. Her kiss, though, had been out of this world. Way off the charts for any girl he had ever kissed. If he was a memory, he was certainly a good one.

"I was more than a memory," he told himself, heaving the ice cream mixer up the stairs, careful not to spill the ice water. He was trying to convince himself, with little success.

The young people poured into the house, and the ice cream was delicious, as he had anticipated. Most of the conversations for the next thirty minutes were a daze. He hoped he answered the questions about farming correctly. His mind seemed on auto pilot. Rose stayed away from him, sticking with Robert on the other side of the room, only crossing to the kitchen with her bowls of ice cream when he was clearly engaged in conversation with someone else.

Still, he found himself at nine o'clock beside Edwin's buggy, helping the man hitch up, hoping Rose would speak a few words to him before the evening concluded. Instead, Rose stayed over by Robert's buggy, deep in conversation with the man, clearly trying to forget him. He didn't blame the girl. He had somehow, unintentionally exposed the woman's weakness, and from what he knew of women, they didn't take kindly to such maneuvers.

"Honestly done," he said, talking to himself.

"What did you say?" Edwin asked from across the horse's back.

"Nothing, but I could have said, nice evening, and awesome ice cream."

"Yes, sir." Edwin agreed. "Would you hold the bridle for a moment? I need to go tell Mary goodnight."

"Certainly." Conrad didn't hesitate, standing guard by the horse's head, while Edwin rushed off into the darkness.

"Come over and talk to me." He willed Rose to appear.

As if she heard, her form moved away from Robert's buggy. She must have mistaken him for Edwin waiting for her. He didn't feel like dispelling the woman's misconception.

"Rose," he said, when she was by the buggy door.

There was a gasp. "Conrad. Why are you here?"

"Holding the horse's head," he said. "Edwin went to say goodnight to Mary."

She climbed in the buggy and sat down, silent.

Should he say more? What was there to say?

"You must forget about me," Rose said, speaking quietly.

"How do you know I'm thinking about you?"

"You're here," she said. "We can't go on like this, Conrad."

"Was I more than a memory?" he asked, daring to hope.

"I'm going to get married," she said. "You must forget what I did."

Which was an answer of sorts, but not very helpful. "I was more than a memory," he said, convinced he was right. "We could be something together, Rose."

"I'm sorry I used you," she said, a second before Edwin reappeared.

The sense of losing her washed over him. Yet, Rose had never belonged to him. He should not complain.

"I'm back." Edwin announced, clambering up into the buggy. "Thanks, my friend. Hope to see you soon."

Conrad stepped back, and watched the buggy vanish into the darkness. The lights had blinked out on the first incline of the hill. He should take the hint, but he didn't feel like taking any hints. Yet, there was nothing he could do if Rose chose to marry Robert. Which she planned to accomplish fairly quickly from all appearances.

Feeling injured and rejected, he approached the front porch where Jesse and Esther's shadowy figures were outlined by the lantern light behind them. He called out, "Thanks for the invite and the evening."

"Come again." Esther answered.

He skirted the edge of the garden and crossed the field between the properties. He should have held on to Rose while he had her so close tonight. He should have never let go. Yet, he couldn't have. Hearts were tender things, easily injured and attempts to restrain them futile. Rose would tell no one about their indiscretion—a serious indiscretion by Amish standards if he didn't miss his guess, and neither would he. Rose was right. A great ravine yawned between them.

They were victims of fate, caught in a tragedy which was not of their own making. Conrad entered his house and turned on the light switch. He checked his smart phone. There were no calls. He set the alarm and laid the phone on the nightstand near his bed. He had a trip planned to see his parents tomorrow in Mullen, so he had best turn in for the night. Conrad undressed and climbed in, but he tossed and turned under the covers a long time before he dropped off to sleep.

CHAPTER 41

On Saturday morning, Conrad eased his Ford pickup into the exit on I-80 for Mullen. He had dreamed of Rose last night. A dream where he had been caught kissing Rose in the basement beside the ice cream mixers and had been chased by the bishop in his buggy. Conrad grinned, remembering his muddled dream. He had a difficult time imagining the Amish men he knew chasing anyone in their buggies. In any case, the rest of the night, the dreams hadn't gotten any better. Stormy clouds had raked the sky, along with tormented visions of rocky mountains and waving plains of grass rolling over the beauty of Rose's face.

Rose had been so close and yet so far. He should leave the girl alone, forget this whole joining the Amish community thing. Rose had made her wishes known—clearly enough, yet he couldn't forget her kiss—along with the certainty there had been more to their encounter than Rose was admitting. His desire to know more about her had grown, to draw even closer to her heart.

He knew this while he wished things were otherwise. He was afraid. Iraq had left a mark on his heart which could not be easily shaken. He would only destroy things if he didn't stay away from Rose. The planned weekend with his family, away from the Amish community for a few days, had come up at exactly the right time. As if the Lord knew what he needed before he did. He could walk away now, and Rose would never talk about what had transpired between them. His working relationship with the Amish community would be preserved. Conrad grimaced. Could he walk away? He would have to if Rose proceeded with her wedding to Robert.

The dim lights in the Amish barns glowed along Highway 50. One thing was certain, he liked the Amish community life. Rising early with them, knowing he could as a matter of habit, was a satisfying feeling. They were disciplined and dedicated to the task at hand, as his father had raised him. He was one of them in heart. Almost, but not quite. He teetered on the edge of something big. One way or the other, his life would change.

If by some miracle, some working of forces he could not imagine, Rose would break off her relationship with Robert, and he would join the community, they would date and eventually wed. Each step seemed more impossible, more out of the realm of reason, of common sense, of anything but a wild insanity. Was love insane? He had once heard love was, but this was beyond insanity. Once the last mountaintop was reached—his wedding to Rose—he could never walk away. He would be Amish for life. He couldn't imagine the agony he would create in Rose's heart if she were his wife, and he turned his back on what Rose so loved before she had known him.

Conrad slowed for the small town of Tyron, lying halfway between I-80 and Mullen. The rays of the sun bursting over the horizon turned the Iron Front Steakhouse into a glowing shade of red. Conrad let up on the accelerator until his pickup crept past the storefront on the empty street. This was what he needed, a distraction. Memories were contained in this place. More than he could name. Weekends after the cattle had been tended, traveling down from Mullen with Cousin Fred and his three sisters.

With Fred driving, they had piled into the back of the pickup and driven into town for supper. The steaks were out of this world. Only the Amish cooking came close to what Mr. Preston and his wife, Betty, produced at the restaurant. The couple must be old by now, but he figured they hadn't given up the place. He would drive down to eat tonight with his parents, if they consented, and touch base with the couple.

Conrad accelerated out of town, a place containing a few houses sitting in the middle of the prairie. Weary looking buildings they were, beaten down with time, and kept up by a few hardy souls who were part prairie themselves. This was his world, a place he had left in search for something. The war? The Amish world? An Amish woman? Who knew he would fall in love with an Amish girl?

He saw Rose's face so close, the longing in her eyes, the grip of her hands in his. She was innocence itself, pure and undefiled. Kissing her had been heavenly—divine. His head throbbed. He had felt guilty in the midst of the bliss. He had never felt guilt for giving a girl attention or for ignoring her.

What was Rose doing this morning? He had no right to ask, but he did. Perhaps she had blocked him out of her mind? He wanted to know. Had she cried herself to sleep last night? Was she thinking of him? Perhaps wishing she had never seen him? At least, he had the memory of her to hold near and dear. He would never forget the girl, no matter how far he roamed in life, no matter if he married or didn't marry. Rose would always be in his heart.

Twenty minutes later, Conrad topped the hill and slowed for the view of Mullen below him. This was the sight he had often enjoyed in his youth. Dad's ranch began outside of town and spread for miles north and west. Forgotten feelings stirred in him, memories from the past, from before college, from before he had thought to escape this place. Fate had aligned to drive him home. Nothing else made sense.

Conrad drove through town, past the gas station at the railroad tracks. Minutes later, he was on the other side. He turned on his blinker and bounced to a stop by the low-hung ranch house. Nothing appeared changed from when he had seen the place last—the barnyard clean, the wooden fences repaired, and the cattle grazing in the distance.

"Conrad." The front door burst open, and his mother ran out. She embraced him. "Conrad, you have come home."

He laughed. "Where is everybody?"

"This is a Saturday morning. Working, of course."

"Point me in the right direction, and I'll fall right in." He grinned.

"You didn't visit for us to work you to death." She made a face. "Come in. Let me look at you."

Conrad followed his mother inside the house.

She set out a glass of water. "Have you eaten?"

"No. I left early."

"Then don't move until I make breakfast for you." She bustled about the kitchen, talking as usual while she worked. "Fill me in on what's going on in your life."

"Nothing much," he said. "I'm working out of the Pawnee office and contacting local farmers, many of them Amish."

"Amish." Her face lit up. "I've seen stories about them on TV. There's even a movie out on the school shooting in Pennsylvania from years ago."

"They're nice people," he said.

"Do they speak with you?" She paused in her work. "I heard they don't like the government or take government aid."

Conrad shrugged. "The subject never came up—not exactly, at least."

"Maybe the army is what they don't like. Shooting people."

"They don't like the army," he agreed. "They're a peace-loving people."

"Can you work with them like you do with everyone else?"

"They're people, Mom."

She smiled and scrambled the eggs in the pan. "I suppose so."

"In fact, I rent my little house from a young Amish couple. They have me over for meals sometimes."

"Ah—" She studied his frame. "I though you looked well fed, too much weight for a bachelor's life."

"Mom," he scolded, "I'm not over there all the time, but they do make the most amazing ice cream—homemade ice cream."

"Homemade ice cream." She smiled. "You're being treated like royalty."

"They're hospitable," he said. He wasn't about to disclose more. Not now.

She dropped several slabs of sausage into the pan. "Do you like breakfast like you used to?"

"I haven't changed."

"You look changed."

"How?"

"Happier but troubled too. Have you fallen in love?"

"You would ask." He hoped his ears weren't growing red. Only mothers could get to the point so quickly. Kissing a girl who wasn't his girlfriend would not meet her approval.

She beamed. "Good news, I take."

"Perhaps not?"

"How can falling in love be bad news?"

"She's an Amish girl," he admitted. Mothers found out eventually.

"An Amish girl. Conrad! Are you serious?"

"We aren't dating. In fact, not even close."

"I see. You have a dilemma. When will her rumspringa end?"

"You know about rumspringa?"

"I watch the movies, Conrad."

"She's not on rumspringa."

"What is she on if you have access to her?"

"I'm not seeing her, Mom. We talk. She's dating an Amish boy."

She clucked her tongue. "Are you robbing another man's nest?"

"They aren't married, Mom."

"Almost married?"

"They shouldn't be."

"Conrad! We raised you better."

"I know." He winced. "I kissed her last night, or she kissed me. Somewhere in there."

"You're in trouble then," she stated more than asked. "Boys always come home when they're in trouble."

"Maybe? Can we talk about something else?"

"Conrad, you should be ashamed of yourself."

"I wasn't going to," he protested, "never even thought of—well, maybe I did, but she definitely kissed me. Asked me to—"

She held up her hand. "I don't want to hear more, but this has to stop. You really need to man up and take responsibility for what you're doing. Does the boyfriend know?"

He shook his head.

"Not yet," she said.

"Not yet," he echoed. Assuring her of Rose's silence would only dig his hole deeper.

"Are you going to break her heart?"

"I may have broken mine."

She lowered her eyebrows. "You need to think of her, not yourself. You're a handsome man, quite a good catch."

"Mom!" he protested.

They laughed together. The tension was gone between them. She trusted him. Deep down she did, which was why a boy always came home.

"Have you thought of joining the community?" she asked. "People from our world do join."

"You've been watching the movies," he said.

"Movies are not all lies. Have you?"

"Joining the Amish."

"Yes, Conrad."

"Should I?"

"You're avoiding the question."

"I have," he admitted.

"But—?" she asked.

"Can we talk of something else?"

She gave in, but not without a parting shot. "You've come home to find answers."

"Home is always the answer," he said.

A sad smile crossed her face. "How many years have I waited to hear those words come out of your mouth?"

"Too many," he said. "I'm sorry."

She walked over and wrapped him in her arms and held him for a long time.

CHAPTER 42

Rose knew Esther would visit the moment she had Jesse fed and the breakfast dishes washed. The only surprise was her sister hadn't left Jesse to feed himself and arrived at the crack of dawn. Rose plunged the long-handled dust rag under Edwin's bed and attacked the far corners. She had avoided Esther last night after the fiasco in her sister's basement. Her face still burned with the thought of Conrad's face so close to hers. The shame of her words when she had asked him to kiss her.

"Lord help me." She choked. "How could I have done such a thing?"

She would have to face Robert tomorrow again. Last night, he hadn't seemed to notice anything wrong with her as they mixed in with the hustle and bustle of the crowd of young people eating homemade ice cream. Alone time would doubtless expose her to Robert's scrutiny. The man had to notice, but then again, perhaps he wouldn't. Robert seemed fully absorbed in the purchase of his farm.

Heat burned inside her at the thought of confessing what she had done to Robert. What if she didn't confess? Would he ever suspect? If she agreed to a wedding date at their next time together, Robert would never think to ask. Could she live with herself, married to a man, and having so passionately kissed someone else?

Rose sat on the bed and held her head in her hands. From the sound of the rapid footsteps on the stairs, Esther was on the way up.

"Where are you?" Esther called out a second later

"In here," Rose sent her muffled reply.

The bedroom door swung open, and Esther appeared. "Rose," her sister scolded.

"Go away," Rose said.

"Why did you avoid me last night?"

"How could you leave me alone with Conrad?" Rose shot back.

"Did he—?" Alarm filled Esther's face.

"No, I asked him to kiss me."

Esther's eyes grew large. "You—Am I hearing this right? You—"

"Yah! Can you imagine? I can't, but I did." Rose wailed.

"Which means he must have kissed you. Oh, Rose." Esther did a little jig on the bedroom floor. "This is the greatest news ever."

"How can you—? Let alone say I—" Rose threw her hands in air. "I will have to confess to Robert."

"You will do no such thing." Esther ordered. "You will tell Robert tomorrow this is his last date and chase him out of the front door."

Rose laughed despite herself.

Esther took a deep breath. "What a happy day this is, indeed."

Rose cleared her throat. "I will do nothing of the sort."

Esther stared. "Oh, yah, you will."

"I will not," Rose insisted.

Esther rung her hands. "I can't believe this. What is wrong with you?"

"I'm losing my mind," Rose deadpanned.

Esther came over to sit beside Rose. "Calm down, and let's think this through. Things are going very well, I would say. Faster than I thought they would—I mean, a kiss already."

"Bishop Bontrager would excommunicate me if he found out," Rose moaned.

"For a kiss? I doubt." Esther's voice was cheerful. "A kiss is the most natural loving thing a woman and man can share."

"Conrad is an English man. Are you losing your mind?"

"I'm in perfect possession of my mental faculties," Esther declared. "And deliriously happy for you. You two will make the perfect couple."

"You have lost your mind," Rose said.

"This is the real thing." Esther patted Rose's arm. "True love. Open your eyes."

"If you ever tell Mamm, or Robert, or anyone, I will—" Rose warned.

"Come now." Esther gathered Rose into her arms. "I've pushed too hard. I'm sorry."

"Thank you," Rose whispered.

Esther's shoulders shook as she began to giggle. "What I would have given to be down in the basement hiding in a corner."

"I find nothing funny about this." Rose pulled away.

"Okay. I will be quiet now."

"Not a word to anyone. Remember. I don't think I'll tell Robert, unless he notices something different in me, which I doubt he will. How could I blurt out—Oh, Robert, I kissed the English man Conrad on Friday night while we were making ice cream. Robert would never recover his goot opinion of me. Never!"

"I don't give a hoot what Robert thinks of you," Esther said.

"Well, I do."

"You shouldn't," Esther scolded.

Rose stared at the bedroom wall for a long time. "I can't believe I kissed the man. Asked him to kiss me."

Esther held Rose close for a moment. "Shall I help you finish the upstairs cleaning?"

"Please," Rose whispered.

"Come, we will say no more about this." Esther decided. "The Lord will open your eyes in his own goot time."

"Open my eyes?" Rose wailed. "More like smite me for my sins."

Esther helped Rose to her feet. "Come, you'll feel better soon.

"You're worse than Job's comforters," Rose retorted.

Esther hushed Rose with a finger to her lips, and they set to work cleaning the upstairs of the old house.

CHAPTER 43

Back at his family's home, Conrad pushed open the barn door and entered the musty interior. He walked into the portion devoted to the riding horses, which were not unlike the horses the Amish drove in their buggies. Perhaps this was another reason he felt at home with the Amish. Their horses connected him with his youth.

Conrad smiled as several horses came running toward him.

"You still know me," he whispered, brushing their necks with his hand. "How about riding today?"

Several of them neighed, as if they understood, and Conrad made his selection. Ten minutes later, he had the saddle strapped on and was headed out through the gate. He let the horse trot for a few minutes until he urged him into a gallop. The wind moved through his hair, and he threw his head back to laugh. The herd of cattle ahead of him turned their heads to follow his progress but didn't stir. He belonged here. Perhaps this was his answer. He should return and make his father happy. Forget he had ever met the Amish people. Forget Rose. Leave her life untouched by his troubles. Could he? Try to forget the attraction which had flamed to life standing beside those ice cream mixers in Esther's basement. How was he to walk away from such a thing? Yet, how could he expect Rose to leave her secured future for the nebulous one he offered? She had told him in no uncertain terms to leave her alone. Why wasn't he listening?

Conrad urged his horse onward. How was he to make peace with such conflicting claims? To soothe his tormented thoughts, he rode west over the hills for a few miles before he slowed to a canter and turned back.

"How was the ride?" His mother asked, waiting at the gate.

"Like old times," he said. "Cleanses the soul, the prairie does."

She smiled up at him. "I have an idea. We could go down to the Iron Front Steakhouse tonight."

"Great minds think alike." He chuckled. "Do you think Dad has time?"

"He always has time for his children," she said.

"I know," he agreed. "I'm sorry for the son I was—or wasn't."

"He understands." Her smile didn't fade.

"You're sure?"

"Yes, Son. He still wishes you would have come home and taken over the farm."

"Now, there are sons-in-laws," he said.

"Things can be worked out." She assured him.

"The thought did cross my mind," he said, "but—"

"She must have gotten into your heart." There was no disapproval written on her face.

"Rose did," he admitted.

"I'm glad. Either way, you will always be our son, and I hope she will be our daughter."

"Mom." He laughed. "Things are not there yet."

She didn't look convinced. "You have come home, Conrad. Makes me think you're finding your own way in life."

"Mom, please—"

"How long are you staying?" She changed the subject.

"For the weekend."

"I'm glad," she said, "you've come home."

CHAPTER 44

Rose went to bed early, with the sun sunk just below the horizon, the last light lingering in the sky before the surrender to the night. Her head throbbed. Mamm had looked worriedly at her while they did the supper dishes.

"I need a goot night's sleep."

She hadn't lied. She did need a goot night's sleep. The problem was obtaining the night's rest. Rose climbed into bed and pulled the quilt up under her chin to stare at the ceiling. The troubled thoughts wouldn't stop. What if Robert noticed something unusual about her tomorrow? Mamm had. Maybe she would get sick by the morning, like *really* sick with head throbbing, eyes running, fever blazing sick. She hated being ill, but this illness would be a relief. By the time she recovered, the thunderclouds might have rolled away. Which was sheer fantasy, one of her many dreams Robert so disliked. How did her feelings for an English man, a man she had kissed in her sister's basement, disappear over the horizon, never to appear again? She was in trouble—deep, deep trouble.

Rose groaned. She had betrayed her own high standards, to say nothing of Robert's trust. Robert was a simple man who didn't dream or imagine things. He really didn't, or he would have suspected her treachery a long time ago, her uncontrollable feelings for Conrad Wisner. Robert would never in his entire lifetime kiss an English girl in his brother's basement ... or anywhere else.

Rose shivered, the strength draining from her. Even with the awful deed done and in need of confession, she still couldn't forget the moment of Conrad-closeness, the handsomeness of his face, the touch of his hand on her arm. She should have confessed to Robert the very evening of her transgression, shouted her sins from the roof tops or from Esther's front porch. No amount of shame could equal the grip of this guilt which had her heart tied in a knot.

Robert would be the one who bore the greater shame. He had waited for a girl he thought virtuous and worthy of his trust. He had turned down opportunities for dating—girls who would have been a hundred times more suitable for him than she was. Robert's eyes would fill with pain when she told him, when the awful, horrid words slithered from her mouth.

"I have feelings for an English man, much more than I have for you. He held me close, and I kissed him."

"You did what?" Robert would ask, unable to believe her. "You kissed the man?"

She would never live down the shame. Robert would cut off their relationship, and she would be ruined. Even if Conrad by some miracle wished to join the community, he would not be allowed with such a scandal on her record and on his. Robert might recover, but she wouldn't, and neither would Conrad. His business with the community's farmers might even be in danger. How could she have placed both of their lives in such jeopardy?

Rose sat bolt upright in bed. She planned the marry Robert. How could a marriage begin with such horrible secrets hidden from view? She flopped back on the bed and stared at the bedroom window as the last light of the day faded away. Sleep simply wasn't coming. Giving up, Rose climbed out of bed to sit near the window. She pushed the drapes aside for a better view outside. The new moon hung on the horizon. How her heart usually leaped with joy at the sight of the new moon, a sign of new beginnings, of hope rising for another month. Yet here she was without hope. Robert didn't believe in nights like this giving anyone hope. Look how right he had been. She had fallen in love with an English man.

Conrad Wisner wasn't real. Robert Schlabach was real. The tears streamed down Rose's face. Why did life keep going on? She wished there would never be another moon in the sky, or another day of the sun rising.

"I'll tell him tomorrow if he asks," she whispered into the night sky. "If not, may these sins be forever buried in my heart. I have to marry the man!"

CHAPTER 45

In the meantime, at the Iron Front Steakhouse, the reserved dining room with its two huge oak tables and chairs was encircled by the Wisner family and their immediate in-laws. Plates of freshly consumed steak had been pushed back, and the party's cheerful voices filled the room.

Mr. Preston entered with another plate of steaks balanced on his hand. "One final round folks, and the night is over. Better eat while the steak is hot."

Conrad's dad, Wesley, raised his hand in acceptance, as did the two sons-in-law. Conrad did likewise, after a moment's hesitation. He was pushing the limits of his stomach's capacity, but he couldn't eat here every night.

Following Mr. Preston, his wife, Betty, appeared with fresh plates, and the sizzling steaks were transferred to whoever wanted a second round.

"What a fantastic evening, as always." Wesley poured on the praise. "Thanks to both of you."

"Don't act like you've been down here in the last year or so." Mr. Preston chided. "I thought you had forgotten about us."

"Never could." Wesley assured him. "We were busy, but Conrad came home for the weekend, and for old time's sake the tradition is revived."

"I will hold you to this promise," Mr. Preston said, his eyes twinkling. "Sure you don't want two steaks, Conrad?"

"No." He waved his hand. "No complaints, though. Excellent, excellent food."

Conrad ate slowly, listening to the happy conversation of his family. He belonged here, and yet he didn't. Something pulled and tugged at this heart, a missing piece which left a hole he had mistaken for something else.

An Amish girl? Would the puzzle be complete with Rose in his life? As if in answer to the question, a craving for homemade Amish ice cream swept over him. Mr. Preston served amazing ice cream. He could place an order, but he wouldn't feel satisfied. Not with the recent memory of spending time with Rose in her sister's basement. The squeak of the turning handles, stirring the ice cream canisters in the ice, returned to haunt him. He finished his steak and stood to his feet.

"Think I'll step outside for a moment."

His mother gave him a smile, but no one else appeared to hear. Once outside, he took a deep breath and surveyed the broad sweep of stars overhead. There was no sign of a moon. He belonged here, and yet he had already left. Inside the restaurant, his family was at peace with or without him. If he needed a confirmation, here was the answer staring him in the face.

"May I find the courage to move forward," he whispered the prayer to the heavens.

The road ahead appeared impossible. Rose dated a real Amish man, and he still wasn't sure he wanted to join the community.

"To a new beginning, at least." He spoke to himself. "To a better one, whatever the beginning may be."

He slipped back inside and met Betty at the counter. "Do you have a flavor of ice cream which compares to Amish homemade ice cream."

"I see you're being spoiled." She shot back. "Let me try, though. How about old-fashioned butter pecan?"

"Let's be brave," he said.

Betty raised her eyebrows but didn't say anything. He took his seat, and she appeared in moments with a heaping bowl of ice cream. "Anybody else want any?"

Several hands went up, and Betty took the orders.

Conrad carefully took a bite. He savored the sweet goodness. Normally, he would have been impressed, but this was not Amish ice cream.

"Pass the test?" Betty asked in his ear.

"Nothing like Amish," he said.

She gave him a playful slap on the shoulder and kept going.

Conrad ate slowly, thinking of Rose, wishing he had been born Amish, or Rose had been born into his world. He wasn't God, and God had chosen. Surely, God would guide the way forward if there was hope for any further moving together of their hearts.

"What are you thinking?" His mother teased.

"Rose," he said.

She nodded, soberly. "I hope things work out for you."

CHAPTER 46

On Sunday morning, Robert sat in church and tried hard to concentrate on the sermon Bishop Bontrager was preaching.

"The day of the Lord will soon be at hand." Bishop Bontrager was proclaiming. "We must seek the face of the Lord and prepare ourselves."

"Amen." Robert muttered under his breath.

He hoped none of the men who sat shoulder to shoulder with him on the backless bench heard. The message of the words had been spoken to him, and to him alone, as a reminder to pay attention to eternal things. Life down here had become very interesting and exciting of late. The closing for the farm was on Monday, and a letter had arrived from Grandpa Beiler yesterday with an invitation to visit Lancaster County and tour several farms there.

"With the new purchase of your farm, why not come out and see us in Lancaster County," Grandpa Beiler had written. "Your wedding has not happened yet, and I could show you the latest farming techniques practiced here in Lancaster, the best farming land in the nation. We would love to have you, even with Grandma laid up with her foot injury. The maid is doing an excellent job, so the home base is covered. Between the wisdom of Lancaster County and your new county extension agent, we should keep you on the straight and narrow."

Maybe Rose would agree to the trip, and they could finalize their wedding date on the long journey across the country. Rose would simply have to get over her constant hesitation about the important decisions in life and accept his guidance.

Robert tried to focus again but failed. His gaze drifted over to the unmarried women's section where Rose should have been seated. He hadn't been able to find her among the lines of single girls the whole morning, which was strange. Rose usually sat on the front bench with the girls her age. She was somewhere in the house. From where he stood in the barnyard waiting for the service to begin, he had seen Rose climb out of Edwin's buggy. She would be happy for him tonight when he told her the news. So much goot news. The closing on the farm and Grandpa's invitation. He wanted Rose's approval. He wasn't ashamed to admit as much. There remained the niggling doubts arising from the differences between the Miller and the Schlabach farming methods. Which was Daett's fault, not his. Rose seemed to understand, but there were still moments when the specter rose to stare him in the face. He had come a long way in the last two months. He had exercised patience with Rose. He was the man who had figured out what Rose wanted and had been rewarded accordingly. The other unmarried men who had expressed an interest in Rose had not been so wise. Here he was, Robert Schlabach, buying his own farm and seeing Rose Miller each Sunday evening. Rose was a little dreamy at times, but under his guiding hand, she was turning into the kind of woman he had always wanted—solid, steady, and certain as the sun coming up each morning. Rose was an excellent catch. He had no question there. She would be marrying him this fall. A little more patience was what he needed.

The image of his farm floated in front of Robert's face— his own acres, his own fields, his very, very own. Rose would be there, working in the kitchen. She thought the kitchen cabinets a little fancy, which was goot. He didn't want a wife with English tastes, but on this point, Rose was a little too conservative. He hadn't spoken with Deacon John yet about the matter. Somewhere, the ordnung must have a clause which would allow him to keep the kitchen cabinets. The cost of removal and replacement for a cash-strapped young couple should suffice. He would bring up the subject tonight. If Rose were to voice her approval of the new house to the women, sort of casually, Deacon John would hear and be more inclined to let things slide. Or better yet, on his trip to Lancaster, he would keep his eyes open, paying special attention to kitchen decor. There must be cabinets like his in Lancaster County Amish homes. He might not know the people, but Deacon John probably did. He would have solid Amish names to drop in his conversation with Deacon John. Surely the deacon would be pleased if he brought Lancaster ordnung standards into their community on the prairie.

The washer and dryer would have to go. No Amish home could have an electric washer and dryer. Not even in Lancaster County. Rose would help him. Rose had to help him.

CHAPTER 47

When the young girls had filed in for the start of the church service, Rose had hung back, taking a seat on the back bench near the kitchen with the older women. She didn't belong there, but no one would say anything for one Sunday. If she sat in her usual place, she would have to send Robert frequent smiles through the entire three-hour church service. The stress would be too much. When Robert asked tonight why she hadn't been in her usual place, she would tell him the truth. Maybe this was a way to force herself to speak—not the unmentionable, but her unease and discomfort with their dating relationship.

Bishop Bontrager wasn't helping matters with his sermon. Her conscience already burned with shame because of her hidden sin, and to think of the Lord's eyes on her. Where had this rebuke been when the urge to kiss Conrad flooded her in Esther's basement?

Rose kept her head down until Bishop Bontrager ended his sermon. The service concluded soon after twelve o'clock. She rushed out to the kitchen and threw herself into the preparation for the noon meal of peanut butter, pickle, and baloney sandwiches.

Once the tables were set, the married men filled one end of the living room and their wives the other. Rose stood against the living room wall while Bishop Bontrager called for a prayer of thanksgiving. After the "Amen," Rose hurried forward with two other girls to wait on the men's table.

"Goot morning." She greeted several of them. "Coffee?

They chuckled. "A goot morning indeed," one of them said. "I heard your young Robert is closing on a farm. Wedding bells ringing this fall? Ding, ding, ding?"

They laughed, and Rose forced a smile. They knew Amish wedding plans were highly secretive. Her silence was expected. Ahead of her, she saw Bishop Bontrager seated among the other ministers. Rose turned to head in the opposite direction, but the other two girls worked the lower end of the table. Rose had no choice but to approach Bishop Bontrager. After his sermon this morning, the man had to see right through her, both for her refusal to set a wedding date, and for her awful transgression in Esther's basement.

Rose kept her gaze down. "Coffee?"

"Yah." Bishop Bontrager's voice was kind. "How are you doing, Rose?"

"Helping with the tables," she said, which didn't answer the question.

"I heard young Robert is buying a farm."

"Yah." Rose still didn't meet his gaze.

"The Lord's blessing be on you." Bishop Bontrager pronounced.

"Thank you." Rose quickly retreated, nearly spilling coffee on a man's head.

She would have to tell Robert tonight. She couldn't deal with this guilt. The hours of the afternoon stretched out across a wide ocean of time. She wanted the moment of doom to arrive, and at the same time, wished the time would never come. How had life become so dark? Sunday afternoons usually went by quickly. This was one of the few opportunities the Miller family had to catch their breath after the rush of the week's work.

When the time came to eat with the other girls at the tables, Rose choked down her food, avoiding conversation when possible. She helped with the dishes afterward, slipping out of the kitchen the moment she saw Edwin drive up with his buggy.

"What a wunderbah day!" Edwin proclaimed from his seat inside the buggy.

"Mary has been smiling at you." Rose teased, clambering up, trying to distract herself.

He clucked to his horse and drove out the lane without answering. The steady clip clop of the hooves filled the air.

"Anything wrong?" he finally asked.

"It's a wunderbah day." She parroted.

"Robert is a decent man," he said.

"I know." She didn't look at him.

He concentrated on driving and, apparently, on memories of Mary, from the smile which crept into this face. Rose didn't break into his reverie. Edwin had noticed and had cared, but no one could do anything about her mess. Confession to Edwin would not help.

Rose hopped down at the end of the Miller's walks and headed upstairs to her bedroom. She lay down but ended up pacing the floor until chore time arrived.

"You okay?" Mamm asked in a worried tone when she came downstairs.

"I have lot to talk with Robert about tonight," she said, as explanation.

"Stop fussing about the new house." Mamm ordered. "Tell Robert you will marry him. Your indecision is at the root of this whole fuss."

It is not, she wanted to protest, but Mamm would only ask further questions.

She worked instead, right up until supper time and washed the dishes afterward. Edwin was still smiling when she ran out to climb into his buggy for the ride to the hymn singing, but he didn't ask any further questions.

CHAPTER 48

During the hymn singing, Robert tried to catch Rose's eye, but she was seated on the second row, which wasn't her usual place. Such things did occur by accident from time to time. Things were going his way, and nothing could dampen his happiness. She would be a goot frau for him, even with her occasional strange behavior. When the last song was sung, he dashed for the barn to bring out his horse.

"Happy tonight, are we?" One of the men teased when he passed him in the yard.

Robert didn't answer, continuing to whistle his merry tune. Everyone knew why he was happy. He was about to purchase a farm and had a wedding coming up this fall.

He hitched his horse to the buggy and drove up to turn his wheels out at the sidewalk. The last bars of his tune hung in the air. He couldn't remember a time when he had been so happy. Through the dim darkness, he could see Rose's form coming down the sidewalk.

"Goot evening." he called out.

She had her shawl tightly around her shoulders and hopped up to sit beside him without answering.

"Goot evening," he said again.

"It is," she agreed.

"How was your day?" he asked.

"Okay, I guess."

"You didn't come down to wait on the unmarried men's table."

"You know I usually don't."

He smiled and clucked to his horse. "I know. I was just hoping you would today."

"I—I guess I should have come, but I—"

"It doesn't matter," he said. "I'm getting to see you tonight and tell you the goot news."

"Goot news?" She was looking up at him.

"Everything went through, and we're closing on the farm this week."

"That is goot news."

"Grandpa will forward the funds by electronic means. Isn't that something? Sending money over the wires."

"Which day is the closing?" she asked.

"Tomorrow."

"You have pulled off quite an accomplishment."

"I thought so," he said. "Grandpa deserves the credit, though, and you."

"Me?"

"Of course." He gave her a bright smile. "Without you I would never have had the courage to look at a farm. Well, at least, not so soon."

She ducked her head.

"You will make me a great frau, even with your occasional strange ways," he said.

"Strange ways?" Horror had crept into her voice.

"Don't be alarmed. I knew you weren't sitting in your usual places all day, but it's okay."

"You noticed?" She sounded choked.

"Of course, I noticed," he said. "Just don't do such things too often. I like regularity in a woman."

"Okay," she demurred, with her head down. "I'll sit in my usual places next Sunday."

"I knew you would."

She stared out of the windshield and said nothing as his horse trotted into the night.

"I hope you have food ready worthy of a celebration, because there is more goot news."

"More news." The alarm was back in her voice. "And food. I have the usual, brownie bars."

"I'm sure the Millers keep pie around." he said. "I want pie tonight. Several slices, with milk."

"What is the goot news?" she asked.

"Grandpa asked me to visit him in Lancaster County. I want you to go along."

"Lancaster County?" The choked sound was back. "When?"

"Quite soon," he said. "Once the farm is closed, which is this week."

"I'll have to think about this and speak with Mamm."

"They won't object," he assured her. "We can make our wedding plans on the long trip out and back."

"We have cherry pie," she said. "We can eat cherry pie to celebrate."

"You have nothing to say about our wedding date?"

"You know how I feel, Robert. I'm dating you, but I need a little more time."

"This fall is coming quickly," he said. "There isn't much time, and I'll have the farm next week to tend."

"I know." Her voice sounded weak.

He hadn't planned to push the subject, but this constant dragging of her feet was getting tiresome.

"We should talk about—" she began. "Talk about— tonight about—"

He silenced her with a wave of his hand. "I know what the problem is. Those kitchen cabinets in the house bother you, but they shouldn't. They're very important to me, even if they aren't to you."

"The kitchen cabinets?" She was staring up at him.

He pulled back on the reins and came to a stop before driving on through a stop sign. "Yah! The kitchen cabinets."

"The kitchen cabinets? Robert, please."

"I want your support on the kitchen cabinets," he said. "If this makes you feel any better, I plan to check around when we visit Grandpa. I'm sure there are plenty of kitchen cabinets in Lancaster County much fancier than ours."

"I can't go along, Robert. I just can't. I'm sorry."

"You said you would think about this."

"I can't," she repeated. "We aren't wed, and the trip would be inappropriate."

He couldn't keep the irritation out of his voice. "We would be in public view the whole time—on the train. There is nothing inappropriate about the trip."

"I can't," she said.

He sighed. "You're the limit, you know. Quite the limit."

"We don't have to—I mean we can call off—"

"I'm not calling off the trip," he retorted. "I'll go alone, but this isn't right. You're supposed to support me."

She didn't answer, her face hidden behind her bonnet.

He finally shrugged. "So, you can't go along. We'll have to live with how things are for now, but I'm having a proper celebration tonight."

"Okay," she whispered.

He glanced backward for headlights on the road and executed a sharp turn on the black top into a small gas station.

Rose gasped. "Why are we stopping?"

The station had bright lights, and Robert parked at the far end where the shadows were the deepest. He handed the reins to Rose. "I'll be right back."

The clerk didn't look too strangely at him when he made the purchase of half a gallon of butter pecan ice cream. "You want it wrapped?"

"Yah," he said. "Double maybe. We have ten minutes to the house."

"Not going to eat in the buggy?" she teased

"Nope." He gave her a grin.

She smiled. "You must have a girl along. Ice cream in a buggy would be romantic."

"Just wrap it," he said.

She tilted her head. "You sure?"

He let his impatience show, and she quickly wrapped the ice cream. He couldn't see Rose's face in the dark buggy when he climbed back in and shoved the ice cream under the seat, then took the reins.

"What did you buy?" she asked.

"Ice cream. A proper celebration with cherry pie."

"English ice cream? Why?"

He clucked to Danny Boy. "You object to English ice cream."

"We could have made some ourselves."

"On a Sunday night?"

"I guess not. I'm sorry I didn't—"

"Could you meet me Monday afternoon at the house?" he asked. "Right after the closing."

"At the house?"

She sounded alarmed once more. What was wrong with the girl? "I know you're busy," he said, "but I want to show you the house again."

"I'll have to ask Mamm."

"You know your Mamm won't object." He pulled back on the reins and turned into the Miller's driveway to park at the hitching post.

Rose hopped out of the buggy without answering.

He climbed down and tied his horse before retrieving the bag of ice cream. Rose was waiting for him at the end of the walkway. He followed her to the house where she soon had a dish ready with a large slice of cherry pie piled high with his store-bought butter pecan ice cream. She settled beside him with a smaller version of his bowl.

He sampled a bite. "Excellent. The English make goot ice cream."

"Does your family make homemade often?" she asked.

"Not really," he said. "I like store-bought almost as much as I did the ice cream your sister made the other evening."

"The ice cream we made in Esther's basement?" Her face looked white beside him. Rose was a bundle of nerves tonight.

"I know you helped." He laughed. "I'm not complaining, but I like store-bought better."

"Did you have store-bought often growing up?"

"No." He took another big bite. "Don't you like store-bought?"

"It's okay," she said.

He let the subject go. There were more important things on his mind. "If I leave the middle of next week for Lancaster on the train, could you check in on the house on Saturday? I mean, not tend to the house, but make sure everything is okay."

"Do you want me to start cleaning?" She looked worried.

"Not yet," he said. "There's no rush. We don't have a wedding date."

She looked away and didn't answer.

"This is excellent ice cream." He smacked his lips.

"I have something I need to say," she said, her gaze fixed on the hardwood floor.

"Surely you don't object to me traveling out to Lancaster?"

"No." She looked startled.

"Then what?"

"I, I—"

"I shouldn't have brought up the lack of our wedding date," he interrupted. "I'm sorry. I'll be more patient."

"I didn't mean our wedding date, Robert."

"Okay," he said. "What? I know you're a little dreamy, but we're working on the problem. In fact, I don't think there's much of one left. I haven't heard anything about moon watching lately."

"No." Her gaze was back on the hardwood floor. "You haven't."

"There isn't a problem."

"You don't think of late that I have been—?"

"Been what?"

"A little strange? Out of the ordinary?"

He laughed. "You have always tried my patience. I do admit, you have, but I'm okay. I really am. I'll prove to you I can wait until you're ready. Even if we have to wait until next wedding season for you to make up your mind. I can move into the house next month, after I have come back from Lancaster, and I will wait. Until you're ready. I promise."

"You would?" She was looking up at him.

"I said I would, and I'll prove myself, so I hope you're satisfied."

"I—"

"You can't object," he said. "I have apologized."

"You have apologized?"

"I think I have."

"I should—" she began.

"Can we have more ice cream," he said. "We're celebrating. Remember?"

"Yah, we are!" Rose leaped to her feet and left for the kitchen.

Robert kicked back his feet and allowed the joy of the evening to sweep over him again. Rose came to things slowly, but she eventually came to them. Of this, he was certain.

CHAPTER 49

An hour later, the empty ice cream carton lay on the floor in front of them. Rose tried not to stare at the cluttered mess. Neither Edwin nor Charles would ever do such a thing. Mamm would have lectured them until their ears were red. Robert had tossed the carton there after he scraped the last of the ice cream out of the corners. Where the man put so much food, Rose had no idea. She had managed a few bites, but Robert hadn't appeared to notice her lack of appetite. He also had failed to follow-up on her attempt to at least express her discomfort with their relationship, a discomfort strong enough, which had led to—

Robert yawned and stretched himself beside her. "What a lovely evening, but I have a full week ahead of me. I really should get going."

Rose opened her mouth for one more attempt at forcing out the words, but they froze on her tongue. Maybe silence was the best option, burying this awful sin deep, deep in her heart, never to see the light of day again.

"What about Monday afternoon?" he asked. "Is there any way you can let me know if your Mamm objects."

"I'll be there," she told him. "Let's assume Mamm can spare me."

He got up and put on his hat. "You have a goot night's rest. What a great celebration this has been."

Rose stood by the living room window and watched his buggy lights disappear over the hill. What was to become of them? The moment for a confession seemed to have passed. Could they go on without her saying anything? Was this even possible. If Robert didn't care, maybe no one cared.

Rose turned back to clean up the mess on the floor. With a sigh, she sat down on the couch afterward, staying there for a long time thinking about things before she slipped upstairs to her bedroom. The path ahead was a blur. She would have to agree to a wedding this fall. Stalling was not an option much longer, even if Robert said he was willing to wait until next year. Marriage would bring this awful drama to an end. She would no longer have to think about Conrad Wisner—unless she could never stop thinking about him. What if she never stopped seeing his face the whole time she was married to Robert?

The thought sent cold shivers up and down Rose's back, and she didn't fall asleep until after the clock had struck twelve in the downstair's hallway.

CHAPTER 50

On Monday afternoon, Rose drove Brownie west toward Pawnee City with a dustpan, a broom, and a wash bucket in the back of her buggy. Robert had said she wasn't supposed to clean the house, but she wanted to, at least, sweep a few corners. She needed to work, to steady her hands. If she cleaned the man's house, perhaps she'd feel closer to him.

"Looks like things are going better." Mamm had said with a smile before she departed.

"We're not rushing," she had mumbled.

Perhaps they acted like an engaged couple, but they weren't. A pickup truck appeared in the distance, and Rose pulled Brownie closer to the ditch. One wheel of the buggy fell off the pavement and rattled loudly. Her hands tensed on the reins. Rose didn't look up until the pickup had almost passed. She thought for a moment the man in the vehicle was Conrad. The truck looked like Conrad's, but the man hadn't been Conrad.

Rose tried to still the pounding of her heart. Was this how things would continue? Would she see Conrad in every English man's face? Worse yet, would she eventually see him again in person? Somewhere! He was part of the community. She couldn't avoid him. Her kiss of shame would burn between them forever.

Rose pulled to a stop at Highway 50, and when the road was clear, turned north. Robert's buggy was parked near the

JERRY EICHER

barn. The closing in town must be complete. Robert owned his farm. She was glad for him. Glad he had succeeded, but not one happy thought rose in her heart which connected her to this place or with Robert. Rose bounced into the driveway to stop beside Robert's buggy. Before she could collect herself, Robert came out of the barn with a big grin on his face.

"What do you think? My very own place, and the ink isn't even dry yet."

She forced a smile. "This is great."

He tied Brownie to the side of the barn. "I'll have a hitching post put up after I get back from Lancaster. Maybe before, if I have the time. Not that I will have a lot of visitors yet, but we need a hitching post."

Rose climbed down and retrieved her cleaning utensils from the back of the buggy.

Robert gave them a brief glance.

"I know you said—" she began.

"It's okay," he said. "You can bring them in, but I want to talk about the kitchen cabinets first."

Rose followed him inside, where Robert headed straight for the kitchen to run his hands over the fancy English cabinets. "I do so like them. Can't you see how beautiful they are?"

"They're English," she said, very quietly.

"I've already purchased the place. I don't want to change them."

"I'm not telling you what must be done," she said

"You can live with them?"

"I suppose so. The issue of money is important with the loan to pay back."

"You agree they should be left?" He was watching her carefully.

"Maybe with time they'll wear and look more Amish."

Robert looked pleased. "I wanted to make sure we were on the same page before I spoke with Deacon John."

Rose froze. "You will tell Deacon John I think they should be left?"

"I will tell him you support me." Robert had moved down the line of cabinets, speaking over his shoulder. "Also, I'll be looking at cabinets when I'm in Lancaster County. I'm sure they have cabinets like these."

"But we should try to keep the ordnung? Surely you agree."

He didn't turn around. "The community writes the ordnung. The Lord hasn't spoken from heaven."

Rose took a deep breath. "Do you plan to join the English when we wed?"

Robert laughed. "Of course not. What a silly question. I'll never leave the community, same as you."

"I agree, I mean, but—"

"We've settled this," he interrupted. "We need speak no more about the matter. With your support and with the names I get in Lancaster County, Deacon John should give me no problems."

"I hope not."

He turned to face her. "Have you never done anything against the ordnung?"

Rose paled. Had the moment arrived to confess her sin? English cabinets were a small matter compared to kissing Conrad in Esther's basement. "There was a light blue dress once—" Rose choked unable to go further.

"See." Robert chuckled. "Everyone breaks the ordnung."

"Robert." She tried again, but he didn't hear her.

His voice spoke from the washroom. "I'll be running an ad for the washer and dryer. I don't have time to run over here for every inquiry. Can I give them your address? I'll leave you the key. You can come up and unlock the door. Show them the product."

"Robert," she said.

He stuck his head out of the door. "Did you say yah?"

Before she could answer, he was gone again.

She followed him. "Robert."

He had his back turned. "Yah."

"We have to talk."

"About what?" He faced her, looking perplexed.

"About—I don't know how to say this—about us."

"Us. Why?"

"We're not doing very well."

"We're doing quite well," he said. "I'm having patience, and you'll give me a wedding date—eventually."

"This has nothing to do with our wedding date," she said.

He lifted both hands. "I know we've only dated for a little while, but I've known my feelings for you for a long time. I admire and respect you. I can wait until you're ready."

"I—" she began.

He kept talking. "I knew you would say yah eventually to a date with me, and my faith was rewarded. I'm the man for you, and you're the wife for me. We have our own place, and when you're ready, we will set the date."

Rose clutched the edge of countertop and forced the words out. "I don't think we can ever get wed."

He didn't seem to hear. "Did you want to do some cleaning in the house now? I have some things to look after in the barn."

"Robert." She spoke loudly this time. "We can't get wed."

He paused in mid-stride. "What did you say?"

"I can't see you anymore," she said. "We have to break off our relationship. We can't live like we're trying to live."

CHAPTER 51

At about the same time, Conrad pulled out of a farmer's driveway north of town, his appointment complete, and headed south. He had an hour before the office officially close, and two more appointments. Which meant that he would run late, but who kept track? No one waited for him back at the house he rented from Esther and Jesse. There was no supper set on the table. Conrad grimaced and tried to concentrate on his driving. There hadn't been supper waiting for him since he left the ranch for college. Rather than supplying answers, the weekend with his family had left him further dissatisfied with his present situation and no clear road forward. He had always known the door was open for his return home, but things wouldn't be the same. Childhood and naïveté could not be recaptured. He needed to move on, but where and how?

Esther was sure of his welcome into the community, but without the issue settled with Rose, he couldn't move forward. She was dating and about to set her wedding date. Their attraction for each other would not remain a secret. Sharp-eyed people would notice. Worse if Rose broke off her relationship because of him? He didn't want to think what those implications might be. He couldn't see a warm welcome awaiting him from the bearded Amish men if he were to blame for a thwarted wedding. Robert Schlabach could make his life a misery, and there were Rose's feelings in the matter. She had made her position clear.

Yet he couldn't stop thinking about her. He hadn't stopped thinking about Rose, even when he forced himself to stop and talk sense into himself. The few moments of respite which came were quickly overrun by emotions which didn't follow his will. He was smitten with the girl. He might as well be honest. He had heard of such things, a love which arrived out of nowhere, a love which gripped the heart and would never let go for a lifetime.

He wished for a lifetime with Rose. He could see this road clearly, growing ever brighter and never fading in glory. They could grow old together, sitting on the front porch watching the moon rise, and their love would remain young and forever new.

He had planned to walk away from home and never look back. He had been fooling himself. He had left home, but he had never left. He had met the Amish, eaten Amish homemade ice cream, sat on a dark front porch watching the moon rising, and fallen in love with an Amish girl.

"Get a grip," he told himself.

Nothing happened. Not deep down, at least. He still loved the girl.

CHAPTER 52

Back at the newly purchased home, Rose was still holding on to the countertop with both hands as the world spun around her. She had no idea how much time had passed. Time seemed to stand still, stunned by the words which had come out of her mouth.

"What did you say?" Robert asked.

Rose gathered herself together. She couldn't back down or her courage would never return. "We are through," she whispered.

"Like in—" Robert's lips were moving slowly. "What does this mean?"

"Something is very wrong with us," she said.

His face was pale. "You mean with me or with the house?"

"I mean with myself."

He clearly didn't believe her.

"Something has happened to me. I don't know what, but something has."

He appeared dumbfounded.

"I know I'm not explaining myself well, but—"

"Nothing has changed, Rose. I still love you with my whole heart."

She forced herself to look at him. "Then why—"

"This is me and my rushing ways," he said, not hearing, his gaze moving over the cabinets. "I'm so sorry."

"No! Robert! This is me. I can't go on, and I can't tell you why."

"I have no idea what you mean."

"Do you want me to tell you?"

"You didn't do anything wrong."

"Yah, I did. Something very wrong."

"Can't we start over?" he begged.

"You're not listening. I'm the problem."

"There must be something, I mean. I already have the house."

"I'm sorry about everything. I really am. I can't say how much."

"We asked for the Lord's will." He moved closer. "This is the Lord's will."

"No, Robert. Dating is about finding out for sure. I know I have found out who I am."

"You're the girl for me,"

"Please, Robert. Just know that I'm sorry, very sorry, but we can't go on like this."

"Like what?"

"I don't want to explain. It'll only make things worse."

"I can change anything about the house you want me to change. Even take out the cabinets."

"This has nothing to do with the cabinets."

"Then what?"

"Me. I told you."

"I want to hear what I'm doing wrong."

"No, Robert. I'm sorry. I didn't intend things to end up like this." She moved away from him, picking up her broom and dustpan.

"You're leaving?" He was hurrying after her.

"We will not see each other again. Not like this. Dating."

"We won't be dating anymore?"

"Robert. We have a problem, and it'll hurt you more if we keep dating and you find out later."

"I don't believe this." He reached for her hand. "Will you let me know when we can see each other again?"

She pulled away. "There won't be another beginning. Not this time. Not with—"

"Rose." Robert followed her to the buggy.

She shoved her cleaning tools under the seat and climbed in to drive out of the lane. Rose turned south and didn't look back.

Rose expected the tears to come, but they didn't. A heavy feeling settled on her stomach, instead, a weight like lead. Mamm would notice her disheveled appearance and would want an explanation. The bare facts could be told, but she had no explanation. Not one fit for Mamm's ears.

Rose pulled into the Miller's driveway and unhitched Brownie by the barn. She had the harness off and Brownie munching a bucket of oats before Edwin drove into the barnyard with his team from the day's work in the fields. She left by the front door without speaking to him, each step across the yard one move closer to her doom.

Mamm looked up from the kitchen sink when she entered and wiped her hands on her apron. "That was a quick trip. Get the house cleaned and things talked out?"

Rose sat down on the kitchen table and put her head in her hands.

"What is wrong?" Alarm filled Mamm's voice.

"I broke up with him." Rose spoke to the tabletop.

"You did what?" Mamm's steps came closer.

"I broke up with Robert."

"But things were going so well." Mamm's hand settled on her shoulder.

"I don't know what's wrong with me."

"You should not have done this." Mamm's voice rose higher. "Why, Rose?"

"Things are a mess. I can't explain."

Mamm's hand tightened, her voice becoming hopeful. "I know you have had a lot of confused feelings. Maybe you and Robert will patch things up later. Did you leave the door open?"

"I told him we were finished."

"You must have nearly killed the man." The weight of Mamm's hand was gone. "Robert loved you."

"I couldn't go on. I just couldn't," Rose wailed.

"There must be more to this than you're telling me," Mamm said. "Let this rest tonight. All can be told when the time is right. Come now. Help me with supper."

Rose nodded and forced herself to stand. Her legs nearly gave out, but she steadied herself against the kitchen table until her strength returned.

CHAPTER 53

Dusk had fallen, and the dim lantern lights were on at Esther and Jesse's place. Conrad stood outside his small house thinking about things. What should be his next step? If there was one. Maybe he was doomed to live in limbo, so near and yet so far from something which pulled and tugged at his heart.

He finally shook his head and went back into the house. Maybe some things could never be solved—like Iraq, like the war, like life itself. A dilemma meant to haunt rather than heal, to hurt rather than soothe the pain.

CHAPTER 54

Rose had the first load of laundry out on the line the next morning as dawn broke on the horizon—a gray, clouding, stormy-looking morning. She was up earlier than usual with the rain threatening, but the truth was, working soothed her nerves since she hadn't slept most of the night. Mamm hadn't said anything more about her breakup with Robert, but Daett had looked strangely at her when he came through the basement on the way out to his chores.

"Goot morning," Daett had called out.

"Goot morning," Rose had replied above the roar of the washing machine motor.

Daett had rummaged through a shelf in the back before he went up the steps. He usually didn't come through the basement on his way out to chores. Obviously, Mamm had told him the news, and he was concerned.

Rose reentered the basement and stowed the empty basket on the shelf above the washer. The task completed, she willed herself up the stairs and back into the kitchen. Her family must have an explanation soon, but from the appearances of things, Mamm didn't expect one this morning. She was busy at the stove, and Rose joined in. She had helped prepare breakfast a thousand times in her life. They could work silently without words.

"I would like to visit Esther's after breakfast." Rose said.

"You can speak to me." Mamm sounded hurt.

"I know. I don't know what's wrong with me."

Mamm looked very concerned. "I never thought you would be the one to hit such a confused spot, especially with Robert."

"I tried hard, I did." Rose couldn't keep the sob out of her voice.

She wanted to tell Mamm everything, but this would lead to the awfulness of what she had done with Conrad in Esther's basement. The words were lost in Rose's mouth before they could take form.

"Did Robert change since you began dating him?" Mamm asked.

"This is my fault."

"You don't have to play the martyr."

"I'm not. I'm messed up. I really am."

Mamm sighed. "You've never been like this, but I'm here when you wish to talk. Breakups can be dramatic."

"I have to speak with Esther. I have to."

Mamm gave in with a nod. "If you don't stay long."

"I won't." Rose set out the last of the breakfast dishes as Edwin and Charles came in from the washroom. Daett wasn't far behind them, and the prayer of thanks was quickly offered after they were seated.

"Why so glum?" Edwin asked, his mouth full of eggs and toast.

Rose ignored him.

"You might as well tell," Mamm said, in Rose's direction. "This can't remain a secret within the family, and obviously not for long in the community."

Edwin clucked his tongue. "Did Robert pay too much for his farm?"

"They broke up yesterday," Mamm said.

Charles's head came up from his plate. "Robert and Rose?"

"You need say no more," Mamm chided. "Let the two of them work things out."

Edwin appeared worried. "Don't tell me Mary is going to pull something like this. Right out of the blue air."

"We are not wise to judge ourselves among ourselves." Daett instructed, his voice rumbling. "Best we listen to the Lord. Everyone is different."

Edwin's worried look didn't vanish.

"Mary is not like me." Rose forced herself to speak.

Edwin didn't look convinced.

"She'll be okay." Rose tried another angle.

Edwin gave her a glare. "Says the girl who broke off her relationship with a perfectly decent man."

"How do you know Robert didn't break off the relationship?" Mamm asked.

Edwin snorted. "Wasn't Robert, and it sure won't be me."

"Enough on the subject." Daett's voice was firm. "We will trust all our ways to the Lord, and He will direct our paths."

Rose managed to finish her breakfast, but most of the food felt like the pieces were hung up in her throat. When they finished eating, the last prayer of thanks was offered, and Mamm brought Daett his Bible. After a little searching, Daett read the Scripture he had quoted from earlier.

"Trust in the Lord with all thine heart; and lean not unto thine own understanding. In all thy ways acknowledge him, and he shall direct thy paths. Be not wise in thine own eyes: fear the Lord and depart from evil."

Daett closed the Bible but didn't offer any further comments. They knelt beside their chairs for the morning prayer. The men left for their day's work, and Rose busied herself clearing the table.

"You sure you don't want to say something more?" Mamm asked.

"I can't," Rose whispered.

"I see something is deeply troubling you."

"I would tell you, if I could." Rose whimpered. "I just can't. Not now."

"What happened Rose?"

The tears came, but Rose shook her head.

Mamm gave in quickly. "You had best go at once and speak with Esther about this."

Rose lifted a stack of plates into the sink, saying nothing. What was there to say?

"I can finish this." Mamm insisted.

"I can wait. This matter is not so important."

Mamm's voice was firm. "Getting peace about this matter. Yah! This is very important."

Rose gave in, slipping on a light coat on the way outside. The wash had begun to move in the slight morning breeze. She must hurry and get back in time to bring in the wash before the rain came. She needed to speak with Esther, but she also needed to work, to feel a routine, to find the hope which came from doing something normal. Insanity was knocking at the door. She had to get relief somewhere. Somehow!

CHAPTER 55

Robert finished his breakfast with a final gulp and rose to leave the house after the last prayer of thanks had been offered by Daett. Once outside, he pulled his hat lower on his head to shield his eyes from the blast of wind out of the east. Rain was coming, but his team had been harnessed earlier and was tied to the fence rail waiting for him. He would work the cultivator until the first of the rain drops lashed his face.

He climbed into the seat and hollered. "Getup."

If any of his family had noticed anything different about him this morning, they had not mentioned their observation. Maybe he was good at hiding things, or perhaps the breakup wasn't hurting like he expected such a thing should. Weren't couples supposed to go through terrible trauma when one or the other terminated the relationship? Likely this was more dreamy-eyed speaking, of which Rose had been inclined. He had probably picked up some of these ideas from being exposed to her. He felt perfectly fine, other than the shame he would experience in facing the community once the news broke.

He was in a fix with a farm purchase just closed, and his wife-to-be jilting him. Daett had yet to say anything about his purchase of the new farm, or his extensive consultations with Grandpa. Daett would have plenty to say when he learned his train had run off the tracks. Things about a man getting ahead of how he had been raised.

Because his train was off the tracks. There was no getting around the truth of the matter. The reality was stark, bare, and open for everyone to see. Rose Miller had left him high and dry. He would be the laughingstock of the community. He and his big plans, his dating of Rose, who everyone knew was one of the most stable and admired girls in the community. No one would blame Rose for the end of their relationship. Failure would solidly mark his shoulders, caulked up to his rush to grab success with both hands.

The reality was he had practiced great patience with Rose and her dreamy ways. He had thought he was changing her, but he had been wrong. Maybe he was better off this way? If he could live through the shame and disappointment.

Word would be out this Sunday.

People would whisper, "Did you hear? Rose Miller dumped him right after the closing on his farm."

How would he face the community? He couldn't, and yet he had to, unless—

Why not? He could keep his plans for the trip to Lancaster County, which he had figured should best be abandoned. The trip would feel strange, going out to meet Grandpa with such a failure on his record. Likely, Grandpa would wish to have his money back on the farm loan but staying home wouldn't change Grandpa's sentiment. Better to face the man, if things must be faced. Rather Grandpa than the community at home. Let things blow over for a few weeks.

In the meantime, he needed a wife. Grandpa might give him a chewing out, but Grandpa also had ideas—goot ones. He'd take almost any girl at the moment, but none of the available young women from the community would touch him. Not for a year or so. By then he would be known as the bachelor who lived alone on his farm. His reputation would be destroyed. He needed answers, and he needed them fast.

His beautiful cabinets were gone. Without Rose to back him, Deacon John wouldn't give much heed to his request to bend the community's ordnung.

"Let's get going," he shouted to his team. "The rain is coming."

CHAPTER 56

With the wind in her face, Rose drove Brownie into Esther's lane and tried not to look toward Conrad's house across the fields. The man wouldn't be at home this time of the day, but her stomach twisted in knots at the thought of seeing him again. He was not to blame for her mess—she was to blame. Pulling back on the reins, Rose bounced to a stop.

Esther came running from the house before Rose could climb out of the buggy. "Rose, what a surprise!"

Rose tried to smile. "Goot morning."

"What's wrong?" Esther reached for her hand.

Rose accepted as if she were an invalid, and climbed down from the buggy, still careful not to look toward Conrad's place.

"What happened?" Esther gripped her arm.

"I broke off my relationship with Robert yesterday."

Esther's face lit up. "What goot news!"

Rose groaned. "I was thinking this was very bad news."

"Now you're free from the man," Esther said, "and you can move forward into the future."

"Esther, please. I beg you. Help me."

"I'm helping you."

"By making things worse. By helping me further into this mess?"

Esther's grip didn't loosen. "You expect me to encourage you to get back with Robert?"

"Not exactly," Rose said. "I need to talk with someone who knows what I've done. Maybe I can fully explain to Mamm afterward."

"We will tell Mamm the truth together!" Esther declared. "This would be the first step toward freeing yourself fully from Robert."

"And destroying me." Rose moaned.

"Mamm won't understand." Esther agreed. "But you're also her daughter. Mamm won't abandon you."

"I'll never live down this shame. People knowing, I kissed an English man."

"Things happen." Esther comforted. "Mamm will be horrified, but I wasn't. I'll speak up for you, and no one else need know more. You broke up with Robert for goot."

"I suppose, this is why I came over. Knowing you would comfort me in my sin?"

"You didn't sin. You kissed a man you loved. Mamm won't see the logic, but I do, and I'm sure Jesse would agree with me."

"Jesse." Rose moaned. "You're making things worse."

"Loving a man is never for the worse. Jesse knows this."

"You've told him." Rose felt her knees weakened, and she held on to the side of the buggy. "The whole thing is a horrid mess."

"I don't see a mess, and I haven't told Jesse anything." Esther assured her. "Doesn't say he won't agree, though, and with me see the Lord's hand moving in mysterious ways."

"I just threw away my chance of marriage to a decent Amish man—for any Amish man. I'll never survive this confession to any further man I date. I'm an old maid now."

Esther let go of Rose's arm to find the tie rope behind the seat, and secured Brownie to the hitching post. "How long can you stay?"

"Mamm said not long."

"Come! We'll make hot chocolate and sit on the front porch and calm down."

"I can see Conrad's place from the front porch."

"See," Esther said, as if this confirmed everything. "We must face things, squarely and head-on, beginning with Conrad."

"I should have confessed a long time ago." Rose whimpered. "Gotten down on my knees and told Robert the gory details."

Esther gave her a glare. "Thank the Lord you had some goot sense left. The man didn't deserve a moment of your attention, let alone spilling your heart."

"Oh, what shall I do?" Rose let go of the buggy wheel and somehow stayed on her feet. Brownie turned his head to look, as if he had doubts himself.

Esther didn't let go of her arm for the walk to the house, where she helped Rose into a seat at the kitchen table. The teakettle was already seated on the warm stove top, gently spouting steam. Esther moved the kettle closer to the fire. By the time she found the jar of chocolate and had taken spoons from the drawer, the kettle whistled a merry tune. Esther smiled at Rose and filled the cups with cocoa and hot water.

"I should be helping." Rose stood to her feet

Esther ignored her to pick up both cups and motioned with her head for Rose to follow her outside. They found shelter from the wind and settled into chairs.

Esther handed Rose a cup and ordered. "Start talking. Tell me everything about how you broke up."

Rose held the cup in both hands and took a long breath. "Well, where do I begin? You know about the kiss in your basement. I knew I should confess to Robert, so I sat in the back with the married women on Sunday morning. I didn't want to see him or smile at him until the horrid words had either been buried or spoken."

"I noticed." Esther commented.

Rose took her time, turning her cup around and around in her hands. "I was so twisted in knots all day. I figured

Robert had to notice and would ask me why in the evening. I figured this would be the time to confess."

"What did you think his reaction would be?" Esther asked.

Rose stared across the fields. "Leave the house, I suppose. Never come back."

"A relief, right?" Esther probed.

Rose reluctantly nodded.

"But he didn't notice?"

Rose looked up startled. "How did you know?"

"Because I know the man."

The tears came, and Esther reached over to squeeze her hand.

"There were no questions." Rose sobbed. "The whole evening, we talked about nothing but his farm, his grandfather, and on top of everything … he stopped to buy store-bought ice cream on the way home."

"On a Sunday evening?"

"Yah, Esther. We needed to celebrate, he said, and I hadn't made ice cream—as if I had known he wanted ice cream and wasn't sick with worry about you know what."

"I know," Esther said.

"I felt like I didn't exist. Which didn't excuse what I did, but somehow this made things worse."

"You don't have to excuse the man," Esther said, a little bitterly.

"Now we're blaming Robert."

Esther didn't back down. "Keep going."

Rose stared at her cup of hot chocolate but couldn't take another sip. Not in the midst of this horrid tale. She continued, forcing the words out of her mouth.

"Robert wanted me to come over to the house on Monday so he could nail down my support for those fancy cabinets and with my help persuading Deacon John to bend the community's ordnung. I didn't know this at the time, but the matter became clear once we arrived at the house. I refused."

"Manipulation," Esther muttered. "I knew the man was capable of a lot."

"Don't blame him," Rose whispered. "I kissed an English man."

Esther ignored her, still muttering. "The proverbial straw which broke the camel's back. I'm not surprised. Serves the man right."

"But—" Rose tried again. "I'm the one who made the mess."

"Love can be a lovely mess, Rose."

Rose stared at the cup of hot chocolate again. "How am I to go on living with myself?"

"You're not hearing me." Esther said, a little louder.

"Yah, I am." Rose insisted. "I know what you're saying. I love Conrad. I know this, and have admitted as much, but this is the problem not the solution."

"You're thinking too much." Esther decided. "You and Conrad must get together and talk."

Rose sat bolt upright and the hot chocolate nearly spilled. "Get together?"

"I will talk to him first." Esther smiled encouragingly.

"No—"

"I will talk to the man," Esther said, quite firmly.

"You can't tell him I—"

"I will ask him how he feels about you and go from there."

"Oh, Esther." Rose sank back into the chair. "Do not do this."

Esther turned her cup slowly in her hands. "I know I have been pushing you in Conrad's direction, so if this goes very wrong, I will take the blame."

"This has already gone very wrong."

Esther seemed not to hear. "I know what I see. The perfect match for my sister."

"No," Rose said again.

Esther leaped to her feet. "Come, time for you to leave. Mamm will be wondering."

Rose stood more slowly. "What am I to tell Mamm?"

"Nothing! Not until I come over. For now, you say you have talked with me, and we're praying about the matter."

Rose felt weak. "You keep bringing the Lord in. I feel like I'm committing sacrilege even trying to pray."

"The Lord is the maker of love, Rose. He wants you to marry a man you love."

"An English man!" Rose shook her head to set her cup down carefully, the contents barely touched. "You're right, though. I really have to go."

"Everything will be okay." Esther reached over to squeeze Rose's arm. "We'll pray."

Rose heard her own voice croak on the way to the buggy. "I'm surprised the Lord is listening anymore."

CHAPTER 57

Dusk fell early on this tumultuous day, with the storm moving in from the north. Robert's fears were settling even as the weather worsened. He was becoming ever more certain an immediate departure for Lancaster County was the solution to his problem. With his certainty rising, he planned to make the announcement when the Schlabach family had gathered around the supper table by seven. Which he did.

"I'm leaving for Lancaster County on the train tomorrow." They had just finished the prayer of thanks.

Daett didn't look too pleased, but he said nothing.

"Aren't you rushing things a bit?" Mamm asked. "First, you're dating Rose, then you're buying the farm, now a trip to Lancaster. You used to move carefully and slowly."

"I'm doing what I think is best." Robert replied.

"You're still young." Daett finally spoke.

"Grandpa invited me." Robert took a bite of Mamm's meatloaf and chewed slowly. His parents should be told about Rose, but he couldn't get the words out of his mouth. He wouldn't tell them, he decided, until he was ready to leave for the train station. This way he wouldn't have to live with their heightened disapproval until he came back, or worse, face their strenuous efforts to prevent this trip after such a total and colossal failure on his part.

Outside the house, the storm which had been threatening all day lashed against the vinyl siding of the house.

CHAPTER 58

On Sunday morning, Rose was seated in her usual place among the unmarried women. Not until the first sermon began did she dare raise her gaze. She expected to find Robert staring at her from the young men's section, but from across the room she caught Esther's smile instead. Esther looked cheerful. She obviously couldn't say the same for herself. There must be rings under her eyes from tossing and turning under the quilt for hours, trying to sleep, trying to forget what she had done.

Rose shifted her gaze back to the young men for a better look but still didn't see Robert. Where was the man? He wasn't usually absent from the church services. Had her rejection so traumatized the man? Horror filled her again.

"You will speak with Robert today and make your peace with him," Mamm had ordered this morning

Rose had repeated Esther's line about being in prayer on the matter. Mamm obviously thought action was required at the moment. If Robert wasn't here this morning, this would only increase the pressure from Mamm when she arrived back home. How did Esther expect to speak with Mamm without making things worse? Mamm's horror would only grow when she learned the truth, which was why Mamm could never know. She must get to Esther after the service and tell her never to breathe a word to Conrad. She would live her life as an Amish old maid. There was no other honorable option. Maybe after the years unfolded, and she was old and worn out from working in other people's homes, she could forget what she had done.

Rose tried to listen to the sermons, but the words wouldn't register—no matter how earnestly she studied the bearded face of the minister. Rose gave up and tried not to think of Conrad, which proved just as impossible. The closeness of his handsome face was burned into her memory, the kindness in his eyes. She would never forget him, not in a thousand years. Not even in the life to come. The Lord perhaps would find forgiveness for her, but she would never forget her sin.

The time ticked past, and Rose stayed frozen on the hard church bench, willing herself not to move or even blink. Remaining motionless didn't help her dilemma, but the action felt right, this shutting down and allowing life to move past her.

The service concluded, and Rose unfroze herself to smile at the girl seated beside her.

"What a timely warning the ministers had for us this morning," the girl whispered.

"Yah, they did," Rose whispered back.

She wasn't lying. The ministers always had timely warnings.

When they stood to enter the kitchen to help with the tables, Esther's voice whispered in Rose's ear. "I need to speak with you."

"Don't share too many secrets," the girl said cheerfully, obviously having heard.

"Out to the porch," Esther ordered, and Rose obeyed.

She was too weak to speak when they stepped outside.

"I have wunderbah news," Esther said, even louder.

Rose found her voice. "You didn't—"

Esther dismissively waved her hand. "We're way past protests. Did you tell Mamm we were praying?"

"Yah."

"Well, the Lord has answered."

"Esther." Rose begged.

Esther appeared not to hear. "Conrad has agreed to visit our place tonight for supper."

Rose stared. "You did tell him."

"No, but I walked over last night after he came home and extended the invitation. After he accepted, I added, 'Rose will also come.'" He appeared interested, happy even. He certainly had no objections."

Rose felt the blood leave her face. "I can't come, Esther. I—I can't."

"You're coming." Esther's hand gripped Rose's arm.

"But the hymn singing. I have to attend."

"Who says? And where is Robert?"

"I don't know. I must have broken his heart."

Esther raised her eyebrows. "The man's heart doesn't break over you—unless I miss my guess."

Rose didn't answer, trying to stay on her feet. "I can't come tonight."

"I'll hint around with his sisters during lunch and find out what's going on." Esther pressed on. "I'll prove to you the man isn't a bit brokenhearted."

"I'm still not coming." Rose felt her head clear a little with the rush of resolve.

Esther's grip on her arm hadn't loosened. "You must. Everything is falling in place."

"But Mamm." Rose tried again. "I can't hide another awful thing from her."

"Don't worry!" Esther declared. "I'll speak with Mamm. Just plan to show up."

Rose tried to breathe. Her knees were so weak she had to hang on the rails of the porch. "No," she said, and a little strength returned, but her heart felt dead, as if hope had fled far away.

"We will see. I'm coming over this afternoon." Esther gave her an encouraging smile, as Rose followed Esther back into the house.

CHAPTER 59

Robert awoke on the train seat with the sun bright in his eyes after his nap. He sat bolt upright, trying to figure out where he was. For a long moment he couldn't remember, but reality came back in a rush. His quick conversation with his parents. The words spilling out. The hired English driver pulling into the yard for the trip to the train station. Loading his single suitcase into the trunk. Mamm's disapproving figure watching from the front porch.

"You tell Grandpa and Grandma howdy for us," Mamm had hollered after him.

Below Robert—the sound had surrounded him for hours—the steady clack of the train tracks decreased as they approached an incline. Outside the window, a distant snowcapped mountain graced the horizon. The scenery would change once they approached the eastern states, but for now, the mountains and the prairies seemed wedded to each other. Robert blinked, remembering Rose's face, her determined look when she broke off their relationship. There had been a deep sorrow in her eyes, as if Rose had wished things could have turned out different. He should have paid more attention to the girl and what she was thinking. Now he was staring failure in the eyes. No question there.

Rose was serious about terminating their relationship. He was becoming more convinced the longer he thought about things. Back home, the rush and weight of the farm work would have kept his thoughts at bay, Maybe even kept his hope alive, but here, sitting on the train, listening to the clack of the steel wheels and the lonesome howl of the horn blasting at the crossings, the truth was sinking in. There would be no repair of their broken fence. Whatever had happened, Rose was finished with him. There would be no more waiting, no more maybes, no more chances in the future. Rose Miller would never be his wife. He had suffered those long months in vain. He had passed up chances to date other girls for nothing. He, Robert Schlabach, had reached for the stars and missed his grasp. He was falling through space with no bottom. His shame would be trickling through the community back home, the whispers blunted by his absence, but he would have to return and face them. He would have to drive home in his buggy alone on Sunday evenings. There was not a girl in the community who was available to date, even if he wished to ask her.

He must do something! But what?

CHAPTER 60

"What are you and Esther up to?" Mamm demanded.

Daett, seated on his rocker reading *The Budget*, appeared not to hear. Rose tried to formulate a proper response, with her gaze cast downward. The afternoon sun sent long rays of light through the living room window, stirring long lines of dust particles high into the air. How could the house be so dirty? She had swept the floor twice yesterday.

"Rose!" Mamm's voice interrupted her thoughts. "I think I need an answer. Esther is being evasive."

Was the truth the best? Rose's heart pounded at the thought of blurting out the whole story in one gulp and without Esther present

"Esther said she would speak with you," Rose managed.

"I want to know now!" Mamm stood her ground.

Rose ignored the order. She couldn't speak about the matter alone.

"I think Rose is right." Daett spoke up.

Both of them stared at Daett.

"You think what?" Mamm asked.

"Esther should be present when we talk about this matter, and so should I."

"Of course. I mean—" Mamm was searching for words. "Rose is your daughter, but I don't think sympathy is what Rose needs right now. She shattered the poor man's heart. He wasn't even at the services today, and Robert never misses a service."

"I couldn't continue our relationship." Rose gulped down the lump in her throat.

"You've been saying this for days." Mamm retorted. "You've yet to give me a decent reason. Every couple has their rough spots, but for you to walk out on a man after he has purchased a farm, and you've basically set your wedding day. You will not live this down in the community."

"I know." Rose felt the blood pound in her head. "I know this all too well."

"You do have a decent reputation." Mamm seemed to comfort herself. "Maybe the fall out will not be too bad. Maybe by next spring? The gardening will be in full swing again, people will have forgotten."

Rose said nothing. What could she say or do? Waiting for the storm to pass would not help. The thunderclouds were heaping up on the horizon.

"When is Esther coming over?" Daett asked, the pages of *The Budget* rustling in his hand.

"She wants to come over this afternoon, and she wants to—" Rose couldn't go any further.

"Goot," Daett said. "Why don't you make popcorn?"

"I will." Rose stood to her feet.

Mamm didn't look pleased as Rose hurried to the kitchen. She found the ingredients and set the popper on the open flame. How was she to eat popcorn during the discussion with Esther? She couldn't, but the others could. She would serve them and let Esther do the talking. Maybe somehow she would survive this storm.

The rattle of Esther's buggy wheels came in the driveway while Rose finished the second popper, dumping the moist white kernels into a large mixing bowl. She added the salt, concentrating, while Daett's footsteps went out the front door to welcome her arriving sister.

Finding smaller bowls in the cupboard, Rose waited until the front door slammed again, and soft voices murmured in the living room, before she went through the kitchen doorway. Esther looked up and smiled while Rose handed out the bowls.

"Sit." Mamm ordered.

Rose sat and studied the floorboards on the hardwood floor.

"Start talking," Mamm said in Esther's direction.

Esther took a deep breath. "You know about the happy marriage Jesse and I have, so let's begin there. I want to remind you I do speak with some authority on the subject, and I do know Rose well."

"Get to the point," Mamm said. "I want an explanation for what Rose has done."

"Let Esther tell the story." Daett spoke up, quietly eating from his bowl of popcorn, with the pages of *The Budget* lying on the rocker beside him.

Esther looked surprised but continued. "I have not approved of Rose dating Robert from the start, and I have my reasons."

"What are those?" Mamm interrupted.

"Let the girl speak," Daett said.

Mamm settled back into her rocker but didn't look happy.

"Remember Wilmer?" Esther asked.

"The boy who drowned," Mamm said.

"Yah. Rose's heart was given to the man."

"They were school children," Mamm said.

"I know." Esther allowed. "All the same, Rose and Wilmer loved each other. Rose never forgot him."

"Is this the reason for her hesitancy to date men?" Daett asked.

"Of course not," Mamm said.

"Was it?" Daett asked Esther directly.

Esther nodded.

"I don't believe this," Mamm said. "We are to forget the past and accept the Lord's will. Rose wouldn't have kept hanging on to Wilmer's memory."

"Rose tried," Esther said, "but Conrad brought all the memories back."

"The English man!" Mamm was half out of her rocker.

"Mamm, calm down." Daett ordered this time. "We will hear the story without going off the deep end."

"Deep end! We're already off the deep end." Mamm nearly shouted, nevertheless settling down.

She didn't look settled down, though. Rose was squeezing pieces of white popcorn between her fingers, letting the pieces fall to the floor. She was acting like a child, but what else was new. She had been acting like a child for a long time.

"Rose was not a goot match for Robert." Esther continued. "She never will be. There has been something between Rose and Conrad from the beginning, from the time Daett invited the man into your house for breakfast."

"Daett did this?" Mamm was up in arms again.

"No." Esther corrected. "Conrad met Rose outside the house before Daett invited him in. They were drawn to each other from the start."

"Rose has rejected Robert because she's in love with an English man?" Mamm looked ready to leap out of her rocker.

"I remember the moment." Daett ignored Mamm. "I walked up on them, with the sun rising on the horizon. I agree, there was something special going on. Maybe this explains why I invited the man for breakfast."

Rose stared. She couldn't believe what Daett was saying.

"What is wrong with you?" Mamm implored. "Conrad is English."

"I know." Daett didn't look too worried.

"I'm not leaving the Amish." Rose managed, but no one paid any attention to her.

"This was the reason Rose finally agreed to date Robert." Esther continued. "She felt so badly about what she was feeling, and guilty, and—"

"As she should!" Mamm declared.

"Guilt is no basis for love," Esther said.

"I agree." Daett spoke up, waving Mamm back into her rocker. "Are the rumors true Conrad may be joining the community?"

"They are," Esther said. "He's thinking about joining."

Daett smiled. "Several of the men said he acts like he is. Perhaps this is the Lord's doing."

Mamm had turned pale. "Stop saying such things, every one of you. Rose will make her peace with Robert when he has had a little time to heal. This time of separation can be a time to mature. As they say, absence makes the heart grow fonder."

"I'm going to be an old maid." Rose kept her voice steady. What other choice did she have?

"Banish the thought," Mamm said.

"I'm sorry if I have disappointed you as a daughter," Rose whispered.

"These storm clouds will pass." Mamm tried to smile. "We will take courage in the thought and say no more about this foolishness concerning an English man."

Rose didn't answer. Mamm was right. She was spinning on a flighty drift into the air as unseen dust particles did, caught in the grip of the sunbeams. Conrad was a sunbeam, a ray of light, and she was caught in his presence. An impossible catching, and a wasted effort. Floating in the air could accomplish nothing.

"Are you okay?" Daett asked, looking directly at Rose.

"Yah." Rose tried to stand. She was okay. Conrad had been a glimpse into the promised land. Like Moses standing on a tall mountain from where he could see the land which flowed with milk and honey, but his feet had been forbidden to enter. As were hers.

"I think Rose did the right thing," Daett said.

Rose heard his words, but at the same time she didn't. Daett couldn't have said what he just did.

"You don't mean this!" Mamm was shouting.

"I do," Daett said, quite calmly. "Rose has done nothing wrong. If Conrad is thinking of joining the community, and Rose feels affection stirring in her heart for the man, she was right in breaking off the relationship with Robert."

"The man bought a farm!" Mamm exclaimed.

"Robert will find a wife," Daett said. "Don't worry about him. Think about your daughter. She shouldn't marry a man she doesn't love."

Mamm was staring, her lips moving silently.

Esther was clasping and unclasping her hands, a little pale herself. "I—I have to say something else. Conrad is invited over to our house this evening for supper, and I want Rose to come."

"You planned this all along." Mamm's voice had gone weak.

"You should trust your daughters," Daett said. "I think Rose should go. She will do the right thing."

"I—I—this is—" Mamm, for once, was out of words.

"Thank you," Esther said in Daett's direction. There were tears on her cheeks.

Rose was sure there were also tears on Daett's face, but afterward she wasn't so sure. Daett didn't cry, and the whole thing had been a dream. She was sure this was a dream. Rose pinched herself, but Esther was still in the living room getting ready to leave, and Mamm was sitting in her rocker. Daett was smiling, following Esther out of the front door.

"Did you put Daett up to this?" Mamm asked, when the two had left.

Rose shook her head, not daring to look at Mamm.

"I can't believe this." Mamm stood, and her footsteps faded into the kitchen.

Rose sat unmoving. How and when was she to get over to Esther's place? She would have to leave in an hour.

"Come help me make supper." Mamm called from the kitchen. "You might as well help even if you're not eating with us."

Rose stood, waiting a second for her head to clear. They would be okay. Somehow, they would be okay. Mamm still wanted her in the kitchen.

Rose took a step forward. She would be seeing Conrad tonight. Rose blocked the thought. She could only handle so much emotion at a time.

CHAPTER 61

Dusk was falling as the train barreled through a small town on the prairie, and Robert felt hunger stir in his stomach. He had been too preoccupied the whole day to think of food.

"I'm hungry," he said out loud.

An older lady walking past paused to give him a kindly smile. "They serve sandwiches and hot chocolate in the diner. Other things as well."

"Thanks." Robert stumbled to his feet. He grabbed his hat from the overhead bin and followed the older lady down the aisle.

They were in the Midwest somewhere. The name of the town shown on the dusty broken sign as they came into town had flown out of his head as quickly as the word had entered. He was a day into his trip, and he was homesick. For the community mostly. He had expected Rose to occupy his thoughts, and she did, but not with the poignant longing of the previously engaged—or the nearly engaged—should invoke.

"Rose," he said under his breath. "Bye, bye, and gone."

Robert followed the older lady into the diner. She turned to motion with her hand toward one of the small tables. "Would you sit with me?"

"Certainly." Robert obliged. She appeared friendly enough.

"We should order first," she said, before he could sit down.

"Of course." He hadn't known, but she didn't appear to notice.

He followed her and ordered a sandwich and a glass of orange juice at the counter after she had placed hers.

"They'll bring the order," she told him.

He nodded, and they made their way back to the table where he had left his hat.

"Visiting back East?" she asked when they had seated themselves.

"Yep, my grandpa and grandma," he said.

Her smile grew wide. "Are you close to them."

"Quite." He thought pensively. "Quite close."

"Ah," she gushed. "The Amish are such family-minded people. Wish my grandson was close to me."

"Is he—" He proceeded cautiously. "Does he live far from you."

"In the same town." She made a face. "Too many things going on, I suppose, to have time for Grandma."

"Grandpa is a great man." The pleasant thought washed over him. "He helped me buy a farm, and I'm on my way to learn a few things from him."

Her face lit up. "How wonderful. "I've heard of such things, but to hear of them with my own ears. You're a blessed people, indeed."

"I suppose so."

She reached over to pat him on the arm. "I know it's difficult to see a blessing sometimes when you're living the blessing, but you're blessed beyond anything I can imagine going on in our family."

"You wouldn't help your grandson buy a farm?"

She guffawed. "The man wouldn't buy a farm. He can barely hold down a job."

Robert stared, saying nothing. This he couldn't imagine.

"Different world," she said, as if this explained everything.

The waitress came and brought their food. Robert glanced at her before he bowed his head. She was sitting still, apparently waiting on him. He bowed his head for a short silent prayer of thanks.

She had tears in her eyes when he looked up. "I knew you would pray," she said.

Robert took a bite of his sandwich and didn't answer. He didn't know what to say.

"By the way, I'm Heidi," she said. "Like the Heidi of the mountains. You know, the blind Grandpa, Peter, and the goats."

He had no idea what she referred to. Apparently, some English thing. "Robert," he muttered. "Robert Schlabach."

"Good to meet you, Robert." She still hadn't touched her food. "What an unexpected blessing indeed."

He nodded, chewing his food. Thankfully, she began to eat.

"Are you married?" she asked. "Obviously not, or she would be along. Dating then? Wedding set perhaps?"

"No." Robert stroked his chin, trying to keep a troubled look from creeping over his face. He didn't want to discuss the subject with her.

Clearly, she had noticed. "Did I say something wrong? Surely you haven't lost—"

This time he laughed. "No. I've never been married. Almost though."

"Oh, a breakup. So, you do have troubles?"

He had said too much already. Robert took another bite of his sandwich.

"I'm so sorry. Your heart must be broken."

He shrugged. "I was disappointed."

"What a strong man," she continued. "You're taking this well."

"I'm trying to figure the matter out."

"I lost my husband ten years ago," she said, the tears coming.

He shifted on his seat. What was he supposed to say? "I'm sorry," he managed.

"He was a good man," she said, wiping her eyes. "A very good man."

He nodded, continuing to eat.

"I'm visiting my daughter in Ohio. We haven't seen each other in a while. Her daughter is having a baby next month."

"Oh." He forced a smile. Babies didn't interest him in the least.

"What do you plan to do with your grandpa, once you arrive?" she asked.

"Tour the Amish community in Lancaster," he said, between bites. "They have the best farming methods, and I have much to learn."

The tears were back. "What a wonderful young man you are. So hardworking and willing to learn."

"I try," he said.

"Sorry again about your broken relationship. I can't imagine why any girl would pass you up."

Neither can I, he wanted to say, but managed a crooked smile instead.

"How long are you staying?" she asked.

"A week or so. Not exactly sure."

"Where are you from?" She tilted her head. "If I may ask?"

"Nebraska."

"There are Amish in Nebraska?" She seemed surprised. "I've been trying to figure out for the last hour if I've ever heard of Amish in the West, because you obviously came from the West."

"The community is small. Nothing compared to Lancaster County."

"Well, I'm glad we met." She settled down to finish her meal. "What a blessing this has been."

He gulped down the last of his sandwich and stood to his feet. "I must be going."

"Maybe we'll see more of each other." She beamed.

"Maybe," he said. He didn't want to answer any more of her questions. Not really, but she had been friendly enough.

He nodded and made his way out of the diner back to his seat. He sat down, wishing this trip was over, wishing he was back home and had never left. Wishing Rose was his wife, and he didn't have to think about finding another one. How was he to get another girlfriend? He had to find one for a thousand reasons, foremost of which was the need for someone to tend the farm with him. Maybe Grandpa would have some ideas when he arrived in Lancaster. At least, the girls there wouldn't know about Rose's rejection of him, but would they date him? There was the brutality of the fact he lived in Nebraska. What Lancaster girl would be up to moving out West? Maybe Grandpa's goot word about the community could persuade one.

Robert sighed and turned to watch the darkened landscape rush past the window. He was dreaming as Rose dreamed. Would he ever escape her shadow? Heidi appeared in his side vision, making her way through the car. She smiled and gave him a little wave. He returned the greeting and settled into his seat, willing sleep to come quickly.

CHAPTER 62

An hour later, Rose drove into Esther's driveway and brought the buggy to a stop beside the barn. There was no light on in Conrad's small home. Neither was there any sign of him or of Jesse in the barnyard. Everyone must be in the house waiting for her, but what did she expect. Rose knew she was late. Mamm's grim face back at the house had kept her from leaving for a long time. Only Daett going out to harness Brownie for her had gotten Rose moving.

"You have a goot time." Daett had handed her the reins.

"Thank you," she had managed to whisper.

He seemed to understand as she drove away from him. How was she to change course, to think differently about Conrad, but somehow she must. She had been wrong in so many ways, and yet—the buzzing thoughts wouldn't stop.

Dizziness overwhelmed Rose, thinking about walking into the house and seeing Conrad. There was time to flee, to race back home with her buggy and try once more to forget Conrad. She had made a mess out of things. Digging the hole deeper was not going to help. Only the memory of Daett's words kept her from turning the buggy around and dashing away.

"Rose!"

She jumped and looked down to see Esther standing by the buggy door.

"I, I, I," Rose stammered.

"Conrad doesn't bite." Esther smiled up at her.

Rose tried to collect her wits. "There's still time—"

"You're coming into the house." Esther was firm.

"Is he in there?" Rose asked, though she was certain of the answer.

"Yah, and you're late."

"I'm still—"

"There's no reason to fear. Come." Esther reached up for Rose's hand. "You should not feel one bit guilty about meeting Conrad."

Rose shakily climbed down from the buggy.

Esther let go of her hand. "Jesse and Conrad would have come out to meet you, but I told them to wait inside."

"Thank you," Rose whispered.

She stood frozen while Esther tied Brownie to the hitching post.

"I made a chicken dish and a pasta salad," Esther said in encouragement, "and ice cream, of course."

"Ice cream!" Rose paled. The memories of Conrad's face so close flooded her mind.

"Don't worry," Esther said. "Jesse and Conrad finished turning the churn ten minutes ago."

Rose's head was spinning. She was going to faint before she arrived inside the house.

"Things are going very well." Esther whispered conspiratorially as if they were in a crowded kitchen after the Sunday morning church service. "Conrad arrived wearing suspenders."

"Suspenders?" Now she was going to pass out. Was the man really serious about joining the community? She still couldn't believe any of this.

"They're English ones." Esther giggled. "With red and white stripes. The poor man must have bought them at the hardware store. At least he's trying."

Rose followed Esther into the house, nearly tripping on the front door sill. When they entered the kitchen, Conrad and Jesse both stood.

"Goot evening." Jesse and Conrad said together.

"Goot evening," Rose replied. She didn't dare look at Conrad.

Esther bustled about the kitchen, and Rose joined her in the final food preparations. The soft murmur of the men's conversation hung in the background.

"Talk to him." Esther mouthed.

Rose didn't answer. Her heart was pounding in her throat.

They transferred the dishes to the table and seated themselves. Rose was careful not to meet Conrad's gaze. She couldn't. Not yet. They bowed their heads for the silent prayer of thanks.

"Amen." Jesse pronounced, and Esther began to pass the plates of chicken.

"How are you this evening?" Conrad was clearly speaking to her.

His voice was gentle, and Rose forced the words out. "Okay, I guess."

"I'm glad you're here," he said.

She met his gaze. His eyes were kind, as she remembered, as if he knew what she had been through these past days, as if he read every torment she had suffered and held her entirely innocent

"It was nice of Esther to invite us," he said.

"It was." Rose nearly dropped the plate of chicken trying to tear her gaze away from him.

"Shall I help?" He reached out without waiting for an answer.

Rose felt the weight of the plate leave her hand.

"How many pieces?" She heard him ask.

"One." Rose choked out.

Conrad transferred a large one and helped himself to a thigh and leg without further ado, as if serving her chicken was the most natural thing in the world.

Rose struggled to breathe, let alone swallow, while they ate. Did Conrad really understand her? Did he know what was in her heart? The tears wanted to come, but Rose held them back.

"What do you think of my suspenders?" Conrad asked, laughing.

Rose took a deep breath and forced herself to look.

"Silly." Esther spoke up before Rose could find any words.

"They aren't Amish." Conrad looked sheepish.

"We appreciate the effort," Jesse assured him.

"They fit you." Rose blurted out, wishing at once she had thought of something more profound, or perhaps loving. She wanted desperately not to offend him.

Conrad snapped his suspenders playfully. "I thought so."

Rose couldn't do anything but stare blankly at the wall.

"Ice cream," Esther announced. "Everybody ready for ice cream?"

"I'm almost done," Jesse said.

"Same here," Conrad seconded.

Esther bounced to her feet. "Ice cream coming right up."

Rose stood to help. Her piece of half-eaten chicken lay on the plate.

"The small bowls," Esther whispered.

Rose nodded her thanks. In her daze, who knew what she would have brought to the table?

"Give him a bowl." Esther added, her whisper barely audible.

Rose stood with the bowls in her hand and waited for a rush of dizziness to overcome her. Nothing happened. She didn't even feel lightheaded. Apparently, she was going entirely numb from the overload of emotions.

Walking over to the table, Conrad gave her a smile when she handed him a bowl. "I was hoping you would come earlier and help with the ice cream making."

The emotions started in her stomach and worked up into her head burning like fire. Rose waited for her legs to collapse, but instead she stayed on her feet.

Conrad was still smiling up at her. "I'm glad you're here," he said.

"I—I was running a little late," Rose stammered.

"I really enjoyed the evening of the youth gathering," Conrad said. There was not a hint of guilt in his face, or of anything but kindness and a touch of sadness.

Rose's face burned, and Esther filled the embarrassing silence with a chirpy. "Homemade ice cream is extra special when Rose helps."

"I agree very much," Conrad said, setting his bowl on the tabletop with a soft clink.

Rose felt her whole body turn cold. "I'll try to come early next time." How presumptuous could she be? Next time? She snuck a quick glance at Conrad. He seemed pleased.

Rose seated herself. There was no way she could serve Conrad ice cream. She waited while the men helped themselves. Esther slipped her plate of half-eaten chicken off the table and out of sight. A bowl appeared before her, followed by a dish of ice cream. If the men noticed Esther serving her, no one mentioned the fact. Rose forced her hand to move, and the bite of ice cream sat on her tongue cooling the rest of her face.

"Like it?" Conrad turned to tease.

"Delicious," she managed to say. In reality, she could taste nothing.

"I helped make the ice cream," Conrad informed Rose.

"You only turned the churn," Esther chided.

"The ice cream is very special." Rose forced out the words.

"Thanks," he said.

They finished eating and bowed their heads for a prayer of thanks again. Rose stood to help with the dishes, but Esther waved her away, speaking loudly. "Jesse is helping me tonight. You go out on the porch with Conrad. The moon isn't rising, but the stars are out."

Rose froze. What was Conrad going to say to Esther's bold proposal?

"Coming?" He clearly asked her, already on his feet.

Rose nodded, unable to speak. She couldn't turn the man down. Daett approved of this, she told herself repeatedly.

Conrad led Rose outside and lined up two chairs facing his house.

Rose sat down and tried to think. What was she supposed to say?

"Lovely evening," he commented.

"It is," she agreed.

"I'm glad you came." He laughed. "I must sound silly. I've been saying this all evening."

"I'm glad I'm here," she said. Pain and joy gripped her heart, tussling hard with each other.

"I don't understand everything about the community," Conrad was saying. "I'm just—"

Rose waited. He seemed at a loss for words.

"I'm assuming a lot at the moment," Conrad finally continued. "Which can be dangerous, so perhaps we should speak plainly?"

Rose still couldn't say anything.

"You had nothing to do with what your sister is up to?" he asked.

"What is Esther up to?" Her voice squeaked.

"I'm sorry," he said. "I wasn't trying to imply anything untoward. Forget I said anything."

Rose waited a long time. If she didn't speak now this moment might never return. "What you think is true," she began. "Esther is trying to put us together romantically."

"I thought so," he said.

"I'm sorry," she whispered.

"You are?"

"I had no right to play along with my sister's schemes."

"Yet you did."

"Yah. I'm here."

"I'm confused," he said. "Could you explain?"

"I have broken off my relationship with Robert," she said.

"Because of what happened at the youth gathering?"

"Maybe. I don't know anymore. I do know I'm not trying to—"

"I didn't say you were," he said. "Yet you came tonight."

"I can leave if you want me to." Her face must be blazing red in the darkness from the shame of this awful conversation.

"I don't want you to," he said. "I want something to come of this, of what we feel, of what we have felt since the first day we met, but I don't know how to proceed."

"Makes two of us," she whispered.

He looked pleased. "I do have one question though. Was I not right?"

"Right about what?" Her face must be flaming again.

"I was more than a memory." His voice was gentle in the falling dusk.

"Yah," Rose admitted. "You were. I know I feel plenty, but—"

"Why the hesitation?" he asked.

"We're impossible, Conrad. Our situation is impossible. I'm Amish and you're English."

"You really think so?" he asked.

"I can't expect you to become Amish for me. I can't leave the community."

"What if I join?"

"Would you be happy?"

"I don't know," he said. "I think so, but I don't know yet."

"I wouldn't want you unhappy."

"Even if I was with you?" he asked.

Rose couldn't believe this conversation, and yet, Conrad was right. They had best be honest. "Not if it's only me. A man must love his world, not just his wife."

305

"You're correct," he said, not looking at her. "I've already caused you great damage. You've called off your wedding plans. I'm sorry."

"You didn't do anything," Rose protested. "I did the calling off, and I asked you to kiss me. Remember?"

"A quite pleasant experience," he said.

"Don't tease," Rose begged. "I can't take this."

His hand reached out for hers, and Rose clutched his fingers. "I'm not teasing," he said. "I'm quite serious. Why are we impossible?"

"I just told you." Rose pulled in a long breath.

"What if I change?" His voice was gentle.

"The heart must also change. You weren't born into our life."

His fingers tightened on hers. "What if I like your life?"

"You do?" She dared glance at him.

"I might," he said.

She let go of his hand. "I can't do this. Not encourage you. I just can't."

"Let me find my way." His face begged. "Let me walk this road with you."

"We can't date," she managed to say.

"There is Esther's garden." His eyes twinkled.

Rose sat in silence for a long time before she spoke. "I will do this. I don't know exactly what this is, but Daett has given his permission. I can't turn away from the door the Lord has opened."

"Thank you," he said, her hand still in his.

Rose's heart pounded in her throat. Had she promised something she couldn't deliver? Had she only dug her hole deeper?

"Look," he said, pointing upward. "The stars above us. Aren't they awesome, so full of the glory of God? What an imagination our God must have."

"He does have an imagination." Rose shivered, but not from the cold. There had never been any conversation like this with Robert.

"The heavens declare the glory of the Lord," he quoted. "Day and night declares his speech. There is no land or language where his voice is unheard."

"Are you a preacher?" She attempted to tease.

He laughed, and Rose joined in.

"You really are joining the community?" she asked a moment later.

He nodded. His face barely visible in the starlight. "I'm thinking of beginning the journey."

"Are you doing this just for me?"

He smiled at her. "You won't leave the subject alone, will you?"

"I can't."

"I think the peace of the community may be what the Lord will use to heal my soul."

She stared at him. "You don't look wounded."

"Inside," he said. "I have wounds I didn't know I had until the peace of your community touched me."

They sat in silence, the sweep of the stars above them.

"You think my motives impure?" he asked.

"No, I'm just unworthy of you."

"You're not," he assured her. "You're a worthy wife for a much better man than me."

"Don't say such things," Rose said.

He looked troubled. "I'm not from your world. We speak much more bluntly."

"Neither am I of yours," Rose reminded him, "and you said nothing wrong."

"I'm not asking anything of you, Rose. I'm just telling you what my plans are, and we'll go from there."

She didn't say anything, her heart pounding again.

"Are you okay?" he asked.

"I'm okay with anything but promises," she said. "Well, not everything but—"

"I understand," he said. "Thanks for tonight. I can't stop thanking you. I know a little of what you must be going through and the courage you have. I'm honored with your presence."

"Now I'm crying." Rose gulped.

His hand sought hers again, and she responded, grasping his fingers.

"Don't make me put fully into words my feelings for you, Rose," he said. "They are quite true and real. Yet, I know we must take one step at a time. The first would be to take your sister out of this—although not entirely. I think we need her garden. Can you come an evening a week or so, work in the garden with me? We could talk."

"You want me to—?"

"Very much, Rose."

"But we can't."

"We can, Rose. Find the faith in your heart to take one step at a time with me? If we fail, I promise I will bear the blame."

"I'm to blame," she cried.

"Yet you will come."

"Of course."

"Thank you," he said.

Rose held on to his hand, the strength of his fingers wrapped around hers. The tears came, long streams gushing down her cheeks. Rose dug for her handkerchief and dabbed them with her free hand. He said nothing, holding her hand in the darkness, the stars twinkling brightly above them.

He waited a long time, until the cool night air had dried her cheeks.

"Ready to go inside?" he asked.

"Can you help me turn the buggy around. Esther doesn't need to know I was crying."

"With great pleasure," he said, and led the way across the yard.

Esther and Jesse were out on the porch when Rose drove past. She leaned out of the buggy door to wave. She couldn't see their faces, but she was sure Esther was smiling. A great happiness rose inside of her, but there were also thunderclouds on the horizon. The greatest one was Mamm, and yet she had to face the thunder and the lighting.

Rose arrived home fifteen minutes later and unhitched to lead Brownie into the barn. She pulled off the harness by the light of the stars and shoed the horse into the barnyard. Mamm was sitting on the couch when she entered the house, with Daett on the rocker.

"Have a goot evening?" Daett looked up with a smile.

"Conrad is thinking of joining the community," Rose blurted out. "And he has a definite interest in me."

Mamm's face was dark, but she didn't say anything.

"You follow the Lord's leading," Daett said. "Be careful."

"I will," Rose promised.

Mamm finally found her voice. "You say Conrad is joining the community. This is only because of you? How can you encourage him to do such a thing, Rose? You know how unstable such men are. He'll steal your heart and have you out in the world the moment the wedding vows are said."

"I trust him," she said.

"The man just waltzes in here and steals your affections." Mamm was becoming more agitated. "He is taking advantage of your broken heart."

"My heart is not broken." Rose tried to speak calmly. "I am done with Robert."

"Exactly!" Mamm declared. "What is wrong with you, Rose? Have you lost your mind?"

"I hope not." She wasn't fainting, Rose comforted herself. Where was this courage coming from?

"You practically had a wedding date with Robert." Mamm's voice reached her through a fog. "Of course, your heart is broken."

"I should not have encouraged Robert. I see my mistake."

"Your mistake is encouraging this English man." Mamm's voice rose higher. "He has nothing but impure motives."

"Does loving me count as an impure motive?" Rose asked.

Mamm fanned herself. "I can't believe I'm hearing you say such things, Rose. How do you know the man loves you?"

"Just sit down." Daett motioned toward Mamm. "We can't fight over this. Rose knows what she is doing."

"If you didn't support her." Mamm looked accusingly at him. "Did you know the devious plans of this English man, when you invited him into our house."

"I knew nothing of his plans." Daett protested. "I liked the man. I liked him from the beginning and loving my daughter enough to join the community sounds like a right noble motive to me."

Mamm was fanning herself, appearing speechless.

Rose wanted to hug Daett, but she wiped her tears instead and whispered, "Thanks."

"We should all go to bed," Daett declared. "It's late."

"The man is English," Mamm said.

"He wouldn't be English if he joins the community," Daett replied. "This is not a new thing. Many have joined."

"I've never seen one join this community."

"Let's go to bed. A goot night's sleep on this and some prayer for the Lord's help and guidance will be in everyone's interest."

Rose fled up the stairs. She stood in front of her bedroom window for a long time, looking at the stars before she prepared for bed and climbed under the quilt. Daett was on her side. Never had she imagined such a thing.

CHAPTER 63

Late on Tuesday morning, Robert stood up from his seat on the gently rocking train to retrieve his hat and single suitcase from the overhead luggage compartment. They were still in motion but had passed the town limits of Lancaster moments before. Gliding into the depot, Robert saw his grandpa waiting for him on the small platform with his horse and buggy tied to a nearby lamp post.

The train jerked to a stop, and Robert was the first in the aisle of three debarking passengers. The conductor stood at the door, smiling at them. "Welcome to Lancaster."

"Thanks," Robert muttered.

Grandpa Beiler hurried toward him with his hand extended for a firm handshake. "How are you doing?"

"Glad to be here." Robert grinned.

Grandpa looked happy. "The trains do get tiresome, but you're here."

"I am." Robert agreed. "Thanks for coming to meet me on such short notice."

"For you, anything." Grandpa beamed. "Come. We have a full week ahead of us."

Robert followed Grandpa's broadbrimmed hat across the parking lot and heaved his single suitcase into the back of the buggy. They climbed into the buggy to head down the street. The roar of the steady stream of passing automobiles filled Robert's ears.

"Busy around here."

"The city of Lancaster for you." Grandpa grimaced. "The whole countryside is becoming almost as bad."

"I guess one could get used to the congestion."

"You do." Grandpa agreed. "Yet there is no question we are running out of land for our people, which is why your trip is such a timely exhibition for me. I have been spreading the word about our trip west and the possibilities. You'll have plenty of questions to answer on Sunday from curious young men looking for opportunities in other communities."

"Goot." Robert stirred on his seat, thinking of Rose and what Grandpa didn't know.

Grandpa was smiling broadly. "You'll be sort of a celebrity. Fresh in from the wild west."

"How are things going with Grandma?" Robert changed the subject.

"Quite well," Grandpa said. "The maid will be with us for another few weeks. Her name's Nancy. I hope you don't mind the extra company, but I wouldn't be free to roam the countryside with you otherwise."

Robert grunted. "You're doing much more for me than you should. I'm grateful."

Grandpa laughed. "Glad to help out. How's the lovely girl of yours? Rose? Wedding date set in concrete?"

Robert winced, looking away. "There's no wedding date."

"Oh my," Grandpa said, but there was no rebuke in his voice. "Haven't you asked?"

"She broke up with me." Robert stared out at the passing landscape. Here was the moment when Grandpa's sharp words of rebuke would appear.

Grandpa clucked his tongue instead. "Sorry to hear the news, and the farm just bought. What happened?"

"I'd rather not talk about Rose."

"No hope then?"

"I don't think so."

"Anything to do with that English man, the county extension agent?"

Robert jerked his head around. "Conrad Wisner?"

"You sound incredulous."

"What?" Robert searched for words. "What does an English man have to do with Rose breaking up our relationship?"

Grandpa shrugged. "Just saying, but I'm not surprised. I saw an attraction between the English man and Rose when we visited."

"You're accusing Rose of indecency?"

"I'm not accusing anybody of anything." Grandpa pulled to a halt at a red traffic light. "Just telling you what I saw. Sometimes the Lord interferes with our plans, for our own goot."

Robert stared, his head spinning. "You're saying Rose and Conrad Wisner, the county extension agent—"

"I know what I saw," Grandpa said. "Sometimes those things are passing fancies which amount to nothing, but in this case, they might not have been."

"So they—"

"I'm not saying anything," Grandpa said. "I'm giving you a reason for why Rose might have broken up with you. One which places little blame on you. Maybe Conrad caught Rose's attention, but she was trying to stay loyal to you."

"I don't believe this!" Robert declared. "I was there the whole time."

Grandpa slapped his back. "You're a young man, and I'm an old man. There is a difference."

"I—" Robert tried again.

"I would cry my tears and move on," Grandpa advised. "You do have a farm."

"I do have one." Robert's mind was in a daze. "Rose and Conrad. Rose would never leave the community and Conrad is English."

"Exactly," Grandpa said, which brought Robert's mind back to the present.

He blurted out the question. "Where am I supposed to find a wife on such short notice? It took years for me to wrangle a date out of Rose."

Grandpa was grinning. "This is Lancaster County. There are a few more available girls, and you do have a farm. This trip might be for more than one reason."

"Rose wouldn't—" Robert's head was still spinning. He couldn't get his mind around Rose and—

"I'm not trying to cast a shadow on Rose's character," Grandpa said. "We're all human and things happen."

"Did anyone else notice this thing between Rose and Conrad Wisner?"

Grandpa shrugged. "I didn't ask."

"But Rose in love with an English man?"

"Let's not put it quite so bluntly. Let's say she was troubled by her feelings for him, feelings which doubtless caught her completely by surprise."

"Surprise," Robert muttered. "I would say more than surprised. Impossible."

"Either way," Grandpa said. "Time to move on for you, I think. Don't hang on to the girl."

An automobile roared around the buggy, the occupants waving with great glee. Grandpa waved back, and Robert forced himself to smile.

"Just keep your eyes open," Grandpa said. "There will be youth gatherings you can attend. Where the Lord closes a door, perhaps another one will open ... and you have a farm. Something which most of these young men around here only have in their dreams."

Robert didn't answer, trying to absorb what he had heard and what he was feeling. Life with Rose was over. He had known, deep down he had. But moving on? Did he actually have the courage? Ask another girl for a date and have her reject him?

CHAPTER 64

Rose was working in the Miller's garden when Esther drove her buggy into the driveway. Rose looked away, half wishing her sister hadn't appeared. Mamm hadn't gotten over the shock of the events from Sunday. Rose didn't blame Mamm. Rose didn't blame anyone but herself. Nothing made sense about what she had done. Only Daett's approval and the garden brought peace, the soil gentle under her feet.

Rose pulled a few weeds, not moving toward her sister, while Esther tied her horse and hurried toward her

"I knew you'd be hiding." Esther scolded.

"Mamm had a fit on Sunday night when I got home," Rose told her.

"I figured," Esther replied. "Is Mamm okay?"

"No. You know she isn't."

Esther made a face. "I'll convince her, just give me time."

"There's no convincing Mamm. I'm not half convinced myself."

"I'm fully persuaded!" Esther declared. "I'll have better success with Mamm."

"Here comes Mamm now," Rose said.

They turned to face the fast-approaching figure.

"Esther." Mamm raised her voice at the edge of the garden. "You have a lot of explaining to do."

"Don't be too hard on her," Rose objected.

"Stay out of this." Mamm ordered. "I want to hear what Esther has to say for herself."

Esther put on a brave face. "This is what I have to say. Conrad is a decent man and a perfect match for Rose, but I'm sorry we kept things behind your back for so long. Looking back I should have told you sooner."

"Yah, you should have!" Mamm still hadn't calmed down. "How about never keeping me in the dark again."

"I should have told you." Esther repeated. "My excuse is I was too busy trying to persuade Rose. I couldn't handle another argument at the same time."

"You were behind this whole thing?"

"Mamm," Rose warned. "Esther couldn't have done anything if my heart hadn't been in on the matter."

"I'm not convinced," Mamm said. "I think Esther put things into your head."

"She didn't," Rose tried again. "This would be more helpful if you concentrated on aiding us as we move forward."

"Aid you!" Mamm's eyes blazed. "Aid my daughter in running away with an English man. I will not!"

"Rose is not running away," Esther said.

Mamm appeared not to hear. "I will gladly help you get things patched back up with Robert, the minute he comes back from Lancaster. Daett and I will even make a trip over with you to visit him."

"We're way past getting Robert and Rose back together." Esther jumped in.

"Stay out of this." Mamm warned. "You have done enough damage."

"Esther speaks the truth." Rose stuck up for her sister. "I'm not getting back with Robert even if Conrad were to vanish."

"You expect me to believe you?" Mamm glared.

"It would be helpful if you did." Esther replied.

"Hush!" Mamm ordered.

"Daett seems to have at least a little sympathy for my position." Rose grasped at straws.

"Yah, he does." Esther's face lit up.

"You will settle this with me." Mamm faced Rose. "Leave Daett out of the equation."

"I'm going to convince you we're right." Esther continued undaunted.

"I don't think you can." Mamm's face turned into a thunder cloud. "I don't want my daughter marrying an English man."

"Conrad wouldn't be English once he joins the community." Esther put on her best smile.

"Don't try to charm me! Once English always English!"

"The Lord can change the leopard's spots, and an English man's heart."

"Don't play with my mind," Mamm retorted. "Rose is seeing nothing more of this English man, either here or over at your place."

"My garden." Esther's face fell. "What about my garden?"

"Don't play on my sympathies," Mamm said. "You and the English man are perfectly capable of weeding your garden."

"Can you give me some time, at least?" Rose begged. "Time to sort things out and time to talk with Conrad."

"Talk with him!" Mamm looked ready to leap halfway across the garden. "You need to stop talking with him."

"Rose is right." Esther jumped back in the conversation. "My garden is the perfect place for them to talk in peace."

"Your garden!" Mamm looked confused. "Why is your garden at the center of this conversation?"

"I want to meet with Conrad again and speak with him." Rose gripped the hoe with both hands.

Mamm contemplated Rose. "You've changed, haven't you."

"For the better." Esther jumped in again. "This is the Lord's will."

"You're not convincing me," Mamm said.

"You will know the tree by its fruit." Esther pressed on. "Rose has done nothing wrong and will do nothing wrong."

"She has broken up with her promised one. I would say Rose has done plenty wrong."

"What is dating for if not to find out the Lord's will?" Esther reminded Mamm. "You know the community believes this."

"How can the Lord be in this?" Mamm's eyes blazed again. "My daughter is in love with an English man?"

"Conrad won't be English once he's Amish." Esther rung her hands. "Think Mamm, think."

"I am thinking," Mamm shot back. "I am thinking of all the trouble this will bring. The scandal to our family. Deacon John will be stopping in this Saturday evening if he finds out what is going on."

"Deacon John will understand." Esther hesitated for once. "I think he will, if—"

"Yah if," Mamm said. "Don't you think Robert will have a thing or two to say about this once he finds out Rose is in love with an English man. We might all be in the bann in a month or two."

"Mamm, you exaggerate," Esther said, but Rose could see Mamm's words had hit their mark with her sister. Horror was filling her own soul at the thought of the bann. Was this where her heart had led her?

"Can you trust me a little?" The words slipped out in a whisper. "Haven't I always lived a proper life?"

Both Esther and Mamm were staring at her.

The tears were pressing. "I know how this looks. I know the danger I'm placing everyone in, but I would like to give love another chance. Impossible though this seems. I lost the boy I loved. I cannot go on until I know for sure this is not the Lord giving back to me what he took so long ago."

"Rose," Esther said, reaching for her hand.

Mamm said nothing for a long moment. "Wilmer. This is about Wilmer."

Rose nodded numbly, the tears flowing down her cheeks.

"Can you give her the chance?" Esther begged. "Please."

"You ask too much," Mamm said. "There's too much risk. You could both be wrong, and Rose's heart may lead her astray."

"Has mine led me astray?" Esther asked. "I'm her sister."

"You married an Amish man," Mamm said.

Esther sighed. "Please, Mamm, just give Rose a chance. She has never willfully made wrong choices, and she has lived her life in the fear of the Lord. We will ask the Lord to be with her, and if things go wrong, I will take full responsibility. I will tell Deacon John I was to blame."

"You would take your sister's heart in your own hands?" Mamm asked.

"I would leave her heart in the Lord's hands," Esther said. "I would beg of you to do the same. English men have joined the community before, and Conrad is an honorable man. Daett agrees with us."

"You ask a hard thing." Mamm admitted. "Yet you also speak the truth. Rose has been nothing but a faithful daughter to me."

"Thank you." Esther whispered. "Thank you so much."

"Don't gush," Mamm said. "My heart is not yet made of stone. Now, I have to get back to work."

"I know." Esther was smiling through her tears.

Rose said nothing, unable to speak. Mamm had given a little, but this was really Daett's doing. Mamm would never have backed down otherwise. Not even an inch.

CHAPTER 65

Halfway across the country, as dusk was falling, Robert sat at Grandpa's table laden with a full Amish supper of mashed potatoes, gravy, fried steak with a steak sauce, and a full salad. Robert had forgotten how hungry he was for home-cooked food after the long train trip in from Nebraska.

"Ahhhhh," he said, leaning toward the table to fully take in the delicious aroma.

"There's also pecan pie," Grandma said from her chair, where she had been sitting supervising the supper preparations. "Nancy makes excellent pecan pies."

Robert nodded. He hadn't paid much attention to the maid since arriving at the house. Now he looked at her, and she tilted her head saucily. "I try."

"You're taking goot care of Grandma," he said, which didn't quite fit the conversation. She didn't seem offended, giving him a warm smile.

"I think we're ready for the prayer," Grandpa said.

Robert closed his eyes, but not before Nancy gave him another tilt of her head.

"Amen." Grandpa announced after a long moment of silence.

Robert looked up again.

Nancy's hand was right there, passing him the bowl of mashed potatoes. "How was your train trip?" she asked.

His hands nearly slipped on the bowl. "Okay." He managed.

"I hear there's a girlfriend." Nancy passed him the steak plate.

"There's no girlfriend," he said, and the room became silent.

"Robert!" Grandma looked quite alarmed.

"I'll tell you later." Grandpa shushed her.

"That's why you came by yourself," Nancy was smiling, looking triumphant.

"I would have come by myself anyway." He gave her a glare. "We aren't married."

"Not much you can do on a train," she said, "in a bad way, at least."

Robert felt heat gathering under his collar at her plain talk. Grandpa was looking at him as if to say, *you're in Lancaster County now*.

"These are excellent mashed potatoes." He forced the words out, passing the bowl on.

Nancy's eyes twinkled. "Am I to believe you're a man who can taste cooking before it arrives in your mouth?"

"The steak looks excellent," he corrected.

"The steak is excellent," she said. "I tasted the food."

Her words and her eyes made Robert dizzy.

"I no longer have to taste her food." Grandma spoke up. "Not that I didn't trust Nancy from the start, but you never know."

"Nancy is an excellent cook," Grandpa said, as if to settle the matter once and for all.

Robert tried to straighten out his thoughts. The newness of the place, the country, the girl hovering over him.

She passed him the sauce next, followed by the salad. He tried not to look at her, but Grandpa was grinning, obviously enjoying his discomfort. Was this a setup or something? Had Grandpa known about Rose? How could Grandpa have known? He hadn't even told his own parents until the night he left. They couldn't have written a letter this quickly.

"What was the name of your girlfriend—I guess, ex-girlfriend now?" she asked.

"Rose," he said.

"Such a pretty name. Was Rose a pretty girl?"

"Ah, Nancy, take things easy on the boy." Grandpa chided.

"Just curious," she said. "Sorry."

"Rose was pretty," he said. "Too pretty for me, apparently."

"Modest," she said. "Modesty is quite becoming."

"He owns a farm," Grandpa's said, his eyes sparkling.

"He does?" Nancy stared.

"He comes from Nebraska," Grandpa said. "Things are done differently out there."

"He owns a farm?" Nancy was still staring.

"I do," he said.

"You want more steak?" she asked.

"Of course." He grasped the edge of the plate.

She stayed close to him. "Tell me about Nebraska. Must be more interesting than plain, boring Lancaster County."

"Lancaster County boring? I thought Nebraska was boring."

"Lancaster County is boring," she said.

"You want me to argue with you?" He couldn't believe his quick comeback.

Her laugher bubbled. "I think you like this place."

"Don't you like Lancaster County?"

"Not in the way you like Nebraska."

"How do you know?"

"I just know but tell me. What are your plans while you're in Lancaster?"

He took a moment to answer, enjoying her rapt attention. "Grandpa will be showing me around, getting me up-to-speed on Lancaster farming methods."

"A farm and no more wedding." She mused. "You do things differently in Nebraska."

A shadow crossed his face. "Not by my choosing."

"Sorry," she said. "You just told me."

"It's okay," he mumbled. "The truth must be faced."

"A man of truth," she said. "I like men of truth."

"How about the pecan pie," Grandpa said.

Nancy jumped up to return from the counter with the pie. She sliced a large piece and offered to slide the pie on to his plate. Robert nodded, watching her hands move so close to him. Lancaster County was different. There was no question there. He glanced at Grandpa, who was not looking at him but was smiling.

Robert took a bite, taking a moment to chew before swallowing the gooey sweetness. He glanced up at Nancy who had her head tilted at him.

"Excellent," he said. "Excellent pie."

"You had better say so."

Warmth flooded him, and he took another bite.

Nancy sent a sweet smile in Grandpa's direction. "Do you want a piece of pie?"

Grandpa chuckled. "Of course."

Nancy gave him the pie plate but didn't offer to cut the piece. Robert thought about her hands moving in front of him. Rose had never affected him this way, but Rose had never offered to cut a piece of pie.

"You don't look too heartbroken," she said.

"Nancy!" Grandpa chided.

"The past is the past." Robert met her gaze. "Should we not look to the future?"

"We should." She agreed.

"Aren't you going to eat a piece of pie?" Robert asked.

"I already tasted a piece earlier."

They finished their pie and had another prayer of thanks. Robert didn't lift his head to check, but he could feel her eyes fixed upon him from across the table.

With the amen said, Grandpa pushed back his chair. "Grandma has the room ready for you in the basement if you wish to retire, Robert. Long trip and everything."

"I think I will." Robert hit his knees on the edge of the kitchen table standing up.

"When do I get to hear more about Nebraska?" Nancy asked.

"Robert needs his rest," Grandpa said. "We have a long day ahead of us tomorrow."

Robert gave Nancy a quick smile. "Why don't I take my suitcase down and be right up. I'll help you with the dishes and we can talk."

"You sure?" Nancy's face glowed.

"I am," he said.

"Young people," Grandpa muttered, but he didn't object.

When Robert returned the kitchen was empty except for Nancy bustling about. "What can I do?" he asked.

"You'll sit right there and talk to me while I work." She pointed to a chair.

"I can do something." He grabbed a few dishes.

"Okay scrape them in here." She gave him a spatula. "I'll fix hot water and you can wash."

"I can try," he said.

"Start talking." She ordered. "What is the prairie like?"

He couldn't believe how much he liked the sound of her voice.

"Talk!" She glared at him.

He hid his smile. "A little flat but not like the real prairie fifty miles north and west of us. The wheat grains there stretch for miles into the horizon in the fall. Spring and fall are a delight to behold, working in the fields as we do. Summers not so much. Can get dry and hot—windy."

"Sounds interesting." She stood by the sink running the hot water, staring out of the window into the dark. "I think I would like the prairie. No trees. Nothing to hinder the view of the eye. I've never seen such a sight in my whole life."

"There is my farm, of course," he said. "From the first time I saw the *For Sale* sign in the yard my heart was set on the place."

"Tell me. Every little detail."

He didn't look at her, savoring the sense of her presence. "We tested the ground on our first visit, Grandpa and I. The soil is certainly not Lancaster quality, but goot for our area. The acreage is a little large for farming with horses, but with a few extra, I should get the crops in with no problem. Nebraska is big into cattle. All of the fields lend themselves to cattle farming. I'll start with several and grow as the place is profitable. Grandpa gave me the loan, which he wouldn't have done if there was no hope of making the farm pay."

"You're quite capable." She was looking at him, her eyes shining. "What about the house?"

The vision of his English cabinets flittered in front of his eyes and the words came easily. "We have to turn off the electricity, of course, and the washer and dryer have to go. Thankfully the hardwood and tile floors meet the ordnung. There is no carpet to pull up, and the kitchen—well, I suppose a man isn't supposed to see much in a kitchen, but the cabinets are English and quite lovely."

"What a buy for a young couple."

"The place is." He agreed. "I hope the deacon doesn't say the kitchen cabinets violate the ordnung."

"I'm sure they don't," she said. "If you like them, they must be perfectly okay, and quite wunderbah. I'd—I mean, I'd love to see them for myself. The deacon won't ask you to tear them out. Surely not! The expense—and for a young couple."

"I thought so," he said. "I would love to show them to you. I think you would like them."

"I'm sure I would." She poured soap into the filled sink and stepped aside. "Here you go."

Robert took a deep breath and plunged in his hands.

"You wash dishes, and you own a farm," she said. "You have such courage to come out on a trip by yourself, and so soon after your heartache."

"The Lord has his ways. We're wise not to question the Almighty."

"You have the Lord's wisdom," she said. "You'll be a preacher someday. Mark my words."

He reached for the first dish. The glow from the warm water spread up his arms and into his whole body. Rose had never spoken such words to him. "Do you have a boyfriend?" he asked.

"I've had my chances." She demurred, "I dated a few months back, but no one at the moment."

"You should be married," he said. "You'd be quite a catch."

She gave him a glare. "Look who's speaking now. I have my reasons."

"And the Lord's ways," he said.

"Of course." Her laugh was soft.

"You should visit Nebraska sometime."

"The sooner the better." She smiled.

The warmth from the water had reached his head, and he listened in a daze to the sound of her voice chattering while he washed.

"I was born in Lancaster County. Always been here. A beautiful place full of beautiful people. Don't get me wrong. You couldn't ask for a better place to begin life and grow up as a young person. There are so many solid and wonderful people who surround and support you in the faith. But I have always wondered about other lands. Somewhere out there. I didn't quite know where. Mamm and Daett don't travel much, but we have visitors from time to time. I do a lot of maid work for young mothers, and they tell me stories of other communities. Your grandpa has been to Holmes County, Ohio, and the vast Amish communities in Northern Indiana, and to your community. He gets around, so I leaped at the chance to serve as a maid when the accident occurred. I ask him questions when I can, but he doesn't have time to fully satisfy my curiosity."

"Nebraska is a wunderbah place," he said.

"And your farm." She moved closer to him, her dish towel brushing his arm. "I can't wait to see the place."

They finished the kitchen dishes and walked outside to sit on the porch swing. Lights twinkled everywhere from shuttered businesses and English homes, with headlights from the highways casting eerie shadows on the low hanging clouds.

"I'll be here for a while," he said. "We should do more of this." He couldn't believe his daring.

"We could," she said.

He saw the side of her face in the dusk, gazing across the Lancaster landscape, not looking at him. "This is the Lord's will," he said.

He felt her hand slip into his, and he tightened his fingers.

"I agree," she said.

They sat for a long time before his tiredness crept over him. She seemed to know when the moment had arrived and stood to hold the front door open for him. They parted at the kitchen doorway with a quick brush of their fingers and whispered "Goodnight."

CHAPTER 66

On Friday evening, Conrad drove north out of Pawnee on Highway 51. He had worked late finishing paperwork at the office. The week had been exhausting, caused by a weariness beyond the stress of work. His emotions wouldn't stop gyrating from moments of euphoria to despair. Had he over promised? Had he stepped into a girl's life and destroyed her peaceful existence only to leave her high and dry once the dust settled? Rose was serious. He had always known she was, and so was he. He loved the girl. Loved her in a way he had never loved any woman. Why the doubts? Had he seen too much dying in Iraq, too much snatched away in front of his eyes? People who lived a good life, fellow soldiers who had wives and children waiting for them back home. There had been no one waiting for him, yet he had been spared while others had given life and limb for the cause.

Was he fleeing his past, to succeed only in dragging Rose down with him into ruin? Nightmares had haunted him this past week. Buried memories he had succeeded in suppressing. Humvees, their heavy metal bottoms distorted, lying on their sides, burning. He could feel the heat of the flames again, hear the screams of his comrades crawling away from the licking fire, the air heavy with the sound of chopper blades, chariots arriving to the rescue, surrounded by the heavy static of gunfire.

Rose had never been where he had been. Neither had he experienced her life, but the world of the community was heaven on earth compared to the battle he had experienced in Iraq. Why the fears? He knew of hurdles and how to overcome them. He knew of commitment. Once he was fully a part of this place, there would be no more jumping into a pickup truck and driving off to where he wished to go. He would have to learn how to drive a horse and buggy. He would be faced with other tasks, like harnessing a horse and tilling the soil with horses. There was his college education? As an Amish man there was little need for anything beyond an eighth-grade education. Unless there was?

Conrad turned right at the stop sign and accelerated again, trying to dwell on the present. The Lord was helping him. He had to believe. Look how things were shaping up. The Amish were quite open to the latest farming information he possessed, which came from his access to a higher learning center. What he valued in life would not be forbidden. He could update his chosen field through continuing education classes, and everyone would benefit. Obviously, life with the Amish would always be a bit of a mystery. Like Rose was a mystery—like why she was willing to love him, to possibly marry him, if things proceeded to their natural conclusion. She was a jewel. He had no question there. Rose was worth the impossible, if necessary. He wanted this. He wanted to find healing and fulfillment here.

Peace came as he thought of Rose working in Esther's garden. She might already be there, hard at the task, waiting for him. He had never had a girl wait for him—let alone in a garden. What better place for their love to blossom and bloom than where tender plants burst into life. He would not be leaping into the Amish world. This path had been laid out for him from the first time he had laid eyes on Rose and her father had welcomed him into the Miller's home for breakfast. The rightness of the whole thing had been cemented in place with Jesse and Esther taking him into their lives, spending time with him around the supper table eating cherry pie and homemade ice cream. This was a new beginning, the first uncertain steps toward another world. Hopefully leading the two of them, officially together.

Conrad smiled as he crested the hill, and his small place nestled beside Esther and Jesse's farmstead came into view. The garden was hidden behind Jesse's barn. He couldn't see anyone until he was almost at the driveway. They were busy at work—both of them. Esther looked up to wave, but Rose kept her back bent over the row of green beans. Fear gripped him for a moment. If Rose had suffered anything like what he had gone through this week? Different torments perhaps, but torments nonetheless. Had Rose changed her mind? Was she waiting to tell him their journey was over before they had taken the first real steps? He wouldn't blame Rose. She was faced with dating an English man with a past. Even if he joined the community, he had not been born Amish. At best, he would always be an ex-English man.

Conrad parked his vehicle and gathered his courage. He climbed out and waved, calling across the field. "Howdy."

Rose looked up, smiling.

Joy leaped inside of him. The path forward was still open. He closed the pickup door, leaving his lunch pail on the hood of the truck.

"Goot evening." Esther called out as he approached. "We thought you would never get here."

"Sorry," he said, "but I'll have to be even a little later. I have my tools at the house."

"Use mine." Esther waved them about. "I'm leaving."

"You don't have to," he said.

"Jesse told me he can use my help in the barn with the horses once you arrived. He's trying to shoe them, and most of them are still new to us. Your timing is perfect."

"Sounds like a plan." He grinned.

Esther gave her sister a quick squeeze on the arm and handed him her hoe. "Here you go."

"Thanks," he said, and Esther left.

Rose hadn't looked up again, since the brief smile sent his way when he drove in. He whacked at a weed. "Nice evening for gardening."

She peeked up past her bonnet. "How are you?"

"Okay, I guess. I had some late office work."

She smiled. "Were you up early this morning."

He made a face. "If I wasn't, I should have been. The Amish get up before dawn."

"I guess we do." Her attention focused on a tough weed hidden under a tall tomato plant.

"Shall I?" he offered.

"Sure." She stood. "I think the roots are entangled with the plant."

He bent down. "I'll be careful."

She tucked her loose hair back under her bonnet and moved back a step.

"Kind of snarled." He tugged gently. "A big weed."

"I must have missed the thing last week."

"We were busy with other things."

Her look was grim. "I don't want to think about my troubles at the moment."

"To a better and brighter day." He lifted the pulled weed high in triumph.

"May all our troubles be gone," she said.

"Yes," he agreed, "but they won't be, I suppose."

She ducked her head, searching for another weed among the tomato plants. "What did you do today?"

"Made trips out to see farmers and had grumpy conversations."

"Are unpleasant conversations normal in your job?"

"Not really."

She was down on her knees in front of a plant, digging with a smaller tool plucked from her apron pocket.

"Persistent things," he said. "A little like me, I guess."

She smiled up at him. "You're no weed. You should go talk with Deacon John."

"So soon?"

Her smile faded. "Unless you don't want to."

"Oh, no." He couldn't get the words out fast enough. "I'm quite unfamiliar with the ways of the community."

"I'm not trying to rush things, but—if people see us together—even here. Perhaps Deacon John should know of your plans."

"I want to—I mean—whatever steps I should take."

Her face was troubled. "Are we living a dream?"

"Then I hope to never awaken," he said.

Her face softened, and a tear formed. "I'm walking, not much more. I think I'm awake, but half the time, I don't know."

"The Lord will help us," he said. "The wounds of the past will heal. We have been given a great gift—a new chance at life."

Her breath came sharply. "I know I'm dreaming."

He reached across the tomato plants to touch her arm. "I'm here, Rose. I'm real."

Her hand lifted touching his fingers. "You are. You came from nowhere. The morning with the sunrise and the wash in my hands, and—"

"I came," he said, "but I was led, I think. What else makes sense?"

"But you're real." Her fingers brushed his, letting him go, looking down again. "We should keep working."

"When should I make this visit to Deacon John?"

She didn't look up. "Normally, people go on Saturday afternoons."

"What do I tell him? How madly I am in love with you?" He held his breath until she looked.

"Tell him you want to wed me next Sunday."

They laughed, their voices soft in the garden.

"You should tell him you want to join the community," she said, "and say you plan to begin attending the meetings."

"Any chance he will object?"

"Deacon John won't turn you down, unless he happens to drive past here and see us together first."

Conrad took a quick glance up and down the road. There was no sight of a buggy.

"The community people will figure things out—eventually," she said. "There's also the problem of what Robert might say when he returns from Lancaster."

"Are you trying to scare me away?"

"Just being honest. I come with my own troubles." She pulled out another weed.

"I'm—whatever the steps are." He searched for words. "When should I start wearing suspenders?"

She glanced down the road. "You do need proper ones this time, and a buggy is coming."

"Should I run?"

"Too late."

He gave a quick wave at the passing buggy, which contained an older lady, her face peering out of the buggy door.

"I think the ship has set sail," she said.

"A long, long time ago."

Rose's eyes were tear-filled, looking up at him.

"I think I'm visiting Deacon John tomorrow afternoon," he said, gazing after the retreating buggy, now a dark speck in the distance.

She wiped her eyes. "I'm sorry. This has been a rough road."

"Robert would have been an easier journey for you."

"I don't think so," she said.

"You can still turn back."

"I know," she said, "and so can you."

"I have brought you sorrow."

"You bring the rainbow," she said. "A beautiful rainbow in the rain."

His chest tightened. "I love you, Rose. I really do."

"You'll have me crying again," she warned, glancing toward the barn.

Conrad looked over his shoulder to see Esther hurrying toward them, hollering, "I was afraid you would be gone. You have to stay for supper."

"You're staying," Rose said, before he could object.

"I think I will."

"Why is my sister crying?" Esther glanced suspiciously at him.

"I'm happy," Rose whispered. "So very happy."

Esther's smile was quick to appear again. "Thank the Lord! Now Rose is helping me with supper, and Jesse could use your aid in the barn. He has the last mare to shoe, a tough cookie—and in my condition—but she shouldn't be a problem for you."

"Esther." Rose was staring worriedly at her sister.

"I'm fine," Esther said quickly. "Conrad needs to learn our ways unless I'm missing my guess."

"I guess I should be learning about horses." he agreed.

Esther gave him a glare. "You should if you are to properly care for my sister."

Conrad chuckled and headed for the barn. He could hear Esther's whispered voice rising and falling behind him, obviously instructing her sister. He would have to learn the language, but there was plenty of time. They would move slowly, the two of them, headed through uncharted waters, but the Lord was in this thing. The ending could not be anything but good.

"Get all the weeds pulled?" Jesse teased as Conrad entered the barn door.

"Quite a few of them," he shot back.

"I suppose you did." Jesse winked at him. "How about standing at the mare's head and holding on to her halter. She likes to lean back and observe the process."

Conrad took his place, admiring the muscle lines on the black neck. "What is your word for horse?" he asked

"You mean in Pennsylvania Dutch?"

"Yep."

"*Gaul*," Jesse said, grunting under his breath. "You're serious then."

"I'm very serious." He hung on to the halter, as the mare tried to turn her head. "Don't move, gaul," he ordered.

Jesse's laugher filled the barn. "You'll have to practice the accent."

"There's plenty of time," he said, stroking the mare's neck. "Plenty of time."

CHAPTER 67

Rose didn't look over her shoulder on the short walk across the yard and into Esther's front door.

"Tell me again, what you said just happened." Esther ordered from behind Rose.

Rose spoke over her shoulder. "Millie Yoder just drove past and saw us working in the garden."

Esther didn't sound too alarmed. "We knew this would happen, eventually. Shall I be with you on Saturday afternoon when the deacon visits?"

"He's coming, isn't he?"

"You know he is. Millie imagines things even when there isn't anything to imagine. We have to put our best foot forward."

"I told Conrad he should talk with the deacon soon. If Conrad goes tomorrow afternoon, the deacon might not visit."

Esther's hand patted Rose's shoulder. "I'm so glad you've finally come around."

"Mamm will have a fit if the deacon visits."

"Daett will talk her down. You know he will."

"Daett," Rose said the word softly. "What would I do without Daett?"

"Or Conrad." Esther added.

"One day at a time." Rose turned to face her sister. "Help me walk this road carefully. No more risk taking."

"No more risk taking," Esther agreed, but her face was way too cheerful. Esther was born to take risks and wouldn't stop now.

"Please." Rose begged.

"I'll try." Esther gave Rose a quick hug. "Let's forget about thunderclouds and make a delicious supper for our men."

"We're not—like dating even." Rose objected.

"But you are," Esther said. "Come, we have to get busy."

They worked quickly, the slicing and stirring of vegetables into water mixed with sauce. There was bread from the cupboard and warmed in the oven. Rose found the jam and butter in the refrigerator. She set it out, pausing to clear her head. This was another meal at Jesse and Esther's place, but different this time. There was tension in the air, which hadn't been there before.

"We have to calm down," Esther said, as if she read Rose's thoughts. "We're friends like always, enjoying a meal together. We can't let this change us."

"I know."

"Then relax."

Rose tried and found a sense of peace deep in her heart. The Lord was guiding them. What else explained Daett's willingness to stand up for this sudden turn of events in her life? Esther gave Rose another hug, and the tension in her shoulders was gone by the time Jesse and Conrad came in from the barn.

"Supper ready?" Jesse stuck his head into the kitchen. "I'm starving."

"Sit down." Esther gave him a bright smile. "Did you get the mare shod?"

"Yep!" Jesse pulled out a chair. "I had excellent help."

"He means you," Conrad said, seating himself.

"I'm sure he means both of us." Esther sent another smile his way. "You'll get the hang of the horses quickly."

"I grew up around them—just not plow horses."

"The soup is ready." Esther waved her hand about. "A meager supper, but we won't starve. There are peaches and cream for dessert."

"Food fit for a king." Conrad grinned. "What more could friends need around a dinner table?"

"Exactly what I said." Esther motioned for Rose to sit and did likewise. "Shall we pray?"

Jesse nodded and bowed his head to pronounce the amen moments later.

Rose gathered her courage and reached for the dipper in the soup bowl. "How much?" she asked Conrad.

He looked a little surprised, but quickly gave her a smile. "One for now. We'll see if I live first."

Rose carefully transferred the dipper of soup to his bowl. "Esther's soup is excellent, I can assure you."

"Any vegetables from the garden?"

"Not yet, but they're fresh vegetables of sorts, canned from last year's garden."

"I was only teasing," he said. "Fill my bowl."

Rose transferred another dipper before she filled her own bowl. Esther gave her an approving smile. She was serving the man and warm circles raced around her heart, feelings that had never been there with Robert. Which was strange. Robert was Amish yet he would have frowned at the silliness of her filling his soup bowl. She would never have dreamed of doing such a thing for the man.

"Excellent," Conrad was saying. "Is this a staple Miller soup recipe?"

"An Amish recipe," Esther informed him. "Though I suppose each family adds their own customs. Mamm always threw in a few extra spices, so we never knew exactly what the recipe was in the final product. I do much the same."

"Excellent." Conrad said again. "How many spices did you throw in on the side."

"A little pepper and salt," Esther said. "I'm glad I got the soup right."

"You did," Conrad assured her. "I think I'll have another dipper full."

Esther glowed with happiness. "There's also warm bread and jam."

"The soup is so good I didn't want to spoil it," Conrad told her. "But we'll have bread and jam."

Rose made sure the bread plate was within his reach, but she let Conrad dip out the soup on his own this time. He gave her a smile while he did so, and the warm circles raced around her heart again. Her own soup went down easily, and Conrad was right. Esther had seasoned the familiar soup to perfection.

After the prayer of thanks, Rose stood to her feet and reached for the dirty dishes close to her.

"No. You don't help," Esther ordered. "Jesse will help me. You two, outside."

"But—" Rose began to protest.

Conrad's look stopped her. "I would love a few moments on the front porch with Rose."

"Of course!" Rose nearly choked. A few moments? She would gladly spend a few hours with Conrad, but Mamm was likely worried already about her stay at Esther's house for supper, so she must leave before too long.

Conrad led the way outside and repositioned two chairs on the porch, so they faced outward. The sun had sunk below the western horizon behind them leaving the eastern sky with only a faint glow of light.

"No rising moon tonight," Conrad said, seating himself. "Seems like there often is one when we sit on Esther's front porch."

"There's a new moon," she said, remembering.

"Really?" He stood again. "Shall we go see?"

"Sure." Rose followed him willingly down the steps and out toward the garden again. Once past the edge of the house, they could see the sliver of the new moon hung a few degrees above the low cloud bank, standing out clearly among the red and gold of the sunset tinged sky.

"Quite beautiful," he said. "A promise of new beginnings, I always thought."

"The moon is beautiful." She agreed.

"Meaning?"

"Nothing, I guess."

"You mean us, don't you?"

"Yah, but the same moon will rise higher tomorrow night. I will comfort myself with the thought."

"To ever higher and higher," he said.

She reached for his hand and leaned her head against his shoulder.

"I'm sorry, Rose. There should be no sorrow in this world, but the Lord has decided otherwise."

"You're not to blame," she said.

They stood motionless for a long time, looking at the setting moon until the clouds moved higher to engulf its brightness.

She dared to look up at him, tracing the outlines of his handsome face with her gaze. Conrad—her—whatever he was at the moment. She loved him with an intensity which took her breath away.

"Come," he said.

She didn't protest, her hand in his for the short walk back to their chairs. They sat down facing toward the dark eastern horizon.

"I grew up north of here," he said, "in the rolling open hills. On many an evening like this before I went to bed, I would gaze out of the window and wonder where life would take me. Even what the girl I would love would look like."

"Not like me," Rose said.

She could see him smile into the darkness. "I don't know. She was always a dream."

"I'm not a dream."

"You're a beautiful awakening," he said.

"You must not say such things."

"I will if I wish."

"Then in small amounts. I can't bear large doses."

"The Lord leads us," he said, "but I suppose you had best be getting home before your Mamm is too alarmed."

"Just a moment longer, please."

"There will be tomorrow," he said, "and the moon will rise a little higher."

"You'll have me crying soon," she warned.

He fell silent until she stood and let go of his hand. "You can help me turn the horse around."

"I can," he said, and when he did, he drew her close by the side of the buggy wheel.

Rose closed her eyes, allowing the sense of his presence flood her being. He was so close, so strong, and yet so tender. She wanted to kiss him, but didn't dare ask, burying her face in his chest.

"Rose." His voice was quiet above her.

When she didn't respond, he repeated, "Rose."

She turned her face upward, and his lips found hers. She reached for him, not daring to believe this was happening again. He washed every pain away and left nothing but glowing sunlight shining in her heart.

"Come," he said, pulling away after a long moment. "I believe you must go home."

"Conrad." Was all Rose could manage, as he helped her into the buggy, even knowing to hold the horse's bridle until she had the reins taut.

"Good night," he said, his voice sweeping by as Brownie dashed out of the driveway.

CHAPTER 68

Rose stayed in her room upstairs late on Saturday afternoon, even when she recognized Deacon John's buggy pull into the driveway. Rose waited until she heard the deacon and Daett's voice on the front porch greeting each other. She knew better, but the hope lingered, maybe Deacon John wanted to speak with Daett or Edwin? Her heart pounded in her chest. Daett and Edwin had not been misbehaving. She was the one who had been seen brazenly working alone in Esther's garden with Conrad Wisner, while she was supposedly dating Robert and everyone suspected their wedding was scheduled for this fall. No wonder Deacon John's suspicions had been aroused

"Rose." Mamm called up the stairs.

She forced herself to step out into the hall. "Yah."

Mamm didn't say anything, but her face spoke volumes. Rose couldn't blame Mamm. There was nothing like a visit from the deacon on a Saturday afternoon to unsettle any certainty, let alone when you were crowding the fence. She was doing more than crowding the fence. She had obviously broken through.

"The deacon." Mamm mouthed silently.

She must stand firm. She was doing the right thing, even if Deacon John might not be able to see the rightness of her position. Daett would give her support.

"Come," Mamm said out loud this time.

When Rose came out of the stairwell, she forced herself to give Deacon John a smile.

He stood by the front door with his hat in his head. "Goot evening, Rose."

"Goot evening." She croaked.

"Could we speak a moment alone?" he asked.

"Yah, of course."

"I'm right inside." Daett told Rose as she walked past.

The deacon appeared not to hear as Rose tried to keep a frozen smile on her face when they stepped outside, and the deacon turned toward her.

"I hate to disturb your family on a Saturday night." He began. "I know the Miller family is one of the most outstanding and up building families in the community. I'm sorry to imply anything with my questions, so forgive me, please."

"You're not imagining things," Rose said. She would not make the deacon dig for his answers. "Has Conrad been to see you."

"Yah." The deacon stroked his beard. "Millie Yoder also stopped by. Were you—"

"I was," Rose admitted. "I've been working in Esther's garden all summer, and Conrad rents the place next door."

"So this is where this began? With you engaged to—" The deacon let the words hang in the air.

"I should never have dated Robert, not when—and we are no longer dating and were never engaged. Not officially."

The deacon ignored her protests. "This sounds very serious, Rose. What have you done, and with an English man?"

Rose took a deep breath. "I know. I don't know where this road with Conrad will lead us, but the Lord has opened a door, and I cannot but walk through."

The deacon appeared very worried. "Did you talk the man into joining the community, with a promise of marriage?"

Rose shook her head.

"I'm sorry," the deacon said, "but I must ask."

"I understand," Rose told him.

"You're—I'm having a hard time with this," the deacon said. "Again, I apologize. I would have gone to Robert first, as is fitting in these kinds of questions, but Robert is in Lancaster. His Daett said Robert is staying longer than planned. What does this mean, Rose?"

"We broke up, but I didn't know he was in Lancaster," she said.

"But, Rose, you were perfectly matched. Everyone thought so. I know Robert did the last time I spoke with him. Did he change his mind?"

"No. I did."

"You did?"

"Yah. I would say I'm sorry, but in a way I'm not. Things were not working with Robert."

"And Robert was in agreement?"

"If you mean with our breakup? No."

"I don't meddle in these kinds of things," the deacon said. "Love and marriage are ordained by the Lord, and he directs in the dating relationship. Did you believe the Lord was directing you otherwise?"

"I just know it wasn't working," she said.

"If Robert was not in agreement, shouldn't his opinion have given you pause."

"Yah," she said. "I struggled long, but our relationship wasn't working."

"Was there something clouding your decision?" Deacon John asked. "I can be plainer if you wish."

"You mean, Conrad Wisner?" she asked.

"Yah." He looked very concerned.

"I will not deny it," she said.

"How can this be right, Rose? Conrad is an English man."

"I know," she said.

"How can you be doing this? Rejecting a community man for what, Rose?"

"I'm not leaving the community."

"Conrad is not from the community."

"He wishes to join, and he did apparently visit you."

"If this were from the Lord, Conrad would join the community before he—before he—I don't wish to speak too bluntly Rose, but you working with him alone in Esther's garden sounds completely indecent."

Rose felt dizzy. What would the deacon say about their shared kisses, and her asking Conrad the first time? Maybe the time had finally come for a full confession?

"You can blame me," she finally said. "I was at fault. Conrad is innocent."

"He was speaking with you in Esther's garden. Does he know of these feelings you have for him?"

"He does," Rose said. She couldn't say more. Conrad's kiss should not be shared with anyone, even the deacon. Not if she wanted their love to retain the preciousness they had known together.

"How can you—" The deacon sounded totally horrified.

"The Lord is drawing our hearts together."

"Words fail me, Rose. You're bringing great shame to your family. Does your Daett know about this?"

"He does, and he supports me," Rose said.

Deacon John appeared befuddled. "He does?"

"Yah. Do you wish to ask him?"

"You wouldn't lie," Deacon John said, shaking his head as if to clear his mind of confusing thoughts. "Your Daett is a sound and upright man."

"Daett is." Rose agreed.

"What is to happen with Robert?" the deacon asked.

"I don't know," Rose said. "The Lord will take care of him."

"Hasn't he purchased a farm?"

"He has."

"A man with a farm and without a wife?"

"If I have done wrong, I will bear my shame," Rose said, "but my relationship with Robert was never whole to begin with."

"With you seeing an English man?"

"I will not justify myself," Rose said. "If I'm wrong, and Conrad does not join the community, I will take whatever punishment the community sees fit to bestow on me without complaint."

"Do you expect us to take Conrad up with open arms after he has betrayed our trust by trying to steal one of our beloved girls who is engaged to a community man?"

"If I'm beloved, then you can trust me," she said, daring to look at him. "Just a little maybe?"

The deacon didn't say anything for a long time. "I will speak with Robert when he returns from Lancaster and get his side of the story. Perhaps there is something to this which we have not seen yet?"

"I'm sure I have failed him," she said, "and I'm sorry."

The deacon put on his hat. "We will pray for the Lord's mercy. Perhaps we can yet bring healing between the two of you and repair this tragedy."

"As you wish," Rose said, but the deacon was already gone, climbing into his buggy to drive rapidly out of the lane.

Daett's approval had stayed the deacon's wrath. Rose wanted to go inside and hug him, but Daett wasn't the hugging type, and Mamm would throw another fit at such an English display of affection.

She opened the front door and met Daett's questioning gaze to simply whisper, "Thank you."

He smiled and seemed to understand.

Mamm's face was a thundercloud, but she said nothing as Rose fled up the stairs.

CHAPTER 69

Robert sat on Grandpa's front porch swing with the gathered darkness heavy around him. He had been out the entire day looking at Lancaster County farms and answering questions from Amish farmers about conditions in Nebraska. His head was way past overload from the multitude of excellent advice given to him. He would think about the suggestions in more depth later. Right now, his stomach filled with another delicious supper Nancy had prepared and served, he wanted nothing more than to enjoy her presence seated on the swing beside him. They had chatted during supper, and she seemed to understand his need for silence now, to gather his wits about him.

"When are you leaving?" she finally asked.

"Next week sometime," he said. "I have to get back." Nebraska seemed a distant and faraway place after his short immersion in the bustling Lancaster County culture.

"I have enjoyed our moments together," she said.

"Same here." He smiled into the darkness.

"Was Lancaster County what you expected?"

"Not really," he said, "but I didn't know what to expect."

"Who is taking care of your farm while you're gone?"

"No one," he said. "I have to get back."

"I will miss you," she said.

"You will write me and maybe visit soon."

"I can't wait."

"It won't be simple for a girl. Traveling back and forth."

"I'll find a way."

"There might be people going there before long with the interest expressed by the Lancaster community."

She reached for his hand, moving closer to him on the swing.

"Would you consider—"

Her fingers tightened in his. "I think you already know the answer."

"I just met you, and you just met me," he said, "and Nebraska is far away."

"I like Nebraska," she said.

"What will your Mamm and Daett say?"

"We can visit our district for church services tomorrow. Grandpa can manage Grandma for a day. You can meet my parents."

"What if they don't like me?"

"They will like you."

"But if they still object to you—perhaps—Nebraska is far away?"

"They won't, Robert."

She lay her head on his shoulder, and the swing chains squeaked above them as with the gas lanterns lights twinkling in the homes across the fields.

"You're a brave girl," he finally said.

"And you're a brave man." She was looking up at him, but he couldn't see her face in the darkness.

"Not really," he objected.

"I could be trouble for you."

He laughed. "I don't think so."

Her head moved on his shoulders. "I think we were made for each other."

"I agree," he said, and allowed the peace of the night to settle around him.

CHAPTER 70—EPILOGUE

Rose stood in front of the mirror in the old farmhouse, gazing at her image in the flickering light of the kerosene lamp, hearing Mamm rushing about in the kitchen below her. With the last of the night's full moon on the windowpanes, the cooks would be arriving any moment. She shouldn't cry, but she was about to. Her wedding day had arrived, after over a year of tension filled with great joy, knowing the eyes of the whole community were watching her and Conrad. Mamm had distracted herself with Esther's baby, her first grandchild, a boy Jesse and Esther named John, trying to forget what her second daughter was doing. Rose had kept on walking, the door never closing on her relationship with Conrad.

Robert and Daett had saved them a lot of grief. Daett with his support, and Robert with his rushed marriage to Nancy last fall. Everyone's head had been dizzy trying to keep up with events. And when five Lancaster families had arrived to visit, making plans for their move this past summer, little time had been left for people to worry about what Conrad was doing.

He had been doing plenty, learning the language, learning how to drive a buggy, and learning how to live as an Amish man.

"Rose." Mamm's voice hollered up the stairwell.

Rose wiped away the tears and went to the bedroom door.

"You can't be wearing your wedding dress yet."

"Conrad is coming at six." Rose replied.

She had given him careful instructions on the Amish customs for the day, but Mamm didn't need to know.

"We'll have breakfast for him," Mamm replied, "but you can't be in your wedding dress. Not until you've eaten."

"I'll wear an apron." Rose stood her ground. "I'm not changing again."

Mamm gave in with a frown. "As you wish, but don't blame me if you spill something."

Rose went down the stairs and gave Mamm a hug. "He's a goot man, Conrad is."

Mamm's frown didn't go away. "A little too late for doubts, don't you think?"

"I'm not having doubts."

Mamm didn't look convinced. "Don't bolt for the door when you're up with the bishop saying the vows. I've suffered enough embarrassment."

"He loves me, Mamm, and I love him."

"He's an English man," Mamm said. "Love is different in their world. They leave their wives."

"Robert is married," Rose said.

"I know," Mamm said, the air clearly gone out of her protest.

"Don't you like Conrad, just a little?"

"You ask on your wedding day?"

"He's a wunderbah man," Rose insisted. "Daett likes him."

"I know," Mamm said. "You're going to wed the man, so we might as well accept the matter."

"Conrad has come," Rose said, as buggy wheels rattled into the driveway.

Mamm gave in with a sigh. "Go welcome him, and come back inside to eat."

"In my wedding dress?"

"You're the one wearing your wedding dress."

Rose caught her breath. Why not? She hadn't thought through the matter this far, wanting only to meet Conrad with the dress when he came into the house. Why not in the driveway, near the garden where they had first met.

"Go." Mamm ordered. "You can't keep him waiting."

Rose gave Mamm another hug and rushed out the door. Mamm was on her side. Deep down Mamm was. Mamm had to protest out of principle, or perhaps out of fear. Mamm didn't know Conrad like she did, the depth of his loyalty, the fervency of his love, and the solidness of his character.

She ran barefoot across the wet grass, toward the dim form standing beside the buggy.

"Rose," he said, reaching for her.

She flew into the arms. This was their wedding day, and tonight she would be his wife, this man she so loved.

"Rose," he said, his face in her hair.

She clung to him. "I had to come out and welcome you."

"Yah, the end of the journey." He held her out at arm's length.

"The beginning," she corrected.

He agreed, she could tell, by the happiness in his eyes. "Did you see the moon?" he asked.

She laughed. "Of course. The moon has been shining the whole night."

They both turned, hand in hand, to gaze at the full glory of the setting orb slipping toward the horizon.

"The Lord is telling us, giving us a sign." He held her hand tightly. "He will be with us for a full and fruitful life. This is how we will end, as we began, gazing at the fullness of his glory."

"Oh, Conrad." Rose melted into him, knowing now the real reason she had on her wedding dress, why she was standing barefoot on the grass near the garden. "I want to tell you my vows."

"Your vows?" He was gazing down at her.

"I know the bishop will marry us later, ask us his questions, but I want to answer mine here and now."

He took her hands, holding them in front of him, waiting.

"I, Rose Miller," she began, "born Amish, promise to you, Conrad Wisner, born English, my trust, my honor, and my sacred affections. I will love you my entire life. I will live with you. I will give you what is mine, as my heart has, so my hand will give. I am yours, to hold, to have, and to keep forever, while I draw breath, and while you live. I hope to make you happy, to be worthy of your love, to be all you ever imagined a wife would be. In this, I am yours, in life and in sickness (may those day be few—very few) and to all the years the Lord will give us. May I be a blessing and not a curse. I will always love you, for what you are and for what you will become. You will be my husband, and I will be your wife. This I must solemnly pledge, my dear, my sweetheart, my most beloved. To Conrad Wisner. To the man who gave me back my heart, who awakened me from a great slumber, who made me alive when I had given myself up for lost. Thank you, dear, from the very bottom of all the heart I have."

"Rose," he said. "What can I say? My words would sound empty to the presence of such beauty. Thank you, dear. Can I kiss you?"

She shook her head. "Tonight, you can kiss me. Tonight, I will be all yours."

"I don't deserve you, Rose," he said, "but I love you. How this can be enough, I will never know."

"Come," she said, letting go of one hand. "Mamm has breakfast ready. We must eat."

ABOUT THE AUTHOR

Jerry Eicher has written and published over thirty works of Amish romantic fiction, along with his childhood memoir, *My Amish Childhood*. He lives in Virginia with his wife Tina. They have four children and seven grandchildren.

ELK LAKE BOOKS BY JERRY EICHER

WHEN HEARTS BREAK

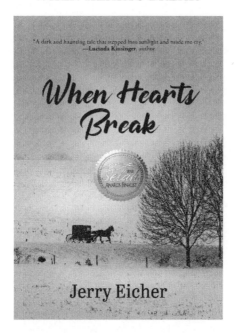

THE AMISH MENORAH

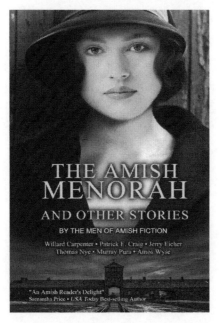

JERRY EICHER

*THE MEN OF AMISH FICTION PRESENT
A CHRISTMAS COLLECTION*

Made in the USA
Middletown, DE
05 March 2022

62193804R00201